EAGLE MAN
AND
MORE
MISSIONARIES

BY

WILLIAM L. MAHER

authorHOUSE™

1663 LIBERTY DRIVE, SUITE 200
BLOOMINGTON, INDIANA 47403
(800) 839-8640
WWW.AUTHORHOUSE.COM

First published by AuthorHouse 07/15/05

ISBN: 1-4208-2655-7 (sc)

Printed in the United States of America
Bloomington, Indiana

This book is printed on acid-free paper.

Table of Contents

Foreword

Why did I write this book? After I saw my biography of a Korean War chaplain in print I began searching for another subject. I considered a former Chief Justice of the United States, who was Catholic, and a female astronaut, also a Catholic. Neither of those ideas clicked.

One avenue of inquiry led to others and I stumbled upon the diary which Father Stan Maudlin, OSB, a Benedictine monk, had prepared over many years. His thoughts and memories tumbled out as he spoke into a dictating machine while traveling around North and South Dakota from 1939 onward.

The diary and his newspaper columns, especially stories about life on the Indian reservations, captivated my interest. Father Stan's yarns may surprise readers. They describe many fine Indian men and women and also show that behind their black robes monks are as human as most of us. The accounts in the diary are not widely known and, I hope, add some liveliness to this book. Unlike the public image of a monk, this one was not a silent Stan, for his writings included many amusing and thought-provoking conversations. For me the diary served a much broader purpose. I saw it like a tree, a Christmas tree, to which I could attach stories which go back years and centuries. For example, a short summary of the life of St. Benedict was a natural part of the book because the religious order which he founded, the Benedictines, is discussed in various ways.

I also connected President Grant's "Peace Policy" into the story because it temporarily hindered the work that done by Catholic missionaries among the American Indians. Thank goodness that the federal government finally came to its senses and ended that repressive program.

I started my research years before the sexual scandals in the American Catholic Church crowded the headlines. That problem is outside the scope of this book. Nevertheless, these are days when Catholics need to read something good about their Church and I hope that this account of the work of lay persons and missionaries, both men and women, will fulfill that objective.

Father Stan was a great help in preparing this book. He was a gracious host when I visited Blue Cloud Abbey in South Dakota and put me in touch with persons who gave me some feeling for that state and life in a Benedictine monastery. For years he provided leads to useful sources of information. Father Stan has reviewed and corrected much of the manuscript and many of his words are quoted verbatim. I did not accept all of his suggestions, but if there are errors they are my fault. I want to thank Father Stan for his encouragement and cooperation.

The professionals at my public library in Jericho, New York assisted my research and I appreciate the efforts of the staff. Char Vance of Focus International Catholic Network put me in touch with helpful people. The University of South Dakota made Father Stan's diary available to me and I am grateful for its assistance. A cover drawing was adapted (with thanks) from the work of Thomas Hatai when he was a student at St. Paul's Indian Mission, Marty, South Dakota.

Lastly, I want to dedicate this book to my family and to thank them for their forbearance. They includes my ever-patient wife Lee, my daughter Maureen (who corrected many mistakes in my manuscript), her husband Vince and their children, Jay and my newest grandchild, Caroline, my son Greg, his wife Sue Ellen, and their children, Christopher, John and Emily. I felt guilty when I carried my typed chapters and a red pen to family gatherings and I promise I won't do that anymore.

fr. stan

Chapter One - Wambdi Wicasa, Eagle Man

"Father, don't you know that God is nice?"

Stanislaus Maudlin heard the question. It was unusual and he wasn't ready for it. God nice? No one in the Vatican or at Saint Meinrad's Seminary in Indiana had suggested that God is nice. What an odd description! Merciful? Yes! He knew that. A just judge? Yes! All-powerful? Sure! But now, in the cramped smoke-filled log house in South Dakota an old Indian man awkwardly asked something the young missionary had not heard before.

Only 23 years old, the Benedictine monk already was an educated and self-assured young man. Still, he wasn't prepared for a subject so obvious and so simple. Just a few months earlier Stan had been in Rome studying for two graduate degrees. Then, early in 1939, the growing menace of Adolph Hitler forced him out of Italy and back to the United States.

It's calving time in South Dakota, the Benedictines at Saint Meinrad's told Stan. Go out there and help! Something exciting is going on, Stan thought, and I want to be there. Yet when he reached the Immaculate Conception Mission at the Crow Creek Indian Reservation, Father Justin Snyder, O.S.B. assigned something awfully mundane. He instructed his new assistant to write thank-you letters to benefactors of the mission. The announcement didn't keep him busy enough and when Father Snyder learned that Stan had studied in Rome, well, he obviously deserved a more important

1

task. "You must know everything," he told the newcomer, "You saw the Pope and all that, so you go down to the fort and teach these people religion."

Stan's first session did not stimulate his students, a handful of old Dakota Indian men from the Saint Joseph Society. As he drove back to the mission, he chided himself, "Oh, boy, I didn't go over tonight. I really didn't go over because these people are so ignorant. I've got to use little ideas, little sentences, everything little so they finally catch on."

He rehearsed more thoroughly for the next meeting. His diary recalled the scene: a tiny log cabin at Old Fort Thompson; "…dusky faces melting into the shadows, with only two coal oil lamps burning, cigarettes glowing in the dark and I am laying God on them once more." But he could not evade the feeling that his impassioned words were not connecting with the oldtimers crowded silently around him.

Out of the corner of his eye Stan noticed how Claude Never Misses sat stoically and quietly flicked the ashes from the Bull Durham cigarette onto his shoes. With one bony leg draped over the other, the Indian's entire body never moved, but conveyed a message - "My God, when is this young man going to shut up? When is he going to wise up?"

Just to the right of Stan sat Clem Wounded Knee. For years Clem had been the catechist, song leader and foundation of the Catholic community on the reservation, preparing others for holy communion, confirmation and weddings. Everyone respected him. Stan knew about Clem's reputation and he hoped that the wise old Indian would turn to his friends and explain, "Look, Father knows everything. Listen now. Come on, come on, wise up!" However, Clem would not volunteer and finally, desperate to spark some interest in the lesson, Stan decided to invite him into the discussion. "Mr. Wounded Knee, what do you think?"

Clem's head drooped and for a short time he remained silent while, typical of a mature Indian, he slowly turned the question over in his mind. As Stan would soon learn Indians don't blurt out answers. "These old people are so gentle," he recalled, "They don't want to put you down, they don't want to show up your ignorance." Clem hesitated to express his thoughts, but at last he looked at Stan and "...in the watery kind of an old man's eye, I saw a gentleness which finally came out in words." Stan had discovered something about the Indians in the Dakotas - they were not only wise and patient, but also willing to accept an ignorant young white man. He could be comfortable among these people.

Clem's answer was another question: "Father, don't you know that God is nice?", stunned the young missionary. In the seminary, when someone wrote "God" on the blackboard the instructor sometimes added some big words: "omnipresent," "almighty," and more. But never something as understandable and ordinary as "nice."

Driving back to the mission that night, Stan stopped his car and stepped outside, alone amid the darkness and silence of the prairie. "I thought if He's nice, I'm going to change my way of praying," he promised himself. "He's not going to kick me out of the house for every darn little thing I do that's wrong. He's going to look down and say `There goes Stan again. I'll have to clean up after him one more time.'"

Then and there the Indians gained new respect in Stan's eyes. He realized that being nice was what the Catholic faith was all about and these old men knew it. From then on he would listen to the inflection in their voices, observe their body language, in summary, pay close attention to his new friends.

Clem's question had changed the direction of a young missionary's life. "Now in your lifetime, somebody, somewhere, sometime this is going to happen to you. It will either be an event or a person, even one word," Stan said later in his diary. "It'll pick you up out of the rut in which you might be and shake the dust off you and start you out in a different direction. Just wait and see if it isn't true."

Although most persons called him "Father" Stan was not a priest. His training at St. Meinrad's Seminary took three more years and he spent the first two of those summers at Marty Mission on the Yankton Reservation in South Dakota, teaching the Gregorian chant to Catholic nuns and high school subjects to teen-age Indians. If he intended to spread the word that God is nice, what better place to learn the Dakota language!

In the summer of 1941 Stan was working at the Marty Mission and decided the time had come for him to speak the Dakota Sioux language. He sought out White Tallow, a tiny woman in her late sixties whom everyone called Unci, which means "my grandma", and asked her to teach him. Unci invited him to visit and start the lessons that evening. Her frame house was typical during "the Tipi days", one room and a lean-to attachment. The only furnishing was a stove which she didn't need in the summertime when she lived outside under a covering of tree limbs that her sons had assembled.

After a short time Stan thought he had learned enough to approach a group of Indian men and greet them in their language. Their reaction took him by surprise. They dropped their tools and bent over in laughter. Stan had used what the Indians called "Women Talk" and one of the men teased him with "We hope you're not that way, Father." Unci mistakenly had taught feminine phrases to her pupil and she corrected the problem when he mentioned what had happened.

A diligent pupil, the young Benedictine returned time and again to sit on the floor of Unci's hut and scribble almost every word that she spoke, or at least those that he understood. Later, back at the Mission, Stan read the Bible in the Dakota language and tried to imitate the way Unci talked. On the surface the lessons progressed well, but Unci's pupil was impatient and becoming unhappy.

Still unfamiliar with many Indian customs, the young missionary finally complained, "Unci, I feel a little disappointed. I've known you for several months and I hear you talking about Father Tim and you call him Ihanktowan Hoksina, Yankton Boy. You talk about Father Dan, you call him Zica Tamaheca, Thin Squirrel. But you did not give me a name."

Unci's eyes widened and surprise spread across the old woman's face. Her irritation surfaced as she confronted him. "O han (`Young man'). I've been teaching you Dakota and you never did give me a present. Now, don't you come back for two weeks and come on Sunday afternoon," she commanded Stan. He was learning the hard way about an Indian custom that a visitor brings a gift. Stan was being banished and he knew it.

What would please Unci? She didn't need water, because her sons brought her fresh water from the river. The Sisters gave her clothing. Stan didn't have money to buy anything. But he remembered that every day Unci loved to spend some time praying with her pipe, so Stan began searching for tobacco. He pushed his hand deep into the rear of a desk and pulled out a two pound can of Sir Walter Raleigh pipe tobacco. Probably an overlooked Christmas gift, but perfect for the day when his exile ended! Approaching Unci's house on a hot August afternoon, the appointed Sunday, Stan hurried up a small rise in the prairie and at the top he saw a couple of saddle horses, a buckboard, a buggy and an early model Ford car close to the cabin.

Stan's first impulse was to turn around and head back to the mission. Why allow himself to be embarrassed among a group of strangers? Still, he had brought his gift of pipe tobacco and he wanted badly to make up with Unci. Uncertain about how he would be received Stan nevertheless decided to enter the house. He pushed open the door and saw a number of men and women gathered closely in the 12-foot by 12-foot room. Their backs to the wall, they sat silently, for Stan knew that among the Dakota tribe presence, not conversation, was important. He spotted Unci and gingerly took a seat next to her. The guests greeted the young Benedictine with nods and quiet smiles.

The silence continued until "Wicoicagetopa", whose name means "Four Generations", reached back and pulled out a prayer drum. He started to pray softly and as he tapped the drum in a slow beat everyone remained seated and began to sway left and right. The Indians closed their eyes and the tempo increased. The men stood and began to dance, then the women took their places among them. The room seemed to be moving. Stan remained seated, but somehow he knew a fervent spirit had taken hold of everyone in the hot, but still quiet little house.

Then Unci rose slowly, her feet covered by Dakota moccasins and her body supported by two canes. She straightened her dress and stood up in the middle of the crowd. The old woman looked down and signaled for Stan to rise, "Koska, inaji; hiyu po!" The Indian holy man reached for his ceremonial symbols, his eagle feather and sweet grass. Something distinctive was happening.

The crowd circled around and around Stan. They sang, but he didn't understand the words. It was only later that the young missionary learned that the purpose of the ritual was to identify his Sioux spirit. Yet Stan had no doubt that he had become the central figure in a serious observance. The whirling around accelerated until Unci turned and broke the silence. Another command, "Enashi!," instructed Stan where to stand while the others danced.

The ceremony finally reached its climax as Unci, in the creaking voice of a grandmother, addressed Stan in the Dakota tongue. "Your name now is Wambdi Wicasa," she announced. The title in English meant "Eagle Man."

"In you there is the power of the Eagle, Wambdi. Wambdi is the highest of all creatures. He is close to the Creator. He hears the Creator's words and brings them down to us. But you also are a man, Wicasa. You are barely a man, but you will be a man. So, besides being close to the Creator, you are close to us. You hear God's words and you bring them to us; you hear our words and you take them to God. You are Wambdi Wicasa, Eagle Man," said Unci.

With those words the Yankton Sioux tribe adopted Stan. It was the first of five names that Native American tribes awarded him and a starting point for more than 60 years of his work on the Indian reservations in the plains states.

Chapter Two - A Huckleberry Finn Boyhood

How was an ordinary American boy transformed into "Eagle Man," a beloved Catholic missionary among the Indians - in a lifetime crossed by the histories of Saint Katherine Drexel, President Ulysses S. Grant, the Indian maiden Kateri Tekakwitha, the Indian leader Sitting Bull, President Lyndon Johnson, and the missionary Father Pierre Jean DeSmet, S.J.?

For most persons who follow a religious vocation the process starts in the local church and the family. However, Stan's family was unusual. His father was a loving but stern Catholic man who had been raised as a Methodist and whose English forbearers reached the United States more than two centuries earlier. The more light-hearted side of the family, his Irish Catholic mother and Grandma Hester, traced their American roots back to 1890.

He was not baptized Stanislaus. Stan's parents christened their first son Irvin James Maudlin and he adopted the name Stanislaus when he joined the Benedictine order of monks years later. From then on everyone knew him as Stan. He was born on December 16, 1916 in the small Indiana town of Greensburg. A couple of years later the Maudlin family moved to the city of Vincennes in the southern part of the state.

Both parents had strong but different personalities and in one way or another each influenced the vocation which their son chose. Being with dad was serious business, but still fun. When Stan sat on a horse at the age of four, he felt scared, yet safe knowing that his dad was standing nearby. Later, at baseball and basketball games what a boost to his confidence to see dad rooting on the sidelines!

In the 1920s Stan's father was a salesman for the first talking movies and sometimes they traveled on business trips throughout the Midwest. It was a happy father-and-son relationship, but at the same time Stan was being taught how a young man must conduct himself in public. Politeness was paramount: "Yes ma'am," "No ma'am," "Excuse me!" Stan broke the rules once; he called an older man by his first name and he never forgot the scolding that his father administered.

As taciturn as Stan's dad appeared he nevertheless was like a god to his first born and proved it once when the family went picnicking. Stan wanted badly to swim in the creek, but his mother had not brought along a child's bathing suit. The problem was solved when she put him in an adult's suit and tied the shoulder straps tightly in big knots, so large that they stuck up above his ears. Stan was in the water, happily paddling around, and he stretched his toes toward the bottom. To his horror he discovered that it was not there.

"Down, down, down. There was no end. I was lost," he described his plunge. "Suddenly a huge hand covered my back. It grasped every bit of the loose bathing suit and lifted me out of the...again I exaggerate, of course...hundreds of feet of water." Up and out of the creek came Stan, coughing, sputtering, crying, as his beloved dad deposited him safely on the bank.

The early years of the 20th century included some happy times for the Maudlin family. Dad owned a store that sold men's clothing in Greensburg. He was an open-minded employer, ready to hear suggestions, but at times proved not attentive enough to advertising and profitable sales prices. A pretty former junior college student went to work there and soon the boss and his new employee married and began their family of six Maudlin children.

Stan's mom was a lively, determined woman who loved animals almost as much as her children. She proved it by riding a neighbor's horse bareback. One time, however, Stan's mother lost control of a frisky mount. "Mom, get off," her kids yelled, but their mom did not give up easily. The horse scampered toward the barn door which scraped her off its back just before the animal dashed into the stall.

The neighbors' boys and girls liked Stan's mother because she knew how to enjoy life. She would rather play children's games than cook. In the summertime, as soon as the Maudlin family finished their potatoes for dinner, she threw a cloth over the table to keep the flies away and led all the local kids for a swim in the creek. Years later, Stan boasted that the Maudlin children had been the cleanest in the neighborhood.

Pick a subject and you knew immediately where Stan's mom stood. She was Irish to the core and Catholic even more so - holy water at the door, religious pictures and crucifixes on the walls. Mom's own mother, Grandma Hester, carried holy water into the house in a gallon jug. "Everything we did in our house was Irish. We had no doubt about it. We couldn't escape it," Stan wrote.

Saturday was Catholic clean-up day in the Maudlin household. "Wash your face. You're going to confession," Stan's mom told her children. Their protests that they had not done anything worth confessing did not matter. "Think of something," she urged. "Don't let the poor priest just sit there. And tell me what he said - I might want to go."

Another event the Maudlin family could not escape was kneeling together in the evening to say their prayers. Stan's mom often rested in bed caring for her youngest child while everyone else gathered around. As the invocations got underway one by one the sleeping children dropped to the floor. "Oh, they're so cute, and praying, too," she exclaimed. But Stan, the oldest of the children could not relax; it was not allowed. "Get hold of yourself," she warned her son. "You'll be a man someday."

One night during the prayers Stan's father won his boy's heart forever while he was leading the family through the Rosary. Then, with Stan slumping badly while he desperately tried to remain awake, his mom launched into her important prayers: the Litany of the Blessed Virgin Mary, Acts of Faith, Hope and Love, the Act of Contrition, etc., etc.

It did not end there. Mom went on, interceding with the Lord for aunts and uncles. One wanted a better job, one needed a husband, another was in the grip of Irish whiskey. Stan struggled to keep his eyes open while his mom continued on and on, petitioning God's help for their neighbors. One of them had sprained something, someone else suffered from poor hearing. Everyone needed a prayer.

On they went until Stan noticed his dad reach out and touch his wife gently. The spell was broken as Stan's father spoke, "Mom, I don't mind your praying for your relatives. God knows they need it. But I have to say this - to hell with the neighbors." Stan could have cheered, even as his mom cried a little, then began giggling and finally everyone hugged each other.

Mrs. Hester lived with the Maudlin family for several years. She was different, to say the least. Sometimes Stan's grandmother would awake in the morning and announce, "Someone is sick!" One of the Maudlin children would ask, "How do you know, grandma?" "I heard the dogs howling at night," she replied. "Go find out who's sick." Well aware of the routine one of the kids made a cursory search around Greensburg and returned to announce solemnly that indeed someone had a cold (even if the report were a fib). The old woman's instincts were confirmed. "I knew it! I knew it!" she declared triumphantly.

Grandma believed that holy water was as powerful as Irish whiskey. Once in a while she demanded that Stan drink a full glass of the sacred water even though for herself she expected better results from the liquor. Grandma was certain that the Irish whiskey could relieve all sorts of ailments, especially hers, and just because the federal government had prohibited the sale of liquor she had no intention of foregoing her favorite brand of medication.

It fell to Stan's father to keep his mother-in-law happy with a supply of the illegal. Father and son drove out into the countryside to visit the local bootlegger, who surreptitiously led them to the edge of a cornfield. As he accepted cash for the liquor the man handed Stan's dad a shovel and pointed into the fields. "Go down through the corn 30 rows, turn right 20 rows," he directed Stan and his dad.

No one except the birds could see the two of them as they maneuvered between the corn stalks, counting row by row along the way. When they reached the appointed spot, Stan's dad began digging and as soon as he heard a dull sound and the shovel struck something solid, he knew that he had located Grandma's treasure. He reached into the dirt, opened a heavy box and pulled out a pint of liquor. At that point Stan understood that he had not come along just for the ride. He began his role in the adventure. When the culprits returned to the car they concealed their illegal prize underneath a blanket. Stan's job was to sit on top of the blanket all the way home.

It was Grandma Hester who indirectly turned Stan's mind toward the priesthood. She had a weak heart and the impressionable youngster noticed how everyone expected the doctor to restore her to good health whenever she became ill. One time, however, the doctor could not cure Grandma and the family summoned the priest. "So the priest had the last word. That's what I wanted to be," Father Stan wrote later.

Even though both grandmothers lived nearby they were not friendly and that troubled Stan. If Grandma Maudlin met Grandma Hester at a wake they spoke briefly and politely, but they did not socialize beyond that. After all, their children were parties to a "mixed" marriage, a son of a Methodist family wed to a Catholic woman, and they lived in the hills of southern Indiana where anti-Catholic feelings were rampant.

As early as age eight Stan learned that some persons just did not like Catholics. He had heard that the men in the Ku Klux Klan hated Catholics and he knew that his Grandfather Maudlin was a member of the secret organization. "He was a custodian at school, so we kids would go over and sit with grandpa and he'd tell us stories and he'd do all this stuff, but once he put one of those white gowns on he was different," Stan recalled.

When the New York Central Railroad brought the Klansmen to Greensburg, Indiana for their convention, a couple of hundred seemingly normal men and women marched down Broadway through the middle of town and on to the fairgrounds. After dark, the Klansmen donned their robes and showed their colors. With their flaming torches reflecting through the bedroom windows of the Maudlin house, they planted a torch in the front lawn of a neighbor's house, a Jewish man who owned a store in town.

The eerie scene was a frightening spectacle. Although the Maudlin family was not threatened Stan and his brother were

11

scared. Stan's father, however, was not and he was determined that the Klansmen would not bother his wife and children. "By God, they won't drive us out," he told his family.

The boy's faith was getting stronger, even while both religions, Catholicism and Protestantism, were tugging him in different directions. The wearying procedure for attending church on Sunday was, according to Stan, "…pretty dumb." It began with Catholic Mass at 6:30 A. M. Sometime before 11 A. M. Grandma Maudlin declared in a commanding tone, "Now we're going to church," to which her grandson replied, "Well, I just went." Grandma commanded, "No, no! Now we're going to CHURCH," and off they went to worship at the Methodist church just half a block away. However, that was not the end of Sunday religious services because about 3:30 P. M. Grandma Maudlin hauled the family away again to attend vespers at the Methodist church.

No wonder that Stan was confused about his identity. He was sure that he was not black and he figured out that he was not Jewish. By that process of elimination he decided that he was Catholic and he reached that conclusion in part because he was enrolled in a Catholic grade school. In a Protestant town that meant that Stan had to run along the middle of the street to avoid the stones being hurled by the non-Catholic kids. The catcalls rained down on all sides. He never forgot the invectives and the wild charges from the older boys that Catholics adored statues and killed babies while in church. He remembered others who were sure that children who didn't attend public schools couldn't be real Americans.

Stan encountered violence and sin often during his missionary work later on, but he was only a five-year old child when he stared into the face of evil for the first time. On a warm Saturday evening he sat alone in his uncle's car parked in the town square. Out of the darkness a figure stumbled from a doorway and veered toward the car. The woman's dress was black and dirty; her stockings were wrinkled and fallen. As the face drew closer, he could see that it was contorted, the hair matted like a mop, the eyes blazing, the teeth yellow and broken.

Instinctively the boy pulled away from the Halloween-face, now lurching up to the windshield and lathering it with her tongue. Then the woman leered in at him until she slipped off into the gutter. A rough hand finally pulled her away, but Stan never forgot how long the ghostly face stared at him.

In happier ways Stan's early years mirrored the tales of Huckleberry Finn. He and his friends were explorers, crawling into caves and strapping carbide lamps onto their heads to find a deeper passageway. When one lamp burned out the boys lighted another, always penetrating farther into the darkness until they could not squeeze through any longer. They knew or at least they hoped that somewhere in the mysterious caverns they would find Indian relics - or perhaps the ancestors of the Indians Stan would meet later in life. Bats whirled around and sometimes when the search became too hot and uncomfortable the boys slipped into a deep, dark pool of water to cool themselves.

On warm days Stan and his friends challenged the steamboats traveling up and down the Ohio River. It was a risky adventure because they chose to swim into the middle of the stream directly in the path of the oncoming paddlewheeler. Spotting them a short distance ahead the captain usually sounded a blast on the ship's whistle, but the kids ignored the warning and treaded water. The captain became irritated as his ship bore down on them. Then another blast on the whistle. Still, the youngsters refused to move, paddling in place, daring the ship to run them down - until at what seemed to be the last second they suddenly slipped off to the side to ride the waves from the passing vessel.

The water attracted the boys to all kinds of sports. On other occasions they would jump off a cliff, swinging far out on a 60-foot vine until they loosened their grip and dropped into the creek below. What fun on a steamy summer day! Stan often would stretch out on the ground beneath his grandmother's grape arbor, reach up and eat the fruit until his stomach almost burst.

Like children everywhere Stan enjoyed every moment of the Christmas season, especially when he accompanied his father as they cut their own Christmas tree and dragged it homeward through three feet of snow. Perhaps, however, it was the spiritual mood of those early celebrations of the birth of Jesus that set him on a course to become a Catholic missionary.

Picture the Mass at midnight on Christmas Eve: cold outside and warm inside, candles blazing, ruddy faces, the buzz of an expectant congregation in a crowded church. Stan stood proudly in the front row of the Men and Boys' Choir, an eager sixth grade student resplendent in a red cassock, white surplice and a big red bow that his mother had sewn. Family and friends were watching. Everyone awaited the signal from Sister Carletta, O.S.F. to start the familiar Christmas hymns. When the ceremonies began and she instructed the choir to sing in a whisper they did; when she told them to increase the volume the rafters rang. Years later Father Stan compared that joyous scene with the Midnight Mass that he celebrated in a crowded two-room log house at the end of Jackrabbit Trail.

In 1928 the Maudlin family suffered a tragedy, so serious that they had to move to live with Stan's aunt in North Vernon, Indiana. The clothing store had failed and Stan's father not only had to declare bankruptcy but also lost his house before the unhappy process ended. He took odd jobs, including a stint at the Briggs & Stratton engine plant in Indianapolis, yet he earned barely enough income to sustain the family.

One morning when Stan's father had taken a job hauling coal, the responsibility for feeding his brothers and sister unexpectedly fell upon Stan. He was 11 years old and had started to save some of his earnings from caddying and mowing lawns. Stan's dad had explained, "That money is yours, my boy. I want you to start saving for whatever you are going to do later. Don't spend it for foolishness." The problem that day was not foolishness. There was simply no food in the Maudlin house and no money to buy any.

Stan's savings were hidden in a bureau in his aunt's bedroom. Stan's mother led her son there and explained the family's predicament, "Daddy is gone and he won't have any money till tonight. Pretty soon Mary Jane, Eddie and Bobby will be up and I don't have any money till tonight. Could I borrow a dollar from you?"

He agreed, of course, and at the same time learned something about responsibility. Years later Stan recorded his feelings in his oral diary: "If your mom ever asks you that you'll know how it feels. But it sure made me know that even I could give something to my mom and dad and sister and brothers. I figured out ways to use second hand things. And we finally made it!"

Stan acquired new friends in North Vernon. Becoming one of the neighborhood crowd was easier after his mother released $3.00 from the savings account so that he could buy a bicycle. One of his best pals was Eddie Eder and they often went over to the Muskatetuck River to go swimming. Stan was very particular about the route to the River because he wanted to be sure that they passed Helen Dowd's house.

She was about Stan's age and he was certain that she would be looking out a window as he and Eddie strolled by. However, there was no sign of Helen's smile and curly hair. Eddie snapped Stan out of his disappointment with an announcement that rivaled the impact of Clem Wounded Knee's statement that God is nice. Eddie declared that he was going away to school at Saint Meinrad's. "What's that," Stan asked? "That's where you study to be a priest," his friend replied.

Unplanned, unrelated events can shape the course of a child's life. Stan had watched a priest play golf one day and an idea emerged. Gosh, he thought, a priest can really be a regular down-to-earth kind of person. Although Eddie's idea stunned Stan it was not the first time that someone had mentioned the priesthood. When he was in grade school a Franciscan missionary who was passing through North Vernon had talked with Stan and had assured him that if someday he became a priest, "I will guarantee you two things if you do become one - you will always have a job and love every minute of it."

Just a few months after that conversation Eddie announced that he was getting ready to leave for school. Stan had delayed telling his mother about Eddie's idea, but that evening, after hauling out the ashes and bringing in coal for the night, Stan hesitantly mentioned that he wanted to attend Saint Meinrad's. His mother reacted immediately. It was a great idea, she said, and she instructed her son to pack his clothes for the trip. But then she thought it over and decided that Stan should first talk to their pastor, Father August Sprigler.

That was not the answer that Stan wanted. He was uncomfortable around the pastor. Father Sprigler was a tall and huge German-American man, made more foreboding by an enormous foul-smelling pipe. Stan avoided meeting him the next day, but finally when his mother decided that she would tell the priest if her son didn't, Stan faced up to the task.

Smoke was billowing furiously from the pastor's pipe as Stan, standing ramrod at attention, described his plan for the future.

"Good boy, good boy! Is there anyone else going with you?" Father Sprigler inquired. Stan reported that Eddie would join him. The pastor continued, amid growing clouds of smoke, "I think you're a smart boy, too, so you won't have to wait until you have finished the eighth grade. You come to see me this summer and I will teach you some English, some Latin and some mathematics, and you can make it this fall."

Stan raced away to tell Eddie the good news. Eddie's father operated the local pool hall and Stan found his friend there, surprisingly glum. The more Stan spoke jubilantly about their plans to attend Saint Meinrad's together, the more Eddie's head drooped. Finally he could avoid the subject no longer and blurted, "I told my mom and dad and I can't go."

Eddie's mother had flatly refused to let him think about attending the seminary until he had finished high school. At that point, however, word had circulated around North Vernon that the Maudlin boy was going away to school. The application papers had been signed and delivered; it was too late to change the plans. His diary entry, written long afterward, summarized his uncertainty: "What have I gotten myself into?"

One summer day before Stan left for Saint Meinrad's his mother sent him downtown to buy groceries. In their family shoes were used only for church and school. As he strolled barefoot past the store where his uncle Ed Hester worked the proprietor, Moses Gumbel, stood at the entrance puffing on his cigar. Gumbel was the quintessential Jewish merchant, chunky, jolly, kind-faced.

"Wait, boy," Gumbel called out to Stan. "I understand you're going away to school." The storeowner noticed that Stan was barefoot and when he learned that the boy had just two pair of shoes, Gumbel chuckled and said, "Ho, ho, that's not enough. Come in." Gumbel then instructed Stan's uncle Ed to outfit his nephew for the trip to Saint Meinrad's. Women who were shopping in the store began to congregate around Stan and offer suggestions. Did the boy need underwear? Should he have stockings? Don't forget a bathing suit! He left Gumbel's store barely able to carry the suitcases and clothing that the generous proprietor had given to him.

Chapter Three - To Rome and Back Again

Father Thomas Schaeffers, O. S. B. greeted Stan on his arrival at Saint Meinrad's and took him directly to the gym. Stan was not prepared for what happened next. Father Schaeffers put boxing gloves on his dazed new student and led him on to the stage, where another equally surprised youngster awaited him.

Physical activity was the school's way of introducing the approximately 115 new students to each other. A series of boxing matches gave everyone a chance to cheer the winners and jeer the losers and, like it or not, Stan had to go through with his bout against Thomas Kilfoil. Tom was a street-wise kid from Vincennes, older than his opponent, and the fight did not go well for Stan.

The first year at Saint Meinrad's was one overwhelming event after another. The newcomers, mostly small-town boys, were as frightened and confused as Stan. They were "scoops" who were paddled and ordered around at any time at the will of any sneering upperclassman. Perhaps worst of all for an active teenager like Stan was being the last person served at the dinner table. Any older student could shout, "I will put on your plate what you will eat," and that determined how much the scoop would eat. The words were a command, not a suggestion.

The freshmen grudgingly accepted their humiliation, but how eagerly Stan and his classmates awaited their chance to dish out the punishment when at last they became seniors! However, it did not happen; by the time Stan entered his fourth year the school had eliminated hazing and he secretly was thankful.

Because Father Schaeffers was best but awkwardly described as a man with "...a smile happily coming from him all over", the students considered him a shelter in their stormy surroundings. He fascinated his young charges with stories about the American Indians, all drawn from the fiction of someone who had never visited the United States, the German author, Carl Mai. Father Schaeffers was short and heavy-set and Stan watched from the choir while the priest played the chapel organ with unrestrained energy. Bouncing and squirming at the keyboard the priest was like a jockey clutching an almost uncontrollable mount.

Father Schaeffers' appearance was less significant than his influence on Stan's career. It was he who suggested that Stan enter the Benedictine seminary at Saint Meinrad's. The subject arose without warning during a casual conversation when the priest, Stan and Ed Eder, who had joined his pal at the school, went out on a rainy afternoon to inspect a dam that had just been constructed. It was Good Friday, but even on that day they felt that it was important to find out whether the water level had risen sufficiently to pass over the spillway and form a new lake nearby.

As they sloshed through the mud on the way back to the school, everyone knew that complete silence was required that day. Yet Stan, not yet 16 years old, nevertheless spoke and revealed that the encouraging words of the Franciscan missionary in North Vernon about becoming a priest had hit their mark. "Well, after all the work that we have put in on this lake, I will hate to leave here," he said.

Father Schaeffers asked why his young friend felt compelled to leave. "When I'm ordained the bishop will surely want to send me to a parish somewhere," Stan replied. The priest in turn responded with two brief questions: "Why stay with the bishop? Why not join Saint Meinrad's Abbey?" Then they dropped the topic and resumed their silent walk. Nevertheless, the conversation had changed the direction of Stan's aspirations for a religious vocation.

Stan's plans for the future became uncertain just before Christmas in 1932. Father Stephen Thuis, O.S.B., the rector at Saint Meinrad's, told the student body that the Bishop of the Diocese of Indianapolis had telephoned and reported that the Diocese had gone bankrupt. It could no longer pay the tuition of its students who were attending the school. The announcement bewildered everyone and even worse was the instruction which followed: Stan and other students from that Diocese were told to gather their sports equipment, pack their trunks and prepare to leave permanently.

The tuition and board at St. Meinrad's were too much for the Maudlin family to pay. Stan's parents had moved to Indianapolis and opened a small restaurant close to a tool and dye plant, but they were barely making ends meet. That night as Stan lay on his bed pondering his fate, another boy shook him and said, "The rector wants to see you."

What did Father Thuis have in mind? Stan was apprehensive and then puzzled when the rector greeted him with a surprising statement: "I understand that you want to join Saint Meinrad's." Stan had never acknowledged an interest in entering the Benedictine order. His silence prompted the rector to qualify his first remark: "Well, Father Thomas Schaeffers told me that you probably want to join Saint Meinrad's."

More silence followed until Father Thuis got to the point and stated, "Therefore, you leave your clothing here, your books here, and you come back in January and continue and Saint Meinrad's Abbey will pay your tuition." Stan did not tell the rector, but he made up his mind to stay only because of his friendship with Father Schaeffers. The following summer Saint Meinrad's Abbey formally accepted Stan for training in the novitiate of the Benedictines under the tutelage of Father Henry Brenner, O. S. B.

Stan sized up Father Brenner pretty early. The monk was, according to Stan's diary, a man who "....simply exuded the peace and the freedom and the imperturbability of a Benedictine. A man for whom the gospel was indeed a revelation of redemption, not a burden of responsibility of - what other word can I use - but a burden, it was a freeing thing."

Hampered by such poor health that he could never take his meals with the students, Father Brenner nonetheless served as their novice master and protected them from duties that he felt were more than they could handle. The curriculum at Saint Meinrad's was rigid and even though Stan was a good pupil, he was inquisitive enough to be disappointed that the rules forbade the seminarians from learning about other authors and theological viewpoints beyond what the instructors taught. There were times when he wondered whether he truly had a religious vocation, especially if it meant that he must leave his family for good. Through it all there was one happy note: Tom Kilfoil and Stan became friends after realizing that they were among the few from an Irish background among a largely German-American student body.

Amid such uncertainty, four years of high school passed and Stan remained in school as most of the sophisticated boys dropped out. It was the "clodhoppers," as Stan called the sons of farmers, unpolished and seemingly untalented, who stuck it out until ordination and whom he recognized later as great servants of the Catholic Church.

Stan's life took a different direction during Lent, 1937. He was now a college student in his junior year at Saint Meinrad's and during the evening meal he was sitting with his friends in silence awaiting the customary prayer service. Someone tapped Stan on the shoulder and whispered, "The abbot wants to see you after supper." Again, a worry; had he done something wrong?

After everyone left the dining room, Stan nervously followed the abbot down the hallway. "I have been looking at your grades in college," the abbot said. "I would like to send you to Rome to get a degree in theology and sacred scripture. Tell your folks that you will be gone for about seven years."

Stan understood that his family probably could not afford to visit him in Rome and that he could not return to the United States until he had completed his training. The hard truth was that he would not see his father and mother and his brothers and sister for a long time. Still, he was happy about the opportunity that awaited him in Europe and he knew that his family was proud of him. When his departure date arrived on October 20, 1937, Stan's father asked two neighbors to drive everyone to the railroad station and see Stan off to Rome. The crowd that piled into the cars was filled with mixed emotions.

At the last minute Stan's father beckoned him back into their house. He closed the door and asked his son to kneel. Standing there silently Stan's father placed his hands on his son's head and prayed over him for a long time. "I am the oldest and he didn't know whether he'd ever see me again," Stan remembered. Drawing on that prayerful moment as an example, almost 60 years later Stan outlined the five important elements of how a father should bless his child.

The first part is a meaningful touch - holding hands, an embrace. "It is tender but it is strong. It is calm, but full of energy."

Second is the spoken message. A father's words come from his memory of the child, previously tiny and growing, now vigorous and full of promise. "Your words are not words strange and copied. They are prayed in the language of the family...`Daddy loves you!'"

Third - attach a special value to the one you are blessing. For example, "My girl, you have made us all so happy. Wherever you are and whatever you do, you will always be in our love."

The fourth dimension - the words of prayer should ask for a special future for the child. "My girl, my boy, I pray that you will always be healthy and happy and that you will always be a friend to everyone. I pray that your guardian angel will always protect you and bring you home safe to us."

The fifth point is forward looking. The parent makes an active commitment to assure that the blessing comes true. "The child who is blessed must know that daddy and mamma will never forsake him or her."

Dispatched by the special blessing from his beloved dad, Stan reached Rome safely and wrote that the atmosphere was "...like a hatch door being opened to the sky." The education at Benedictine Collegio di Saint Anselmo was liberating. His mind began to explore conflicting and challenging ideas about theology, a far cry from the one-book-per-class and recitations that he knew at Saint Meinrad's.

Unfortunately, he overdid it, forcing himself to spend night and day in the library. Nervous exhaustion and the Lenten fast caught up with Stan one afternoon in 1938. Other seminarians had taken the afternoon off to tour Rome, but he remained behind to study Hebrew. By the time the students assembled in the chapel at 5:30 P. M. Stan felt that the room had begun to whirl around him. He started to sweat heavily and his muscles began to quiver. Then he pulled himself to his feet and struggled into the garden where the fresh air provided some relief. The problem probably was associated with

Meniere's disease, an imbalance of the inner ear, which afflicted Stan several times throughout his life. Doctors told him later that there was no cure.

When the same symptoms overwhelmed him the following week, Stan felt himself under attack by an uncontrollable fear of crowded places, such as the stalls where the students knelt and prayed during religious services. "I was too stupid to know my limits," Stan explained in his diary. The solution, he decided, was to restrict himself to a rear seat in the church and the classrooms, and his friends could not understand why.

Ten years passed before Stan acknowledged that his trouble was he tried to do everything perfectly and that was impossible. The right doctor or counsellor might have helped him to relax, but the seminary in Rome offered no assistance. The puzzling illness, the first of several to beset Stan during his life, persisted into the fall of that year. At that point his Benedictine superiors said that he must return to the United States.

Away from the pressures of his studies, life was more enjoyable. Stan traveled to the Benedictine monastery in Einsiedeln, Switzerland and professed his religious vows as a sub-deacon. Fresh air and long quiet hours in the countryside did wonders. His health and state of mind began to improve noticeably, but not completely. Christmas in Rome was inspiring; amid clouds of incense Stan and other seminarians in the Benedictine choir sang while the abbot carried a statue of the Christ Child in a joyful procession.

The late 1930s was a turbulent period throughout Europe. The oppression of Adolph Hitler's Nazi regime reached everywhere and it finally touched Stan and two other seminarians when they were traveling by train in Germany. Several Nazi soldiers entered the railroad car and saw the students in their dark, full-length religious habits. The chance meeting triggered a barrage of insults about the United States.

Stan suppressed any German expressions that he may have heard at St. Meinrad's and simply pretended that he could not understand what the soldiers were saying. The tension eased when the conductor finally came to the rescue and hurried the three Benedictines away from the soldiers and into a car which was reserved for women and babies.

The plan to send Stan back to the United States accelerated after an urgent telephone call from the American Embassy in Rome in January, 1939. The message warned all Americans: Get out of Italy as soon as possible. Neighboring Germany is on the brink of war. Women and children had priority on the ships crossing the Atlantic Ocean so Stan's departure was postponed. Perhaps he secretly was pleased, for the delay allowed him to spend two weeks skiing at Einsiedeln and another week visiting Paris. Then, only about six months before World War II erupted, he arranged passage from LeHarve to the United States on the "Isle de France." Stan did not realize it, but he was en route to a career as a missionary to the American Indians.

Chapter Four - Sitting Bull and Father DeSmet

Stan returned to Saint Meinrad's early in 1939, but too late to join the classes in the spring semester. Perhaps that was fortuitous because he continued to suffer from periods of acute anxiety and couldn't concentrate on studying. His Benedictine superiors decided that instead of more studying the young man needed something physically vigorous, an environment in which he could regain his health, and what better activity than wrestling calves on a mission station out on the prairie! So they put Stan on a train bound for Chamberlain, South Dakota where he would continue on to the mission at Stephan.

Had Stan known about a circular that the Catholic Church distributed in France many years earlier he might not have been so eager to serve. The paper was intended to encourage missionaries to work in the United States, but it was hardly inviting. It read, "We offer you: No Salary; No Recompense; No Pensions; But Much Hard Work; A Poor Dwelling; Few Consolations; Many Disappointments; Frequent Sickness; A Violent or Lonely Death; An Unknown Grave…"

In heading westward from Indiana Stan followed in the footsteps of many missionaries, including the Benedictines, Jesuits and others, who traveled into the wilderness to carry the story of Jesus to the native Americans. The earliest arrived in the mid-17th century; they were Jesuit priests Claude Allouez, Pierre Marquette and other French clergy who brought a distinct French influence across the Canadian border into the American territory that is now Minnesota and the Dakotas. Four of those men became the first Catholic bishops in the region.

The experiences of these trailblazers formed the road map for those who followed. They ingratiated themselves with the native population by living among them, even amid the scorching heat, violent electrical storms and the chilling Alberta Clippers that howled in from northern Canada. The pioneering missionaries traveled with the Indians as they tracked the herds of buffalo. As a result these priests blended into the tribes and many Native Americans trusted them and gradually accepted their preaching about Catholicism.

The 19th and 20th century priests who served the Indians may have been guided by the spirit of an instruction that the Vatican issued in 1659 to missionaries who were traveling to China: "Do not draw invidious contrasts between your native people and those of Europe. Do your best to adapt yourselves to them."

Unfortunately, other white men, especially trappers and traders, introduced the Indians to firearms and liquor and the evils associated with them. Lawne Tatum, a Quaker who worked among the Native Americans in the 19th century, developed an opinion that "The Indians are largely what the white people have made them…They have learned and practiced many of the vices and few, if any, of the virtues of civilized nations." Such were the difficulties that faced the earliest representatives of the Church.

One of the greatest examples in the 19th century of missionary zeal, despite the hardships, was a Jesuit, Father Pierre Jean DeSmet. He was one of 15 children and although not very tall was so strong that his classmates at school in Belgium nicknamed him "Samson."

After Father DeSmet came to the western United States he experienced a calamity while riding his horse one day and his reaction revealed both his humility and sense of humor. He was trying to pass underneath the low-hanging branch of a tree, but it hooked his collar. The horse, however, continued under the tree and beyond it, leaving his rider swinging in mid-air. Father DeSmet wrested himself loose and wrote later, "A crushed and torn hat, an eye black and blue, two deep scratches on the cheek, would in a civilized country, have given me the impression of a bully issuing from the Black Forest rather than a missionary."

Beginning with his first trip up the Missouri River in 1840, Father DeSmet roamed the plains and waterways for several decades, traveling sometimes among the Yankton Sioux, Potawatomi, Pawnee, Blackfeet and other tribes, and accompanying local traders and soldiers, most of whom were Catholic. Shortly after arriving in the Dakotas he headed westward into uncharted territory on what would become an annual trek to the Flathead tribe in Oregon. Many Indians welcomed the foreign priest and smoked the calumet with him; in fact, on his first voyage up the Missouri River the Indians carried him into their village on a buffalo robe, an visible sign of their respect. His rapport with them was such that he baptized many Indians, 174 on one day and 160 on another.

Father DeSmet's writings contained a vivid example of the hardships that he and other early missionaries endured. It was part of his report of a visit with Pananniapapi, known as "Struck-by-the-Ree", the leader of the Yankton tribe. The chief had waited 22 years to be baptized and when the missionary visited him to administer the sacrament, Struck-by-the-Ree housed the priest in his "guest-lodge," hardly an inviting title for a rat-infested cellar built from timber and covered with earth.

After describing how he fought off nighttime attacks from the rodents, Father DeSmet wrote, "During this labor, I felt assailed by another enemy, the flea. If he is not so formidable as the rat, he is more importunate and he attaches himself to his prey in a most tenacious manner. Often one is deceived into the consoling belief that he has put his finger on him, but - `he is not there.' To be brief, I was awake and up all night, making play with my hands, fingers and nails to defend myself against the fleas, and their comrades in evil-doing, the mosquitos [sic], and bedbugs, the ants, the spiders, et omne genus muscarum. As you perceive, Father, all is not gold that glitters."

Tahun Sapa, called Yellow Hair, an Indian who claimed two wives, accepted Father DeSmet's preaching and was baptized. There were consequences to becoming a Catholic and he described them in a letter to Father DeSmet: "You have made me poor. I had two wives. Before you baptized me you told me to dismiss one. Now my arm is broken and I cannot split wood and I have no second wife to do the work and my only wife is sick, so you made me poor. But if you had told me to dismiss both, I would have done it, because I want to be on the road to the Great Spirit."

Storytellers passed along tales about Father DeSmet's prowess. When the Crow Indians began to doubt his powers their chief decided to confront their visitor in full view of the warriors. He ordered him to approach a buffalo bull and place his hands on top of the animal's head. Not only what the priest believed, but his courage as well were being put to a test. If he refused the challenge or the buffalo killed him the Indians would could safely assume that the priest did not represent any supernatural authority.

Father DeSmet had no alternative; he must accept the risk or otherwise lose credibility with the Crows. The Indians watched skeptically while the "Black-Robe" advanced toward the bull. As he reached the animal it lifted its shaggy head and fixed a glassy stare on the missionary and the cross that he was wearing. Transfixed by daylight shining off the cross, the buffalo stood motionless as the priest rested his hands on its head. For the Indians that was proof enough of the priest's God-given powers.

A missionary's life in the 19th century was lonely and very little of it was easy, as Father DeSmet recalled, "I spent three years without receiving a letter from anyone. Two years I was in the mountains without a roof or a bed; six months without a shirt on my back and for days and nights not a bite to eat."

Father DeSmet's reputation for hard work and persistence spread from the distant plains to Washington, D.C., where President Abraham Lincoln asked for his opinion about Indian affairs. The missionary's advice was frank and, speaking about the work of government officials, he wrote, "What is the reason that so many fine words and pompous promises come to nothing, nothing, nothing?" Because Father DeSmet was so beloved by the Native Americans, the federal government commissioned him to assist in negotiations with the tribes. Peace talks were successful in several instances and led to treaties which avoided a lengthy war at an estimated cost of $500,000,000. No wonder that Senator Thomas Benton, acknowledging the priest's relationship with the Indians, declared, "Father DeSmet can do more for the people of the United States than all the armies with flying banners."

Some time later several Indian leaders traveled to the nation's capital and asked President Ulysses Grant to encourage more Catholic priests to serve in the West. Sitting Bull, the famous chief of the Hunkpapa Sioux tribe, became so impressed with the zeal of the missionaries that he urged the President to authorize their work among the Indians. "My people, the Sioux nation, want a Catholic missionary. They are good men," he said. "They are the best servants of the Great Spirit. They know our people well. Let them be agents of the Great Father. They will serve him as well as they serve the Great Spirit."

In 1868 the Peace Commissioners in Washington appointed Father DeSmet to meet with the Sioux chieftains and try to settle their differences with the government. He surprised white men and Indians alike when he announced that, instead of inviting the Indians to visit him within the protecting walls of Fort Rice on the Missouri River, he would travel into Sioux territory to locate their camp.

While amazed at his courage, many whites doubted the Jesuit's prudence. They knew that Sitting Bull was attacking military forts and white people throughout the region and they were well aware how dangerous it was to venture very far beyond an Army post. His friends were worried, but Father DeSmet assured them that 1,000 children in Belgium were kneeling every day before the altar of the Blessed Virgin Mary and praying for his safety. "My intention is, if I can possibly effect it, to penetrate into the interior among the hostile bands. I know the dangers of such a trip. I have no motive other than the welfare of the Indians and will trust entirely on the kind providence of God," he wrote.

Father DeSmet departed from Fort Rice in a horse-drawn carriage with a large black crucifix attached to the dashboard and an escort of 80 friendly Sioux warriors. Accompanying them were Major Charles Galpin, an Indian trader, and his wife, a Hunkpapa Indian, who acted as an interpreter. They traveled across the plains for several days yet made no contact with their quarry. Nevertheless, word had reached Sitting Bull and other chiefs that Father DeSmet was en route to their campground near the junction of the Yellowstone and Powder Rivers. The Sioux leader sent a message, "Tell the Black-Robe we shall meet him and his friends with arms stretched out, ready to embrace him. Say to the Black-Robe . . . 'We have made room for you in our hearts. You shall have food and water and return with a glad heart. We wish to shake your hand and to hear your good words. Fear nothing.' "

Finally, about two weeks after the expedition left Fort Rice, a dozen of Sitting Bull's warriors were seen riding toward Father DeSmet's party. Were they hostile or friendly? When the priest heard them singing happy songs he knew the answer.

The Indian chief decided to ride out on the prairie to greet his guest. He and about 400 of his braves put on the most colorful apparel and war paints and galloped off toward Father DeSmet and his party. But as Sitting Bull came closer he noticed something which alarmed him. A large flag was unfurled in the Black Robe's party. Were the white men setting a trap? Sitting Bull had to know the answer, so he spurred his pony forward and then around the priest, his escort and this strange emblem.

On one side of the flag was an inscription that Sitting Bull did not understand. The writing contained the name of Jesus Christ. On the reverse side of the flag was a circle of golden stars around a picture of a woman, the Blessed Virgin Mary. Sitting Bull wondered whether this strange symbol was a flag of war. After examining it carefully he decided that it was not. Instead, the Indian leader interpreted the bright emblem as a sign of peace. It was safe for Sitting Bull to ride ahead and extend his hand to greet the Black-Robe.

Widespread singing ensued among the Indians and the magnitude of their greeting brought Father DeSmet to tears. However, the possibility that their visitor might be harmed still existed. Many Sioux hated white people because Indians whom they knew had been slain or wounded in battles. One chief in particular, White Gut, plotted to murder Father DeSmet.

Sitting Bull, however, was determined that no one would hurt his visitor and no one did. He dispersed the troublemakers and amid cheers and songs, the Black-Robe accompanied by Sitting Bull, Black Moon, Gall and Four Horses rode into the great camp of the Sioux, where no white man had dared appear for the last four years. Five thousand Indians had assembled and watched the Sioux leader escort Father DeSmet directly to the chief's own lodge.

In a huge amphitheater that the tribe had prepared specifically for the occasion, Father DeSmet planted his banner of the Blessed Virgin Mary and spoke to the huge crowd: "The flag which now stands in the center of this circle is the holy emblem of peace. But on this occasion I deem it most necessary and now will leave it in the hands of your chiefs that you may regard it as a token of my sincerity and good wishes for the welfare of the Sioux nation. I pray to God that you will look upon it as a blessing to your tribe. It is to Him that you must look for all blessings and from Him all blessings flow."

The Jesuit continued, "This cruel and unfortunate bloodshed must be stopped . . . I now in the name of the Great Spirit and in the name of all that is holy and good do here in the presence of your chiefs and braves and of you all who are assembled to meet me, beseech you most solemnly, one and all, to bury all your bitterness toward the whites, forget the past, and accept the hand of peace which is extended to you."

Sitting Bull responded, admitting that the sight of the unknown banner far off on the plains had worried him, and added, "Father, you pray to the Great Spirit for us. I thank you. I have often besought the kindness of the Great Spirit, but never have I done so more earnestly than today, that our words may be heard above and all over the earth….Welcome, Father - the messenger of peace. I hope quiet will again be restored to our country."

Father DeSmet stayed barely a couple of days, just long enough to present to Sitting Bull a crucifix made of brass and wood and to teach the Indians some colorful accounts from the Bible, such as the stories of Daniel in the lions' den, the raising of Lazarus from the dead, and the crucifixion and resurrection of Jesus. The good will that arose from his visit resulted in the Treaty of Laramie, which the Peace Commissioners and representatives of Sitting Bull signed only two weeks after Father DeSmet departed from the Sioux camp. The Treaty created the Great Sioux Reservation, which included the Dakota Territory west of the Missouri River.

Sitting Bull remained a warrior for several years but after meeting Father DeSmet he changed his attitude about white people. In the past the Indian leader had sworn to kill the next white man whom he encountered, but when he watched the Catholic priest walking among a multitude of fierce warriors the Indian leader stated that he never had met a braver person.

The Sioux leader understood that the Catholic Church represented something that his people needed, namely, education. He told the Indian students in the mission school on the Standing Rock Reservation, "I am glad that the Winyan Wakanpi (nuns) are teaching you and the Sinasapa (priests) are helping, too. I saw these white faces. They have a spirit that is very powerful and mysterious. I want the sisters to tell you about it."

As for Father DeSmet, even though he was a man who once dined with the French, Spanish, Russian and Belgian ambassadors on the same evening, he admitted that he was comfortable among the Indians. "I did the best I could among the great personages, but I remain of the opinion that I shall always be more at my ease sitting on the grass and surrounded by savages, each making his jokes and at the same time eating with good appetite a fair rib or roasting a piece of buffalo or fat dog," said Father DeSmet.

It is easy to appreciate the lasting influence that Father DeSmet had on the plains Indians and the missionaries who followed him. An historian, Stanley Vestel, wrote, "He was affable, even-tempered, laughter-loving and without any of that lust for unnecessary martyrdom which so often interfered with the success of Jesuit missionaries. For many years this saintly man longed to found a mission for the Sioux and had visited them wherever he could. No man in North America had more influence with them than he did."

Chapter Five - Leading Toward Ordination

Barely a generation after Father DeSmet began to inspire the Indians another missionary, Bishop Martin Marty, O.S.B. led many German-born Benedictine monks to establish mission churches in the United States. Although decades apart, the careers of the Bishop and Stan were nevertheless linked, for the novice missionary spent his first night in the Dakotas in the mission where Bishop Marty had worked many years earlier.

Life, albeit existence, was far less comfortable for Bishop Marty when he arrived at Standing Rock Reservation in 1876. His quarters were so cold that while a fire burned at the rear of a stove a pan of water froze at the other end. Sometimes he said Mass underneath an umbrella which deflected rain coming through the roof of his log cabin.

Such discomforts, however, did not deter the Bishop from carrying the word of the Lord to the Indians. Matters were stressful when Bishop Marty began his work. It was a dangerous period, barely two months after Sioux warriors under Sitting Bull's leadership had wiped out Colonel George Custer and his troops at the Battle of Little Bighorn. Chief Kills Eagle was eager to follow up the Indian victory by attacking Fort Yates and the Army was poised for revenge. The Bishop averted a bloody clash when he rode out to meet an advancing war party and convinced the Indians to lay down their arms.

The first Benedictine in the Dakotas, Bishop Marty established mission schools at the Standing Rock and Devil's Lake Reservations. The Catholic Church provided the land for a building and the students ate food which they grew themselves, an accomplishment which not only fed them, but perhaps boosted their self-esteem.

When Sitting Bull met Bishop Marty he praised the benevolence of the Church and its representatives. The Indian leader assured the Bishop, "You come from America, indeed, but you are a priest and as such you are welcome. The priest does nobody any harm; we will give you food and protection and will listen to your words." The Indians used a descriptive expression to describe Bishop Marty: "He did not bend the grass when he walked." It showed how much they admired this dedicated man.

The word of God was powerful, but sometimes the Indians accepted religion for reasons that were more practical than spiritual. Stan learned that lesson in his early days on the reservations. He asked why they became Catholic and some replied that they would "go in that little house over there and they would get some water poured over them and they would be given food, beans and salt pork and flour. So grandpa would say, `Let's go over and get some of that, too, and then we'll get some more beans and salt pork and flour, absolutely.'" Once a particular religion became more popular on a reservation - for whatever reason - it attracted more and more Indians who reasoned that God must be affiliated with that specific faith.

At the beginning of his training in the Dakotas Stan started preaching in church, but under a tight rein. That was what Father Baumeister, S.C.J., Stan's mentor, wanted. He spoke English poorly and therefore he allowed his protege to deliver the sermons at Mass. However, this "old school" pastor set the ground rules. In deference to typical European customs he insisted that his young assistant speak from outside the communion rail which was below the altar because he had not yet been ordained a priest.

During 1939 and 1940 Stan learned the meaning of the ancient Benedictine motto "Ora et Labora" (in English, "pray and work"), laboring during the summer on the Yankton Reservation at the mission named after Bishop Marty and studying and teaching at Saint Meinrad's Abbey the rest of the time. The work was physically demanding, one sweaty day after another of hauling loads of coal over the muddy gravel roads leading to the Marty mission and weeks of helping the teachers and the students to construct a school there.

Father Sylvester Eisenman, O.S.B., not only built the school at Marty, but also remained in charge. Serving as principal, counsellor and foreman for 750 Indian students required a disciplined person and he was it. Father Eisenman succinctly described the goal of the nine priests and other missionaries with whom he worked: "We Benedictines on the reservations are working to put ourselves out of a job. We are working to give to you students the skills, the wisdom, the tools by which you can control all of the influences that impinge on your life."

Each day's tasks began at breakfast when Father Eisenman, issuing orders in his authoritative style, recited the work assignments to be performed that day by the staff and students. Their daily schedule was split almost equally between physical labor and vocational training. There wasn't much room for originality, but Stan managed to introduce something new and different when he taught the Indian nuns to sing the Gregorian chant during Mass in their chapel.

In the summer of 1939 Stan played an unintended starring role in an administrative faux pas. Still a seminarian, his job was to drive the Benedictine Abbot Ignatius on an official visit to Saint Michael's Mission. Such appearances displayed all the pomp and ceremony of an entrance by the king himself. The sequence of preparations included a telephone call to alert the host school or church about 15 minutes before the dignitary was scheduled to arrive. That was time enough to line up the children, position the banners and strike up the band.

All that had been completed when Stan, chauffeuring the Abbot's shiny blue Cord car, pulled up in front of the pastor, Father Alfred Baltz, O.S.B., dozens of dancing, clapping children, and Father Alfred's three goats. The goats supplied the milk that the pastor believed soothed his ailing stomach. Stan jumped out and rushed to open the door of the car for the grand exit by the Abbot.

At that regal instant the goats surged forward and leaped onto the front fender. Before anyone could intervene or even shout they were up on the hood and then like tiny reindeer on to the roof of the Abbot's prized automobile. The Abbot was a precise and quite proper man and the look of irritation that spread across his face and then focused on Father Alfred was almost beyond description. A broom stood outside the door to the pastor's house and with one swipe it flung the goats back to the ground. Handerkerchiefs appeared immediately to erase the tiny hoof marks from the Abbot's car, but it was already too late to preserve the dignity of the occasion.

Those summers of 1939 and 1940 were Stan's first exposure to how missionaries, both priests and sisters, administered mission parishes and boarding schools for Indian children. They were strict, but usually loving persons and when the abbot appointed Stan the superintendent of a school years later, his experiences at the Marty Mission proved invaluable.

On May 26, 1942 with Stan's parents present observing an ancient ceremony which took three hours Right Reverend Bishop Elmer Ritter ordained some 30 new priests, including Father Stanislaus Maudlin, O. S. B. At his first Mass he remembered Moses Gumbel, the store owner who had outfitted him for his first trip to St. Meinrad's. He was Reverend Maudlin, but from then on until early in the 21st century everyone called him by his informal title, Father Stan. The next year his superiors sent him on his first permanent assignment: to live in Belcourt, North Dakota and to minister to the Chippewa Sioux on the Turtle Mountain Reservation.

A Blackrobe among the Indians

Chapter Six - In the Turtle Mountains

Native Americans revere the Turtle Mountains as a sacred place. Hundreds of years ago as the Indians struggled to understand God and the puzzle of creation a legend developed about how those mountains originated from a turtle, whom the Indians believed was the savior of mankind.

As the story goes, the turtle rose out of the water, bringing the human race up from the depths. A muskrat deposited a small amount of soil on the turtle's back and the soil multiplied to form the mountains, which the Indians still honor as holy ground. A whirlwind arrived from God, the legend continued, and created a spring in the Turtle Mountains. A long serpent, which represented evil, lived under the ground near the spring, but the whirlwind sucked it out of the soil and hurled it away. Water bubbled up, pleasant to drink and full of healing properties, and that spot on the Reservation became recognized as a holy spring.

To many Native Americans the soil was Mother Earth and all new creation came from Mother Earth. Father Stan realized how deep was this idea when he and an old Indian man were driving toward the Black Hills. They traveled for many miles and no one spoke until they approached a large field on the side of the road. Out in the middle a tractor dragged a piece of heavy equipment that turned over the soil. Clouds of dust arose and swirled off to the east. The Indian murmured something that his companion did not understand so Father Stan asked him to repeat it. "That's not right. No man should scratch his mother's face that way," the man said.

The conversation reminded Father Stan how the Native Americans honor "Mother Earth." Often as he watched a woman prepare soup or stew he noticed that the cook walked to the back door and threw a spoonful on the ground outside, which was their way of thanking God for the meal.

Even as the middle of the 20th century approached, many of the Indians in the Turtle Mountains lived in humble and crude surroundings, often one or two room log cabins. When a family was building a cabin the boys cut the logs and their sisters forced mud between the pieces of wood. It hardened and protected them from the piercing winds of winter. Tar paper and sod covered the roof.

The inside of their little buildings usually were more cold than comfortable; when the logs began to snap and creak during the night they knew that the temperature outside had dropped to 30 or 40 degrees below zero. If more firewood was needed, an axe stood outside each entrance to the cabin. Out in the bush running water came from a spring and smoke floating up from kitchen stoves instead of telephones invited neighbors to join them for a meal.

Another missionary, a contemporary of Father Stan, captured the difficulties of everyday living on the plains when he wrote, "In winter there are the inevitable blizzards with their forever raging winds that rip at the roof and windows and doors, disrupting travel and mail and telephone service and electricity for days at a time and settling through the buildings with sifted snow. I don't know how many times I have had to shovel out my house and churches and dry out my vestments and clothes and books and papers, wipe off the altars and statues and wash the snow stained linens. Not much is ruined that cannot be salvaged, save the damage to the buildings themselves; since some of the snow in the attic is impossible to reach it gradually melts and rots their ceilings and walls.

"At the Indian Mission, for instance, the wallboard in both the church and the hall is in hazardous shape. At my other white parish in Naper, Nebraska, in the Archdiocese of Omaha, the walls in the church are covered with tin, so it's not so bad, it just creaks and squeaks in a high wind; but here in Herrick we have plaster — since I have been here much of the plaster has fallen and I have had to patch it several times.

"I have repainted the sanctuary twice and much of the paint has again peeled away. It is almost impossible to caulk all the cracks and holes, as I have tried to do, and a prohibitive cost to replace the doors, since they won't stay shut any more, and the windows, since the frames are rotted, too — within the last few weeks two of them blew out completely and I have cardboard in them now."

Father Stan understood what it was like to survive in this climate because he and the other priests in Belcourt lived in a log cabin with four rooms. Yet he preferred to call the atmosphere "cozy." Others might suppose that with their dirt floors these little buildings and their occupants were dirty, but early explorers claimed that they were the cleanest persons they ever met.

"It didn't take long after coming to a reservation that you realize that you are in a different world," Father Stan wrote. "You are in a world of spirits, a world of generations, a world that thinks back on the past and feels responsible for the future. You live in a world of the ancestors and a world of children." The lifestyle of the Native Americans might be different, but monks were still monks and they wore their Roman collars when they taught in public schools and put on their robes when they got behind the wheel of a school bus.

Father Hildebrand Elliot, O.S.B., who had preceded Father Stan at Saint Ann's Church in Belcourt, lived in the same wooden house with his new helper. It was a quiet place because Father Elliot was not a garrulous person and limited his efforts to raising money, saying Mass and hearing some confessions. The heaviest work fell on the shoulders of his young assistant, who nevertheless felt that the mere presence of a veteran priest such as Father Elliot showed the commitment which the Benedictine community had made to the parishioners.

Just about every other task which a missionary performed - driving the school bus, nighttime sick calls, everything from baptisms to funerals and any activity involving children - became Father Stan's responsibility. He grew to recognize the meaning of a tap or two on the front door a day or two before Ash Wednesday. It meant that someone had arrived and wanted the priest to administer the pledge: "I will not drink alcohol during Lent." The moment was sacred - a man had given his word!

Soon after he arrived at St. Ann's, Father Stan decided that the parish needed a cemetery. He recruited some teenage workers and, although the boys eventually completed the job, they also took time off to search for wild strawberries, pecans and bee hives. Working up to 16 hours a day at jobs such as that proved to be exhausting. Desperate for some peace and quiet, one day Father Stan broke into the priests' house at another parish to escape from 40 energetic Boy Scouts with whom he had been camping at Lake Ypsilon. Another time the priest led some children on an armed invasion of Canada. They tramped through the bush on a hunting trip and unwittingly crossed the border. The Canadian authorities understood their mistake and after some shouting shooed everyone back into the United States.

Now that Father Stan lived among the Indians, he had to learn to communicate with various tribes. That meant studying a new language, Mitef, because the Chippewa people in North Dakota did not speak the same words as the Sioux in Marty. As Father Stan began to minister to the people on the Turtle Mountain Reservation, he found out that a young couple did not even arrange their own wedding. Their parents made most of the decisions and the local priest got involved, too - he selected the date for the ceremony.

In those years, the early 1940s, the Indians had long since ceased to hunt buffalo. Instead, in the fall of each year entire families toiled in the potato fields to earn their living, with the result that during those months the school buses traveled back and forth almost empty. Some Indians performed different work, peeling bark from cranberry trees. After they dried the bark Louis Marion brought a load to Rolla where freight trains carried it out of the Turtle Mountains to the Lydia Pinkham plant. The bark then was treated and sold as a popular natural medicine for women. During the colder months, the men in Belcourt cut "bam" trees into firewood or fence posts and the sound of sleigh runners squeaking in the snow became commonplace as the logs were hauled away. But too much of the work available for Indians was plain drudgery and some became disillusioned.

A slogan passed around the reservations: "Go on Relocation! Get out of Belcourt. There's no future here." All the Indians knew what it meant: Cities such as Oakland and Denver offered prospects for a better life and many families boarded the trains at Rugby and headed westward. However, the grass was not greener in these strange places and within three or four months Father Stan saw a surprising number filtering back to a familiar way of life on the reservations. People called this phenomenon "returning to the blanket," the Indian notion of safety and identity. Consoling these discouraged families added another task to the missionary's job.

Soon after he transferred to Belcourt Father Stan noticed how few persons attended weddings, often just the bride and groom and their witnesses. The family and friends remained outside the church, having decided that they were too poorly dressed to enter. The missionary felt that this attitude must change so he addressed some schoolgirls and said, "Gee, girls, when you get married, let's just have a great big celebration."

What Father Stan didn't know was that after the ceremony in the church the great big celebration did take place back on the reservation. Curious, he followed the wedding party a few times as the couple returned to the bride or groom's home. Each time when he was about two miles from the house, two men stepped out of the bush and fired shotguns into the air. Boom, Boom, Boom!

Further along the road, more men appeared and shot their weapons to signal that the newlyweds would soon arrive. When they did all the people who felt too poorly dressed to attend the church were singing, dancing and ready to swing the bride around. The celebration was underway! Thereafter, Father Stan encouraged more people to attend church weddings, even if they weren't well dressed. It took seven years of continual persuasion before the attendance increased significantly.

In the beginning of his work at Turtle Mountain Father Stan was unaware of the rivalries among native tribes. The Indians in the Belcourt area were different and sometimes hostile to those in South Dakota. However, the naive and self-assured missionary felt that he could communicate with Indians everywhere, but he failed to understand that different tribes spoke in different languages and had different sensitivities. One day he began talking in the Dakota dialect to a group of local men who were standing outside Mr. Mosse's Big Store in Belcourt. He didn't realize that their language was Mitef. As they listened their eyes widened, then grins spread over their faces. Finally Joe Monett warned, "Father, careful now, you're speaking our enemy's talk."

One of the first lessons that Father Stan learned was that it was not always practical to follow the regulations that were taught in the seminary. One of them was that a monk should never be alone with a woman. Father Stan watched Stella Fredrick, young and attractive, emerge from The Big Store in Belcourt. Her arms were filled with bundles and she approached him and asked for a ride home.

A rule's a rule and Father Stan explained as tactfully as he could that he was not allowed to make an exception. "What do you think I am, some woman for the road?" a visibly angry Stella responded as she trudged homeward over the hill. About a week later as he drove along Jackrabbit Trail an old lady appeared on the road ahead. She, too, was burdened with groceries.

Father Stan did not offer her a ride either - until he had traveled about 30 yards past her and applied the brakes. His conscience abruptly suppressed the rule about women and monks. He pushed his gears in reverse and helped the woman into his car. In cases of need he recognized that what he had been taught at Saint Meinrad's no longer applied. Years later, when Stella was dying of lung cancer, she managed a laugh when Father Stan remembered their encounter near The Big Store.

Father Stan usually met people in more cordial circumstances. Among those he befriended on the Turtle Mountain Reservation was a ninth-grade lad named Alec. A skinny boy, Alec had a poor self-image. "I would see him creeping along as if he was just waiting for the next lash," the priest recalled.

Alec's life needed a lift. One afternoon while the students were waiting for their school buses, Father Stan caught the boy's attention: "I kind of banged him against the wall." Would Alec like to go swimming some time? Startled, but flattered, he readily agreed. It was up to him to pick a day for their outing. Alec chose a Sunday in the summertime, a date which could not have been more inconvenient for Father Stan.

At that time in the 1940s a priest could not eat or drink until he had finished celebrating his Masses for the day. Father Stan's normal Sunday routine began before 6:30 a. m. and after his last

Mass ended about 12:30 p. m. he dropped into the nearest chair in the priests' house. At that point all he wanted was a bowl of soup and a nap.

There was no opportunity to rest that Sunday afternoon. The doorbell rang and when Father Stan looked out the window he saw a Model A Ford car with its motor running and a grinning Alec at the wheel. "Smile, darn it," the priest thought to himself. When the boy asked if his newfound friend was ready to go swimming Father Stan stifled a groan. "Once in a while I guess you gotta lie, so I said `Yah.' I no more wanted to go swimming then jump off a skyscraper," he said.

Off they went, driving through Belcourt and past the high school, Alec waving joyfully to his neighbors. His whole attitude shouted, "Look at me! See who I brought along!"

But as they reached a crossroad Alec jammed on the brakes.

"Look, Father! The loup gouroo!" the boy cried. (In Indian lore, as Father Stan explained to many audiences, the loup gouroo is the spirit wolf or the helper wolf.) The priest scanned the neighborhood, but saw no wolf.

"We gotta stop," Alec said. This time Father Stan looked more carefully and still saw no animal or spirit of any kind. Perhaps the boy was so excited that his imagination was playing tricks on him.

"Father, we gotta go back," a determined Alec exclaimed. Without any idea why they were reversing their course, Father Stan agreed, "You're driving. Let's go!"

Alec spun the Ford around and headed for South Belcourt, the poorest section of town. The boy and his mother lived there in a tiny log cabin with a tin stove pipe sticking up through the tar paper roof. As Father Stan and his frantic companion pulled to a stop at the entrance to the house, smoke already was curling out between the logs.

Although the building was ablaze they managed to kick open the front door and saw Alec's mother on the floor. Reaching in among the ash and flames, the boy grabbed the hem of her dress and dragged her outside. The woman's long high-collared dress was scorched, but it may have saved her life. Prayers and Alec's kisses revived his mother and she opened her eyes just as the roof caved in.

"Father, didn't you see the loup gouroo?" Alec asked moments later, somewhat disappointedly. Did an invisible animal signal Alec to rush home to rescue his mom? Did he really see a wolf? Was some spiritual power at work? Priests are supposed to have the answers, but Father Stan could not explain that one. He could only admit that he had not seen the phantom wolf.

"I remember the first kind of dumb thing I did when I was at Saint Ann's. But it sounded like a good idea and I had long ago felt that a good idea should be given a chance," Father Stan wrote about his experiences in Belcourt. So he said `Yes' when Ben LaJimodiere, the night watchman for the local community, approached him about the Boy Scouts. "Father, I'm too old now to keep it up and you are young. So, I've decided that from now on you are the Scoutmaster," Ben announced.

Tying knots, finding the Big Dipper, building a fire in the bush were not in Father Stan's inventory of talents. He had never been a Boy Scout. His only source of guidance was the Scouting handbook and with that and youthful energy he tried to stay ahead of his troop of about 25 eager boys.

The first test of his leadership as Scoutmaster was closer to a disaster than a success. He led his troop on a camping trip to Gordon Lake. The Scouts were supposed to dig drainage ditches and put up their tents, but they ignored instructions and instead ran off for a swim. Mealtime came and the boys ate all the food that Father Stan had brought in his pick-up truck. As the evening fire flickered out they were still eating and nothing remained for breakfast. When at last all of his Troop fell asleep, he knew that they would be hungry as soon as they awoke and they expected him to feed them. His only choice was to drive back to Belcourt and load up more food. The reward for becoming a faithful Scoutmaster was a big bill at the grocery store.

A day with the exuberant Scouts was full of surprises and it prepared Father Stan for the uncertainties of other events at Saint Ann's Parish. One of biggest was the annual picnic. Some of the activities took place in the church itself and Father Stan was assisting in his first post-picnic clean-up in 1943 when Mrs. Fred Davis approached him to warn that a fierce wind was coming in from the west.

Indeed it was; there was barely time to hustle the children out of the building and into a storm shelter. A devastating blow shredded the siding and strained the rafters and the studs which held the structure together. Hail pounded everything and the wind tore openings in the roof. Water piled up two inches deep inside the church and even though it all swished out after Father Stan drilled holes in the floor, the damage was done. When he walked outside he saw how personal the storm's havoc had been - the hail stones had smashed the hood of his car almost level with the engine. Such was his introduction to the annual summer fun picnic at Saint Ann's and the rage of a summer storm.

Chapter Seven - Coaching a Basketball Team

Heading out on a nighttime sick call in the dead of winter sometimes meant following a trail through the woods. Scary sometimes, it was a job that a priest had to do. When Indians became ill and feared that death was approaching they preferred to die at home among their family and friends. To them, especially the older men and women, the hospital was a foreign place, cold and unfriendly. At times like those it meant that the priest had to travel into the bush and out onto the reservation to anoint a sick Indian.

Arranging for the last rites of the Church in the middle of the night was easier said than done. A relative of whomever was ill had to run to the Great Walker or Roussin school where the government telephone line was located. A call was made to the hospital and a nurse there then put in another call to summon Father Stan at Saint Ann's rectory.

The message might be "Father Stan, so-and-so's grandma is dying. Hurry up and come to such and such a place. We'll meet you with a sleigh or a Model A or a horse." However varied the instructions, he became accustomed to being awakened at 2 A. M., slipping pants over his pajamas, bringing gloves and overshoes and setting out with Holy Communion to find a trail through the brush.

After midnight one winter evening the hospital reported that Mrs. Allery was dying in a log house west of Bongie's Corner. The nurse had said, "Father, when you come to a white rag tied to a tree, you'll have to leave your car and walk down toward the lake. It won't be too far. You'll find the house because it's the only one there."

Moonlight filtered through the trees as Father Stan groped through the woods. He tried to suppress an eerie feeling. On other nights he had listened to coyotes gathered near the lake. Were strange eyes watching from the darkness? The packed snow crunched beneath his feet, but he heard another sound - a constant scratching - that frightened him.

Father Stan was certain that a menace of some sort was tracking him. Pretty soon his imagination overwhelmed him; he sensed the hot breath of a wolf at his shoulder. It was time to turn and defend himself. As the priest wheeled around to his left and brought his gloved hands up to fight, the attacker lay at his feet, unmoving. As his feet shuffled, so did his foe - a big and brittle leaf from a bam tree which had attached itself to his boot. Father Stan finally relaxed and ahead saw the kerosene lamp shining in the window of Mrs. Allery's cabin.

He was never sure whether his visit helped a sick person return to good health. A woman with a severe heart condition needed his prayers one night. He visited, administered the last rites and returned the next morning to find her alone, hunched over a wash board and laundering her clothes. "Oh, Father, I'm okay now," she declared merrily. "You blessed me. That's all I needed."

The whole setting of those nighttime sick calls enthralled a young missionary: the rattle of the horse's harness while they sped between the trees, the crack of the whip, the swish of the sleigh gliding over the snow, a big moon above a landscape held rigid at 30 degrees below zero. At last in the darkness ahead there was a light in the window of a little log house, a door opened and the sick man's family greeted him. "Father is here," the word passed softly from one worried face to another. Prayers, cigarettes glowing in the dark, a long and quiet visit, a calming time. For Father Stan it was a rewarding part of the occasion.

On winter nights he sometimes sat in the hospital with the old folks, playing cards or telling stories. One prairie tale told how Father Ouellette received a telephone message on an early spring night: go out to a family north and west of Fish Lake, where the grandfather was dying. The priest had a fast little mare and a buggy, but he was not sure that he could see the trail in the dark. Judge Diam Frederick agreed to help. He took the reins while Father Ouellette prayed and clutched the little vessel which held the Holy Communion. When they reached the edge of Fish Lake the horse stopped abruptly - it would not walk onto the ice. The judge looked left and right, but there was no other passage to the far shore. "It's okay, my girl," the priest whispered to the mare. "The ice will hold you. I've got the Communion with us and it's all right."

Judge Frederick slapped the reins and ever so cautiously the horse stepped onto the frozen surface and while the two passengers held their breath walked slowly several hundred yards across the ice. Father Ouellette stayed with the grandfather until he died. It was sunrise when the priest and his friend headed back and reached the edge of the Lake. Where there had been ice strong enough to hold a horse and loaded buggy three hours earlier there was clear water and waves lapping at the shore. Who could explain how the ice that was there when needed had disappeared so quickly!

Some stories defy explanation, such as the rescue of Father George Pinger, S.C.J. after he was trapped in a snowstorm. He told Father Stan that he had left the highway and was driving across the open prairie trying to avoid the foul weather when the fan belt broke and he had to abandon his car. With no alternative but to walk, he set out through the snowdrifts.

The struggle proved too much. Fatigue set in and he was about to collapse when, according to Father Pinger, "first, sparrows led me. They flew so close to my head it was as if they were saying `stay with us' and I did. Then there was a magpie. It flopped on the ground right in front of me and I tried to keep up with it. Then there was a coyote. He didn't bite me, but he rubbed against my leg and pushed. Then I fell down and wanted to sleep.

"But I heard a noise. It was a car. The coyote had led me to a road and the people in the car found me. I have to thank the animals that God sent to guide me." The ordeal ended in the hospital where the priest lost several frostbitten toes.

Not long after Father Stan arrived in Belcourt he found himself face to face with a far different challenge. Everyone knew that he came from Indiana and that the Hoosier State had a reputation for basketball. People automatically thought that he should be a coach. What they did not know was that Father Stan's most recent coaching experience consisted of guiding his team to a one-point win over Pierre Indian School in 1940 after a one-point loss the previous year.

The first surprise was that the kids at Saint Ann's School had never played basketball. "That's like not being baptized," Father Stan announced and the new coach began to organize a team. The boys had no uniforms, no sneakers, only one basketball and a tough Hoosier taskmaster for their coach. "Harder, harder!", their mentor demanded during practices until finally one of his players, Beef DeCouteau, with tears in his eyes, erupted, "Damn it, Father, we're doing our best." After that he eased up, shouting less and listening more. Yelling was not necessary; his players obeyed his instructions not just because he was a coach, but also because he was their priest.

Word spread around Belcourt that Father Stan knew the game. It was early in the 1940s and many local men had left to join the military services. The public school officials needed him to teach English and coach their team. There was a caveat to the plan; the superintendent said, "Father, we can't pay you. You got that collar on, see…we can't pay priests. Sorry." Father Stan agreed to help out anyway.

Billy LaVerdure was on the basketball squad at St. Ann's School. A bright-eyed seventh grader, he was always looking up at you and grinning, said Father Stan. After the season ended the coach assembled his players once a month to see a movie. As Billy and his buddies, Herman Marion and Joe Dionne, joined a group of boys heading toward the gym to watch the film Billy surprised Father Stan.

"Father, I wanna go home."

"Go home? My gosh, I got a film and you guys want to take off! What is the matter?"

Billy didn't have a chance to answer; one of the other boys piped up, "Well, Billy dreamt last night that his mare had a colt, Father, and the colt has a white star on his head and a left white front foot."

Had a colt been born? Billy had to go home and find out. Nothing could be as important as his dream. Disappointed, but unwilling to quash Billy's hopes, Father Stan released the three boys. "Okay, tell your mom that I said it was okay to come home from school early," the priest instructed his young friend. The remaining kids forgot about Billy and his pals; they enjoyed the show and then Father Stan drove them home. Barely two hours later, as he was putting the school bus back into the garage a model T Ford sped up the hill. Billy's father jumped out of the car, solemnly lifting off his cap as he hurried toward the priest.

"Father, quick, quick, go out to my place."

The story tumbled out in a burst of words. Billy and his friends had indeed returned home. Before checking on the mare Billy asked his mom if they could take the .22 caliber rifle and she refused emphatically. The boys found that the star-marked colt had not been born so, with Billy's dream on hold, they huddled together near a log barn, sitting and talking.

They had overshoes, one pair for three boys, but by throwing the shoes back and forth over the puddles, they had avoided getting their feet wet. Billy's mom didn't know it, but the boys also had the rifle.

As Joe pulled on the overshoes, Herman, called "Dummy" by everyone, took the gun and began cleaning it. Billy was close by. Somehow the rifle fired. The bullet struck Billy and he slumped on the wet grass. When Billy's father reached Father Stan, the priest asked if he had summoned a doctor. "No, Father, the heck with the doctor, go, we want the religion first."

By the time Father Stan drove up to the LaVerdure home, Billy's mom had placed a blanket over her son, now lying face down on the grass. The covering was wet from a spring rain and discolored by Billy's blood. It was too late for a doctor. Father Stan turned the body over and there was one final spurt of Billy's blood as the priest administered a final blessing.

Amid the turmoil and the arrival of a small crowd, no one had paid much attention to Dummy. ("By the way everyone has nicknames up there, that doesn't mean anything," Father Stan explained later. "It's just a nickname.") The boy was thrashing around, groaning, his face covered with the wetness and the coloration of the crushed grass.

There was overwhelming distress in Dummy's mind, Father Stan was sure of that, and even more anguish on Delima LaVerdure's face as she folded her hands and stared down at the body of her dead son. In her agony could Billy's mother console the boy who had just killed her son? The priest knew that he must ask. He walked over to the distraught woman, embraced her and pleaded, "Delima, would you please tell Dummy that you're not mad at him?"

"Father, I already tried," she said. "I went over to him twice and tried to tell him that they are all friends and things like this happen. That poor boy. Father, tell him we aren't mad, these things happen. Father, tell him now. Please, Father, don't let him cry like that." "Lead me, Saint Ann," Father Stan implored silently as he approached Dummy.

Another car pulled up while Father Stan was speaking to the boy. Out stepped the sheriff, chomping on his cigar and striding straight for Dummy. Grabbing him at the back of the neck, the officer lifted the boy off the ground, shouting, "I'm going to get to the bottom of this, you guys fighting this way. Why did you kill that boy? You're going with me!"

The crowd cringed; why didn't the sheriff understand! But Delima LaVerdure refused to let a horrible situation become worse. A trim woman of barely 100 pounds, she faced the hefty officer, nose to nose, and halted his advance. "Don't you touch him. He's my boy's friend," she said. "You get off my land. I didn't ask you here. Get back where you belong."

For three days Billy's coffin, covered with cheesecloth, rested in the little house where he had lived with his family. Neighbors came, Father Stan among them, to express their sympathy. He sat near one of the windows and could hear children playing close to the house.

A shadow, then a smaller one, passed through the open window into the room. Turning, the priest looked outside and saw the mare and nearby a little colt, with a white star on its face and a white mark on its front foot. From then on everyone could remember Billy. The children could ride his colt, feed it, play with it. Billy's dream lived on.

Father Stan called his Saint Ann's basketball team the Eagles. Perhaps he chose the nickname because he was Eagle Man to Unci and the Yankton Sioux. However, the players could not fly to their opponent's gym and often had to travel 50 miles on the road. Somehow Father Stan packed ten boys into his car and off they went, in snow or sunshine. That's when the adventures began. One December day they started a trip toward Dunseith Indian School. As a big V-snow plow approached at high speed, Father Stan maneuvered off to the side of the road. But not far enough, because the plow struck not snow but gravel and hurled it toward the windshield of his car.

The windshield shattered and threw bits of glass and snow over everyone in the front seat. One of the boys wondered whether the team would continue and play the game or return to Belcourt. "Just sit down, Chuckie, and all you guys," the determined priest said. "We're going to play a basketball game." It was an unimaginably cold drive but the Eagles had no intention of turning around.

Another time the team finished a game in Rolla only to walk outside and discover that a blizzard had engulfed the little town. Father Stan could hardly see across the street. He was not sure of the road back to Belcourt. Should he attempt to drive the boys back? Then Ted Delonais walked out of the show hall where the game had been played, saw the team's predicament and spoke up, "Follow me, Father. Just keep on my taillight. We'll make it." They did, with Father Stan's eyes fixed on the red lamp on Delonais' model A truck just a few yards ahead of him.

It could be risky to ride with Father Stan. Just how dangerous became apparent when he was driving a bunch of players home from a pick-up game of softball. There were more boys than seats in the car so he put three kids in the trunk and left the lid open. When they reached Smiley Allick's Cafe in Belcourt all the players hopped out of the car except those in the trunk. What the priest had not reckoned with was the exhaust fumes which had drifted into the car. He hurriedly dragged the three bedraggled boys into the fresh air.

Every game presented a different problem. The Eagles were playing basketball in the new gym at Rollette and the bleachers were packed with girls cheering for the home team. George LaFrombois of the visiting Eagles was dribbling the ball up court but Father Stan sensed that he was distracted. Saint Ann's star player was moving slower and slower, his eyes searching for someone in the fifth row of the bleachers.

Suddenly an opposing player swooped past George, stole the ball and scored an easy two points. Father Stan quickly waved his arms and called a time-out. He pulled George aside and asked what happened. "Look, Father. Up there," George answered. "She's tiny. Ma kani cute."

After World War II ended Father Stan organized a basketball team of ten men who were military veterans. They went from town to town playing on Sunday afternoons. After one game everyone decided to have coffee before heading home. When they entered a local restaurant the proprietor ignored them and continued reading his newspaper. The eerie silence was not a good omen. Finally he pointed to a sign which read "No Indians or dogs allowed."

Father Stan was furious; the man's attitude was one hundred percent wrong. Besides, he could sense that trouble was brewing so he quickly hustled his players out of the restaurant and out of town. Surprisingly, the proprietor gave up his business a few days later. Some say that he sensed that times were changing after World War II and Indians could not be mistreated that way any more. However, institutional discrimination died slowly - it was not until 1967 that Catholic Indian teams were accepted in the state high school basketball tournament.

Chapter Eight - A Church Burns During Mass

Through his basketball players, their families and a growing number of friends Father Stan learned that besides attending Mass, the Catholic Indians and their neighbors practiced their faith in a variety of helpful ways. For example, Bruno Gladue assigned himself the job of heating one of the churches in the wintertime. On Sunday mornings Bruno and his family left home before dawn and rode three miles to the church in their horse-drawn sleigh. Upon arrival he lighted three stoves in the basement so that the building would be warm and comfortable before other parishioners arrived for the 10 A. M. Mass. Art Longie was the same type of dedicated layperson. Snowdrifts, no matter how deep, could not prevent Art and his horse from reaching Saint Benedict's Church near the Turtle Mountain Reservation because, like Bruno Gladue, he was responsible for warming the building before Sunday Mass.

No one was more devoted than Mary Enno, the organist at Saint Anthony's Church. Mary's two-room log home on Jackrabbit Trail had a little Esty pump organ so she invited the choir to her house for its practices. They rehearsed the music which they would sing at Midnight Mass on Christmas and rehearsed again and again until Mary was satisfied that they were ready.

On Christmas Eve the teams and wagons arrived early at Saint Anthony and Saint Benedict churches on the Turtle Mountain Reservation. Father Stan had already started to hear confessions at 1 P. M. and he would continue until moments before midnight. There were no electric lights, just a number of tall coal oil lamps throughout the building. The sweet smell of burning incense reached every corner. A hush fell over the congregation. Everything was ready to celebrate the birth of the Savior.

At last the first high note sounded from Alex LaRocque's fiddle - the signal that the priest was about to begin the Mass. At that moment all eyes turned to Mary Enno in the balcony and upon her cue the choir burst forth in its well-practiced version of "O Come All Ye Faithful." It began a joyous spectacle which reminded Father Stan of Christmas when he was a child in Indiana.

Three Catholic parishes served the people in the region: the two mission churches, Saint Anthony and Saint Benedict on the Turtle Mountain Reservation, and Saint Ann's in Belcourt, originally a trading post and later a city named after a missionary who had visited that area in the 1830s. Besides the traditional Christmas holidays the people in the area celebrated three important times every year. The first seven days of January were a period for the Indians to visit and patch up any unfriendly personal relationships. If angry persons did not settle their disagreements they were likely to continue. Another important event - family week - occurred in February or March when businesses, churches and schools combined to help the elderly break loose from "cabin fever" at that time of year.

On the last Sunday in July Saint Ann's held its annual picnic and when Father Stan arrived there shortly after his ordination Father Hildebrand instructed his new assistant to supervise preparations for the picnic. The 24-year old priest quickly realized who really was running the show when Mary Jane Davis handed him a list that outlined what he had been assigned to do. Father Stan asked Father Hildebrand to clarify his duties and he was told, "Well, you go around from house to house and you write down the things that the people will be prepared to bring, whatever it is, chickens, potato salad, pies, cakes, you know - everything."

Sisters Cora and Vita were in charge of the fish pond. Others organized the bingo game. Henry Croteau and his friends set up grandstands outside the church. Everything was in readiness, but as Father Stan began to say Mass that Sunday morning he noticed that rain was falling. A gentle rain, but nevertheless everything was getting wet. The crowd had planned on enjoying the picnic and they asked, "What are we going to do, Father?"

Being a newcomer, Father Stan had not learned how determined his parishioners could be. When he replied, "Well, I guess we'll have to wait till next Sunday," Mary Jane Davis and other members of the parish were disappointed and complained: "Impossible! The food is here, it's hot; we cannot put it off, Father."

Father Stan was not prepared for the congregation's suggestion for solving the dilemma: have the picnic inside the church! That, of course, meant clearing everything off the floor and making ingenious use of whatever remained. In the all-white parishes that Father Stan had known back home, the wooden pews were sacrosanct; they were part of the building, screwed into place. But he decided that this was the parishioners' church, not his, and he approved the plan.

The congregation yanked the pews out of the floor and stacked them against one side of the building. Kerosene stoves were moved into position underneath the choir loft. They chose the communion rail in front of the altar as a counter to sell ice cream and candy. Where to put the fish pond was a problem which needed a more creative solution. Someone noticed that there were no tops on the confessionals. That suggested the answer: Put barrels in each stall so that the children could cast their fishing lines over the top and down into the confessionals and pull out their prizes.

Parish life generally was more serious, especially on the first Friday of every month. One woman, the sole support of her severely deformed son, received Holy Communion in her home on that day. The boy, in his early 20s, was so crippled that he slept in a crib, but from there his gaze followed Father Stan when the priest entered their tiny house to speak with his mother and bless them.

"Fadder, could my little boy sometimes go to communion with me?" she asked in an accented voice. "He knows, Fadder. He knows." The son's eyes widened, he laid still and breathless waiting for the reply. The emotion of the moment overwhelmed Father Stan. Before answering the woman, he thought to himself - how could he refuse so humble a mother! Wouldn't Jesus want to come into this little house filled with so much faith and love?

Finally he replied, "I will come back tomorrow." The boy understood instantly and his twisted frame erupted in spasms of joy. The mother and son hugged each other amid yelps of happiness and Father Stan stood back and wiped away his tears. From then on both received Holy Communion on the first Friday of every month until they died within a month of each other and Father Stan said separate funeral Masses for each of them.

Fred Morin was another friend of Father Stan and a faithful parishioner of Saint Benedict's Parish. Like Bruno Gladue his job was to start the furnace in the church on Sunday mornings. Fred lived about three miles away and when his car was running it was an easy drive. However, if his car refused to start during the winter months, he had to leave home in the darkness and walk through the snow in order to reach the church, then split some wood, if necessary, and light the furnace - all between 5 and 6 A. M.

There was no electricity in the building, but a gasoline-powered generator supplied some lighting at night for bingo games and operated a fan which blew warm air from the furnace throughout the church. By 10 A. M., when families arrived for Mass, it was warm and comfortable. One Sunday the church became much too hot and Fred blamed himself for setting it on fire.

The constant putt-putt-putt from the little engine was annoying and Fred asked Father Stan whether he should turn off the generator before Mass began. It was cold outside, with a foot and a half of snow on the ground, but they agreed that the furnace would supply enough heat. Father Stan started to say Mass and by the time he began preaching he noticed a haze in the rear of the church, even though no one complained about smelling smoke. A haze was no cause for alarm because the parishioners frequently went into the basement and smoked cigarettes before Mass. Moments later, as the ushers started to pass the collection baskets, the first wisps of smoke drifted out of the heating vents.

Even when Fred went into the basement to investigate Father Stan continued saying Mass, all the while trying to convince himself that everything was all right. In a few seconds Fred raced back up the stairs and, summoning four or five men, they hurried into the furnace room below. Murmurs led to shouts and banging in the basement and Father Stan, sweating at the altar directly above the furnace, was sure now that something was seriously wrong. Someone opened a side door and, with the rush of air into the church, fire roared up through the walls.

No one panicked when the men began yelling, "Hurry, get some snow!" The congregation knew that was how Indians extinguished a fire in the winter: throw as much snow as possible on the blaze, the snow would melt and convert into steam, then the steam would rise and snuff out the fire. But this fire had a big head start. Father Stan quickly turned from the altar to face the congregation and said, as calmly as possible "Folks, our church is on fire. Everyone go out quietly."

Father Stan struggled with his own crisis. He had been taught that once a priest started to celebrate Mass he must have Holy Communion and finish the service. Smoke and the sweat from his brow almost blinded him. He could barely see the missal on the altar. The burning floor was beginning to shift beneath him. Perhaps this time he could not complete Mass. When flames burst through the floor below the altar Father Stan knew what he must do. He quickly consumed the wine and communion hosts while Donald Bruce, standing outside the communion rail, yelled, "Hurry up, Father, get out of here! Come on! Do I have to carry you out?"

As he hurried into the sacristy to remove his vestments Father Stan was surprised to see his parishioners rushing back into the church. He had lived on the reservation long enough to know that the Indians did not get rattled easily and were experienced in handling emergencies. They must know what they're doing, their priest said to himself. The women quickly stripped the cloth from the altar and took the candlesticks outside. Men joined them and together they pulled the pews out of the floor, screws and all. Others smashed their axes into the floor near the altar and poured shovels full of snow into the hole above the blazing furnace.

None of their firefighting efforts stopped the flames from spreading and after several muffled explosions rattled the windows Father Stan ordered everyone to leave the building. Alex LaRoque, James LaRoque, Art Longie and finally Fred Morin, coughing, their hands covering their eyes, groped their way out into the fresh air. However, everyone had not been evacuated. A woman screamed and then yelled that her husband, John Parisien, was trapped inside.

Father Stan ran to the front door of the church. He stepped inside, but sensed immediately that the heat was so intense that his lungs would be seared if he tried to advance any farther. So he picked up a stick, broke a window and was able to enter the basement. The missing man was not there, so the priest withdrew. Only after he reached the outside did someone notify him that John was safe and gathering snow to put out the blaze.

Within minutes the fire had moved into all corners of the building. Father Stan and his parishioners knew that there was nothing else that they could do to save their church. There was no fire apparatus for miles around and they had no telephone to call for help. Overcome by the futility of their efforts, the crowd huddled outside in the cold watching helplessly and before long the building began to collapse under its own weight. As the burning tower tilted the church bell started to ring. That was the last straw for Fred Morin. He fell into a heap on the frozen ground, wailing, "Look what I have done. The bell is crying. I have burned down God's house." No, Father Stan reassured him, this calamity was God's will.

Father Stan wondered how he could comfort his distraught parishioners. He decided that the best way was to continue his regular schedule, which included a religious study meeting that night at Bill LaVerdure's house. As the evening was ending he reached for his gold pocket watch. His home parish in North Vernon, Indiana had inscribed his name on the watch and given it to him when he was ordained. His abbot in the Benedictines even had to approve the gift, so the watch was something special. However, it was not in his pocket. To put the last nail into a bad day, he ruefully came to the conclusion that the watch must have been lost in the fire.

The LaVerdure family, the Lafromboise family, and other friends who had prayed with Father Stan that night tried to assuage his loss. They promised to replace the watch, and they did. He remembered clearly that, after leaving the smoldering wreckage of the church, he had returned to the log house where the priests resided and sat in a big chair to mull over the unhappy events of the day. Then he left for the meeting at the LaVerdure house.

About two months later Father Stan relaxed in the same chair after saying Sunday Mass. He soon fell asleep and, when he awakened and reached for his handkerchief, his keys slipped out of his pocket and fell down among the cushions. Father Stan's hand searched the chair. At first he found a pencil. Then his fingers probed more deeply and touched a chain that was attached to something round and thin. He wasn't sure what he had found, but the treasure which emerged was the round, gold watch that he thought had been lost forever.

The day the church burned down was hardly typical of Father Stan's life on the Turtle Mountain Reservation. The people grew to trust the young missionary, enough that a late night telephone call to the rectory imploring, "Father, please come over and bless our house. Some evil things have been going on, noises. We can't sleep. The kids are scared," was not an unusual request.

Other callers alarmed Father Stan, such as the young man who claimed to be stalking a woman in Watertown and the woman in Aberdeen who asked for permission to kill herself. He pleaded with her to wait until the next morning and when they spoke again she said," Maybe you won't have to have my Mass for burial. I'm feeling better today."

As Father Stan became better known in the sparsely populated Dakotas and found that his services were more in demand, he decided that it was time to learn to fly. He was 50 years old and piloting an airplane was the most expedient means of traveling the long distances across the prairie. Friends on the Turtle Mountain Reservation raised money for flying lessons and Father John Tennelly, head of the Bureau of Catholic Indian Missions, contributed $100 toward the cost.

After nine hours of instruction by pilot Wayne Riggins, Father Stan was ready for his first solo flight. It proved to be an unsettling experience because the wind direction changed while he was in the air and the airport switched the runway that was being used for landings. He nevertheless reached the ground safely and anticipated that his friends would cut off his shirt tail, a traditional ritual after a pilot flies alone for the first time. However, they respected clerics and his shirt tail remained intact. Father Stan flew for 14 years, renting a plane whenever he needed one.

In 1949 his assignment changed. The pastor at Saint Michael's Mission on the Fort Totten Reservation in North Dakota, an older man, could no longer handle the strain of raising money to pay the church's debt and asked to be replaced. Abbot Ignatius Esser, O.S.B. transferred Father Stan to St. Michael's with a mandate to solve the problem.

At about the same time the Benedictines gave him an additional job. For several years some of the monks in the Dakotas had been petitioning to separate themselves from Saint Meinrad's Abbey. They intended to remain Benedictines, but they also wanted to establish their own monastery. In 1949 Father Stan wrote a paper supporting the idea. Abbot Ignatius took the young missionary at his word and instructed him to join two other monks in finding a site for the new abbey. Father Stan realized that he must leave his friends in Belcourt and on the Turtle Mountain Reservation, but the change was not final. He resolved that he would return, if not soon, then surely in the final years of his life.

Still, those eight years in the Turtle Mountains were among the busiest and happiest of his life. "Maybe it was the personality of the people, maybe it was their flashing smiles, maybe it was the music, maybe it was the conversation, but any time I went into those small houses I felt just like walking into a warm embrace," he remembered.

 BLUE CLOUD ABBEY

Chapter Nine - Benedictines, Past and Present

Centuries before the Benedictines began searching for a permanent home in the Dakotas and long before Bishop Marty arrived in the region an Italian-born monk named Benedict of Nursia founded a Catholic religious order of priests and brothers.

Benedict grew up in the 5th and 6th centuries, a child of a wealthy family whose parents sent him to Rome for an education. But life in the city was not the heartening experience that they expected for their son, a serious young man of 20. The immoral pursuits of his acquaintances shocked Benedict and drove him to flee from the city, leaving behind everything he owned except a few pieces of clothing.

He traveled to the Italian countryside where he hoped that he would enjoy a more spiritual life. When Benedict reached the area called Subiaco, he searched for a quiet place to rest. After climbing a wild, rock-strewn hill he found what he was seeking, a secluded hideaway at the top. The cave was perfect for what Benedict wanted: a place for meditation and solitude.

The stone cavern served as Benedict's home and place of prayer for three years. One of his few contacts with the bleak world outside was another monk, Romanus, who occasionally stood at the crest of the hill and lowered to Benedict baskets of bread and animal skins for his clothing. While living alone there Benedict prayed seven times a day and spent seven hours in physical labor. Despite such isolation, word spread about the young man's intelligence and compassion and a group of monks persuaded him to become their leader.

Benedict's effort to form these men into a religious community was almost fatal. The rules of conduct that he introduced were too strict and his angered new companions offered him a cup containing a poisonous drink. However, ancient records claim that when Benedict made the sign of the cross over the cup it shattered and he withdrew from the group.

Another band of monks joined Benedict near Naples and that association was more enduring. In 525 A. D. these men combined with Benedict to form the Benedictine order of priests and brothers, the oldest religious order in the Catholic church. They built an historic abbey at Monte Cassino in Italy which came to be recognized not only as the birthplace of the Benedictines, but also as the mother house of monasticism on the continent of Europe.

During Benedict's life of 70 years about 1,000 men followed his holy way of living and joined the religious order that he founded. His saintly life inspired thousands more to become Benedictine priests, brothers and nuns in the ensuing centuries. Eventually the Catholic Church canonized both Benedict and his sister Scholastica, who was instrumental in forming the Benedictine community of women. The spiritual and educational work which the Benedictines performed in the Middle Ages and through many turbulent centuries led Joseph Cardinal Ratzinger to salute them: "They are the saviors of western civilization."

St. Benedict sought to assure that the practices of the early Benedictines would differ from the rigid asceticism which was common to other Catholic fraternal groups of that time. He created regulations for daily living and warned against unusual private self-mortification, such as denying oneself sufficient food or sleep or painful self-punishment. A Benedictine's day should be allocated to separate periods for work and study as well as prayer, a regimen that the members of the order practiced continuously into the 21st century.

Each man's personal sanctity was to spring from obedience, humility and most of all the idea of community which would bring each monk closer to salvation. Community, Father Stan believed, was the crucial element in each man's life. "We don't come to a monastery to save ourselves, to save our souls," he wrote. "You can't baptize yourself, you can't forgive your own sins, you can't ordain yourself. There's nothing you can do for yourself. You're saved by Christ; you're saved by others."

The principles that Benedict espoused became the basis of the famous Rule of Benedict which later served as the guideline when other Catholic religious orders were formed. The fundamental requirement, according to Father Stan's analysis of the founding of the Benedictines, was that monks should be involved with the world around them, that is, they should not turn their backs on civilization and move away to live solitary lives in the hills.

"I have the feeling myself that we are called to stay in the structure [of society and the church] and in the structure then reform and redeem the members who are hurt by the structure," Father Stan wrote. "I don't believe it's right to flee responsibility, whether in the world organization or the church organization. I think that we have a responsibility to stay where the evil is happening."

The Benedictines were not an itinerant group, as were some Catholic religious orders, and instead put down their roots in specific locations where they remained. The growing numbers of Benedictine monks extended their presence throughout Europe and constructed more abbeys, including one built in the 10th century at Einsiedeln, Switzerland.

The first Benedictines to cross the Atlantic to the United States were German men, excellent farmers who were willing to work with the people whom they were trying to convert to Catholicism. They intended to establish roots and become part of America and proved it by constructing permanent, well-built schools and other facilities, including their own monastery at St. Meinrad in Indiana. Their priests and brothers ventured to the frontier states to serve as missionaries to the Indians and opened their first school on the plains at Kenel, South Dakota.

By the middle of the 19th century the Benedictines, Jesuits and other Christian missionaries had succeeded in persuading many Indians to give up their pagan practices. Chief Struck-by-the-Ree saw the value of Catholic education and in 1844 asked the Church to establish a mission to instruct the children in his tribe.

However, the Church's influence among Native Americans was jeopardized when in 1870 President Ulysses S. Grant sent the following message to the United States Congress: "Indian agencies being civil offices, I am determined to give all the agencies to such religious denominations as had hitherto established missions among the Indians and perhaps to some other denominations who would undertake the work on the same terms - i.e., missionary work."

These agencies were specific regions where federal employees administered programs for the benefit of the Native Americans. Grant's decision marked a change in the government's policies. Up until that time white men had bullied and suppressed the Indians, but leaders in Washington began to realize that this approach was unproductive and costly in lives and money.

President Grant wanted to civilize and pacify the Indians and he decided that Christianizing them should be a first step in implementing his idea. In order to carry out such a program he needed the cooperation of Christian institutions and clergymen. This new approach from Washington became known as Grant's "Peace Policy." The plan allowed the religious denomination that was the best established in the region of each Indian agency to nominate a representative to supervise the local activities of the federal government. This led to a program by which one religion, and only that religion, could be practiced in each area and only its members could proselytize the natives there.

On paper the idea seemed ideal for the Church because among the 72 agencies Catholic groups were predominant in 38. Church leaders urged that those reservations be assigned to Catholic missionaries. However, Catholics played a smaller role than they expected because 13 religious denominations bid for various agencies and worse yet anti-Catholic bigotry interfered in the selection process. Several Protestant religious groups lobbied to take control over the mission stations which the Catholics had regarded as theirs.

More significantly, members of the Quaker faith gained President Grant's ear and he assisted them in assuming leadership positions in the federal Indian Bureau in Washington. The Grant administration was determined that its Indian policy should quash the warlike tendencies of certain tribes and when the President reportedly said, "If you can make Quakers of them it will take the fight out of them," it revealed whom he preferred to do the job. The government's one-sided approach gave the Peace Policy a new name. People began calling it the Quaker Policy. The result was disastrous for the spread of Catholicism; the federal authorities turned only eight agencies over to the Catholic Church and 80,000 Catholic Indians were relegated to reservations which came under Protestant administration.

This federal scheme of religious segregation was enforced strictly, but not always. A Benedictine missionary attempted to visit Catholic Indians on an Episcopal agency and a government official in Washington ordered him to leave. Grant's policy carried a penalty, too, for a clergyman could be fined $1,000 if he trespassed on a reservation that had been assigned to a different denomination.

A couple of years later, when the Catholics tried to remove a Protestant clergyman at another location, the government changed its mind and decided that the reservations should be open to all religious denominations. It was evident that some Indians preferred assistance from the Catholic Church. Chief Red Cloud met with President Rutherford B. Hayes in 1877 and specifically asked for Catholic priests and sisters to teach his people to read and write. Newspaper criticism and the withdrawal of the Quakers from the program followed and the Board of Indian Commissioners in Washington finally rescinded the Peace Policy in 1881. The federal government no longer told Catholic missionaries where they could travel and preach.

The Church learned a lesson from the Peace Policy - it could not rely on the United States government to help it spread the Catholic religion. It needed its own organization to counteract the prejudices of government employees. Out of that realization came the Bureau of Catholic Indian Missions, which was founded in 1874 and continues to work into the 21st century.

The Church's mission to teach the faith to the Indians received a boost from the Supreme Court of the United States in 1907 when the Court affirmed that Catholic schools could receive federal funds for the education of Indian children. Another milestone, the ordination of Rev. Philip Gordon as the first Native American priest, occurred in 1913.

By 1949, after working the good part of a century in the Dakotas, the Benedictines there recognized that they were a long distance from their monastery in Indiana. They were linked by centuries of tradition to Einsiedeln and many of them had studied at St. Meinrad, but these men wanted their own abbey out on the prairie. But first they must find a location that was accessible to their missions and not too expensive to buy.

The search committee of Father Stan and two other monks inspected land in Aberdeen, Pierre and Yankton in South Dakota, Fargo in North Dakota and other sites, but none was satisfactory. The Pipestone Indian School in Minnesota was a large piece of property and it seemed suitable. The buildings and acreage could be purchased for $1,000,000. The price was considered cheap, but it was still more than the Benedictines could afford.

Abbot Gilbert Hess, O. S. B., Father Gaulbert Brunsman, O. S. B. and Father Stan were driving around one crisp October day, hoping to discover just the right piece of property. They headed north toward Summit, South Dakota and liked the countryside. The monks stopped to stretch and saw a large house and a farm in the distance. The owners, a man and his two sisters, had lived there and worked the soil all their lives and told the visitors that they were not interested in giving up their land. But the family had a suggestion: continue driving to Marvin, South Dakota and talk to Oscar Casperson. He's thinking of selling.

The monks traveled on to Marvin. Yes, the Casperson farm, a sizeable one overlooking a valley, was up for sale, so the three Benedictines inspected it carefully. There were problems; the parcel was so rocky that Father Stan could almost cross the 80 acres by jumping from one large boulder to another. But what appeared to be an impediment to the purchase actually was a hidden benefit - the monks assumed that the land would be cheap because it was so rocky.

Besides, they figured that they could remove the rocks themselves and convert some of the acres into pastures. On the positive side, the Casperson property had three attributes that the Benedictines required: good water and a location which was not only near a suitable highway but which also was within driving distance of the railroad.

The discussion about a purchase became serious and Mr. Casperson said that the transaction was being handled by the First Dakota Bank in Milbank. "Speak to Mr. Benedict there," he told the three Benedictines. Benedict! How could the banker's name be anything but a providential omen!

When the trio of heavily-dressed Benedictines, wearing huge black coats, dark fur caps and rubber galoshes, came through the front door of the rural bank late in the afternoon, visions of Frank and Jesse James almost panicked the tellers into sounding an alarm. It was not necessary, however, after the visitors introduced themselves to a handsome, broad-shouldered officer of the bank. He was Mr. Benedict.

The banker announced that Mr. Casperson's land was scheduled to be sold at auction and the priests would have to submit a bid just like any other prospective purchaser. Father Stan and his companions evaluated the property and decided that they would offer no more than $26 per acre. Once the auction got underway, the only other man interested in buying kept raising his offering price. The bidding shifted back and forth and as the price approached the monks' limit the competing bidder suddenly withdrew without any explanation. Father Stan and his companions had won! It was November, 1949 and the Benedictines finally had acquired a site for a monastery in the Dakotas.

Why did the other man quit? He answered the question many years later during a visit to the abbey which the monks built at Marvin. Father Stan did not remember him; he was just "a face in the crowd" on the day of the auction. "Father, I'm the man who was bidding against you," he described himself, "but as it got up to $24.60 somebody told me that you were priests and that you were bidding on that land so that you might build a monastery there, and that is why I quit bidding," he said.

While the monks were awaiting the auction they decided to stay overnight in Milbank. In those days priests sometimes wangled their meals and accommodations from the nuns who operated the hospital in the town through which they were traveling. A group of Italian sisters ran the local hospital and they were more than apprehensive when the three roughly-dressed men walked in and claimed they were priests.

The sisters fed the suspicious-looking strangers anyway, but they also put in a hasty telephone call to their chaplain. The priest hurried back to the hospital and quizzed the unannounced guests. "Who's the bishop of Indianapolis?" he asked. "When were you ordained, Father? What bishop was living at that time?" And so on, until the chaplain finally exclaimed, "You sons of guns! I was at a banquet. I was there to give a blessing, but sister called an emergency that some strange men had come in posing as priests and I was to come back immediately and unmask them."

The residents of Marvin also were cautious about a band of Catholic monks moving into their little community. Their anxiety intensified, according to a story reported to Father Stan, after a clergyman showed up at the local Baptist church and warned that great evils would befall the citizens if they allowed these intruders, who already were living in a farmhouse on their newly-acquired property, to build their monastery.

Sentiment was mounting against the Benedictines and their hopes when Sheriff "Bud" Thorpe stood up at a town meeting. "I was always told never to judge a man until I could hear him out," he said. "I've never seen these bastards, so I'm not going to listen to them being run down right now. I'm going to leave here and I'm going to wait until I see them and after I see them I'll be the first one to condemn them if they deserve it." Thorpe's statement took the wind out of the opposition.

The monks called their new home Blue Cloud Abbey. The color means "fullness of blessing," but the principal reason why they chose the name was to honor Chief Blue Cloud. The Benedictines knew him as "Mahpiya To," the leader of the Yankton Sioux tribe. Almost three-quarters of a century earlier Blue Cloud had demonstrated his trust in the men who wore the black robes. He had secretly smuggled Bishop Marty onto the reservation at Yankton and, in defiance of government regulations, allowed the Bishop to say Mass in his home. Chief Blue Cloud had known about Catholicism for a long time, having accompanied Father DeSmet to Fort Laramie for a treaty signing ceremony in 1851. The Benedictines remembered that he had donated land for their mission on the reservation in Yankton so it was appropriate to show their appreciation by naming their new monastery in his memory.

Under the guidance of Father Gilbert Hess, O.S.B., the first abbot of the new monastery, the priests and brothers set to work in 1950 clearing the land and laying the footings for the first building. The job progressed well enough that they started living in their own residence the following year. Once settled the monks began to provide for their own needs with a farm that in a short time yielded abundant vegetables, grapes that the mothers of some of the men turned into jellies, and 800 pounds of squash in one harvest.

In time Sheriff Thorpe and his family became friendly with the men at Blue Cloud and the relationship proved beneficial on both sides. Under the Sheriff's leadership the people in Marvin came to accept a Catholic monastery in the countryside and the monks reciprocated by helping to save his sheep when they were trapped in a blizzard. Sheriff Thorpe sponsored an annual trail ride and he usually asked Father Stan to say Mass in his family's pasture.

Chapter Ten - An Unhappy School Superintendent

Father Stan was a good neighbor, but being friendly was not his only role. When he was not out scouting for a location for a new monastery, his main assignment after 1949 was to administer Saint Michael's Mission and school. Located near Devil's Lake on the small Fort Totten Reservation in North Dakota, the Mission brought him back among the Sioux. Still, it soon became the site of one of the unhappiest periods in his life.

His new job included running a boarding school for Sioux children, a task for which he admittedly was ill suited. Father Stan simply wasn't comfortable being confined to a desk and discovered quickly how hard it was to raise the funds to operate a school. The place was $60,000 in debt, so money was constantly on his mind. There was a simple solution to the problem, but one that he wouldn't adopt. The Mission owned 300 head of cattle and Father Stan could have solved the problem by selling part of the herd. But that meant that he would have more employees than he needed and some would have to be fired. He wouldn't go that far.

The federal government was not keen about helping the Catholic schools. It paid each mission a paltry amount for each student who was under 21 years old and at least one-quarter Indian blood, but officials watched the attendance numbers closely and insisted that any boys and girls who lived close to a public school must go to classes there. Even so, not all of the children who were enrolled in mission schools were eligible to receive a subsidy of federal money. The student body on the Pine Ridge Reservation numbered 400 in 1963. However, Washington made payments for only 144 of them. Father Stan cooperated with the government workers as long as it was practical, but rules and regulations frustrated some missionaries. "There are too many federal employees in the Indian service and things here on the reservation stink to high heaven," complained another missionary, Rev. Harold A. Fuller,S.J., when he wrote about "Iron Curtain tactics" at Holy Rosary Mission at Pine Ridge, South Dakota.

Filling seats in the classroom was important, but getting the Indian children to leave home to attend school elsewhere could be a terrifying change. Children complained about mistreatment at some religious schools. "They were whipping me like hell and I didn't know why they were doing that," Jessie Bear recalled his experiences as a student.

Stories circulated about how children who were headed for mission schools, some as young as eight years old, were forced into trucks and the girls were stacked horizontally on the bottom, and the boys placed on a level above them. Frightened and missing their families, they traveled for two days through dust and heat until they reached their foreboding new home. A number of the children ran away, but they were caught soon enough and returned to the mission. The priests and nuns eventually became more tolerant and offered bus tickets home to youngsters who refused to stay. While Father Stan said that misbehavior wasn't a problem at Benedictine schools, the administrators of other institutions sometimes shaved the heads of those who didn't obey the rules.

Convincing the Indian parents to send their boys and girls to Saint Michael's school could be difficult. Attendance was important, not only so the children could learn, but also because the mission's income dropped for every child who didn't show up. However, Father Stan figured out a way to keep the whole family happy. He and Father Tim Sexton built a community center with something for the parents and the youth alike - a basketball court, a bowling alley and a lunch counter. In the evening a half hour of studying came first, then the parents joined in socializing while the children enjoyed themselves.

During the winter the roads in the Dakotas frequently were snow-covered or badly in need of repair so the Catholic mission schools usually closed from before Christmas until Easter Tuesday. They were in session during the summertime, but the government schools were not. The different schedules created an opportunity for the Indian children who wanted to skip school altogether. In the winter, they said, "I go to the government school", even if they didn't, and in the summer some fibbed, "I go to the mission school." However, by the 1960s when the road conditions improved and the sisters were able to attend their classes during the summer, the mission schools remained open throughout the cold weather.

Unfortunately, truancy was frequent and some Indian parents were at best indifferent about whether their children attended school at all, mission or public. Adults who valued education for their family sometimes were ridiculed as simply being out of touch with the culture of the tribes. The perception of formal education suffered because the members of some reservations rejected the idea of educating their children and tried to pull everyone down to the same level of ignorance. Even so, in 1954 among a student body of 218 at Saint Michael's school 205 of the children were Indian and the rest were white. The attendance figures were sufficiently encouraging for Father Stan to open a high school, but it survived only three years.

Perhaps Rabbit Baker, the father of one of Father Stan's fourth grade students, summed up the prevailing train-of-thought. He approached the missionary one day and said, "Father, let me ask you something? We're all Catholics, ain't it, Father?" Father Stan agreed. Rabbit continued, "And we're all going to heaven too, ain't it?" The priest agreed again. Rabbit went on, "And in heaven we're all going to know everything, ain't it, Father?" Happy that Rabbit knew his catechism, Father Stan nodded his approval.

Rabbit was eager to make his point and finished, "Well, then tell me this, Father! When I was growing up I learned that you didn't do a job twice. Do it once and do it good and that'll be right. Now if we're all going to heaven, and we're all going to know everything up there, why'n hell then do we have to go to school all the time and learn something we're going to know anyway? Does that sound too smart?" Father Stan's reply was not recorded.

A grade school education at a mission school was more demanding than Rabbit imagined, as Father Stan learned when he took charge at Saint Michael's. It was hard enough for the Indian students to learn English, but at some schools the teachers also forbade them to speak or even pray in their native language. Father Stan wanted the boys and girls under his charge to retain their heritage so he tried to teach them the Indian prayers, but with little encouragement to recite some forgot them forever.

For 80 years the Grey Nuns of Saint Boniface, from Manitoba, Canada taught Native-American youngsters at the boarding school on the Fort Totten Reservation. They were strong women, each with a distinct personality. The superior of the convent, Sister Andrew, O.S.B. acted as a quasi-mother to the boys.

At more than six feet tall, Sister Ludmilla, O.S.B. was a friendly giant who towered over the little boys and encouraged their appetites. About 3:30 P. M. every day the nun went to the kitchen and the kids knew why. She and Sister Afra Nisch, O.S.B. prepared a basket of huge sandwiches. Then Sister Ludmilla walked through the boys dormitory, holding the basket well above her head. The children trailed behind like a line of squawking ducks and each boy jumped up reaching for the bread but none reached high enough. The scene seemed like a reenactment of the Pied Piper of Hamlin. When the parade reached the recreation room she gave each hungry boy a blessing and his butter and jelly sandwich.

One time Sister Ludmilla was unusually generous, more than she had to be. She had been an employee of the federal Bureau of Indian Affairs before joining the convent and Father Ambrose Mattingly, O.S.B. asked her for a donation toward the church at Fort Thompson. She gave $10. The priest told a teacher about the gift and the woman topped it by contributing $15. Determined to increase the ante, Father Mattingly returned to Sister Ludmilla and mentioned the other woman's generosity. Not someone to be outdone, Sister Ludmilla increased her contribution to $20. One wonders where the bidding stopped.

The sisters at Saint Michael's Mission decided on many of the regulations for the school. One of the rules was that classes never stopped, no matter how bitter the weather might be. If the second and third grade children half-froze while waiting for the bus, the sisters gave the kids a warm bath when they reached school and asked the doctor to check them before sending them to their classes.

Within a short time after Father Stan arrived there he discovered that he had his hands full dealing with the sisters. Some were more experienced than he was and almost every change that he proposed in the educational schedule at the school precipitated a tug of war. For example, he suggested that the students should be told that the buses wouldn't operate when the temperature dropped to 20 degrees below zero. The idea was a novel one and the nuns opposed it. However, he was so adamant that he threatened to leave the school. Finally, a compromise was reached whereby Father Stan arranged to notify the radio stations at Minot and Devil's Lake to make an announcement whenever the weather prevented the buses from running.

One day Father Stan and Sister Pineault, who had seen much in 40 years at the mission school, were looking out the window and watched a former student staggering from one ditch to another as he passed the church. He appeared to be drunk. "Oh, look, one of my boys," the sister said. "He was such a nice boy and look what has happened to him now. What went wrong with him?"

What they saw was a disappointment, but it also triggered a thought in the priest's mind: Perhaps the cause of what went wrong was not "them," the Indians, but instead "us," the clergy and the sisters. Maybe they - the children - needed to spend less time with "us" and more with their families.

Father Stan asked himself why the boys and girls who boarded at Saint Michael's must stay there for the entire school year. Some of them lived within three or four miles of the Mission. Why must they spend holidays there, too? Shouldn't they be allowed to spend Christmas among their parents, brothers and sisters? Were they looking after the best interests of the children?

He decided to try out his theory on the children themselves. Walking out on the playground, where the kids were running around, Father Stan gathered them together and asked if any would like to spend Christmas at home. "Oh, boy, atta go, Father," and "That would be great," settled the question. But when he presented his idea to the staff of teachers they dismissed that suggestion, too.

"Father, what could be worse than that! Think of this: we would not then have a nice Midnight Mass."

The sisters raised a second serious objection: Don't let the students go home, the teachers warned, because they will never return. Father Stan gradually persuaded them at least to try the idea and he reminded everyone that, after all, it was the parents who had the final word about the education of their children. At last, Sister Pineault conceded, "Well, go ahead, Father - but it won't work."

This was a test of the priest's determination and when he watched the students leave for the Christmas and New Year's vacation he too wondered whether he would see them again. Imagine the relief that spread throughout the Mission when most of the children showed up on Monday morning, and several newcomers tagged along with them.

Having cracked open the door to changes in the way the school operated, Father Stan went further and recommended that the youngsters be permitted to return to their families every Friday afternoon and come back on Monday morning. The sisters didn't like that suggestion either. They argued that they couldn't release the students because they needed them to clean the school on the weekends. But after thinking it over, the sisters realized that if the children tidied up the building on Friday afternoons and then left, the teachers could at last take off their shoes and relax over the weekend. With that, they saw the merits of the priest's proposal.

The evolution of Saint Michael Mission from a boarding school into a day school moved forward in 1953 when Father Stan and a friend flew to Duluth, Minnesota to buy five buses. He hired three drivers and laid out four bus routes. About 30 children who lived some distance away continued to board at the Mission, but all of the other youngsters became day students. The monks not only drove some of the buses, but also led the children in songs going back and forth to school.

Operating the buses on icy roads could be nerve-wracking, but Father Stan had even more problems with the driving of some of his fellow missionaries. One morning a snowplow came plunging through the drifts and stopped in front of Father Stan's office. The driver, a huge man named Frank Charbonneau, jumped off the plow and struggled up the stairs. "My, this is nice of Frank to come here and clear the road out for us," the priest thought to himself. Frank had something else in mind.

"Father, you've got to do something about that Father Cuthbert," he said. "Oh, what's the matter?," Father Stan asked. "He had the kids in the school bus and three times within a mile he drove the bus into a ditch and three times I had to pull him out," Frank explained. Father Stan knew that Father Cuthbert Hughes, O.S.B. enlivened the children's trip to school with his jokes and stories, but his driving was so poor that he had to be replaced behind the wheel of the bus.

Father Paul Thoma, O.S.B. was very old, generous, and, in Father Stan's estimation, a terrible driver. It was almost impossible for him to back his car out of the garage without scratching either the fender or the garage door. Father Stan decided that he must warn his friend: "Now, Father, I'm glad that you're able to drive around the reservation and that you go to visit the prisoners in the jail in Devil's Lake. But let me tell you that if you ever have an accident, if someone hits you or you hit someone else, don't sign anything. Don't make any deals with them; you're fully covered by insurance. Don't do anything at all. We'll take care of it later."

Father Paul did have an accident. While leaving a parking space in front of the post office in Devil's Lake, he backed into the path of another vehicle and damaged the right rear fender of his car. When Father Stan heard the story he asked, "You didn't sign anything, did you?" Father Paul answered, "No, no, I didn't do anything."

Father Stan continued, "And you told the police about it?" The old missionary said he did, but added, "They recognized that it was my fault so they let the other man go." The story got worse; Father Paul mentioned offhandedly that neither he nor the police obtained the name of the driver of the other car. The priest volunteered that the driver offered him $50, but he refused it. "No, I was told not to accept any money as payment," Father Paul explained.

Father Stan tried hard, but he conceded that administering a school and its staff was not his strong suit. He feared that he was "deteriorating into a bureaucratic functionary unrelated to the real world of loving people."

Long after the Benedictines reassigned him in 1956 he wrote, "I look back on those years at St. Michael's and wonder how anyone could have put up with me. The work was absolutely incompatible with my nature. I'm sure everyone else was aware of my inability, and this could be said of the sisters. They were the heart of the mission and were the shapers of its past and even its present. Those poor nuns put up with me for seven years and I'll always love them for that."

Chapter Eleven - Drexel Money Builds a School

Leaving Saint Michael's Mission in North Dakota, Father Stan transferred across the state line to the Stephan Mission on the Crow Creek Reservation in South Dakota. It was at Stephan that the generous works of Saint Katherine Drexel crossed the paths of the Benedictine priests. A two-story house which served as a school and residence had been built there in 1886, the result of a meeting in which a contingent of Indians led by Chief Drifting Goose asked Bishop Marty to establish a school. Katherine provided the money, a $15,000 grant from the estate of her wealthy father, the Philadelphia financier, Francis Drexel, who had been a business partner of J. P. Morgan.

The Drexel children, Katherine and her two sisters, grew up on a 90 acre estate amid a lavish lifestyle. A lively girl, Katherine studied the piano, French and Latin, was presented to local society and had received and rejected a proposal of marriage.

All of its material wealth did not detract from the strong Catholic strength of the Drexel family. Katherine slowly began to consider whether she had a vocation to become a nun. To evaluate the idea, she prepared a list of pros and cons and admitted that there were obstacles for her: religious life included few luxuries and a self-analysis revealed that she hated to follow orders from someone she regarded as stupid.

Katherine was still young when she learned that there were not enough priests and sisters available to staff the schools for American Indian children. The Drexel girls traveled to Europe several summers and while in Rome one year she pleaded with Pope Leo XIII to send more missionaries. The Pontiff's reply, "Why not, my child, yourself becoming a missionary?" frightened her so much that she could not wait to flee the Vatican.

Catholic leaders in the United States were familiar with Katherine's interest in educating Indian and black children. Still, it was a surprise that soon after her father died in 1885 two strange men showed up on the Drexel doorstep. The family butler announced to Kate and her sisters, "Two gentlemen are downstairs to see the Misses Drexel." The girls were aware that their father had established a trust for $14,000,000 and they expected that the visitors would ask for money.

"Kate, you go down," her sisters decided. The men were Bishop Marty and Father Joseph Stephan, O.S.B., after whom the Mission was named, and money indeed was what they wanted. President Grant's Peace Policy had failed to assist the Church in educating Indian children, Bishop Marty argued, and he asked Katherine for a grant to build Catholic schools. She agreed to help and started the flow of funds from the family trust to build not only the school at the Stephan Mission, but also other institutions in the Dakotas.

The more poverty that Katherine saw as she toured the west the more determined she became to live the life of a nun. Although she began her trip in the luxury of her father's private railroad car, the scenery changed to horse-and-buggy country by the time she reached the home of Chief Red Cloud, the head of the Sioux nation. She gave the Chief a bridle and left a black-fringed shawl for his wife, but more importantly Katherine made a favorable lasting impression on the Indian leader.

Fortunately for the sisters at the Holy Rosary Mission on the Pine Ridge Reservation, Red Cloud remembered Katherine's generosity. At the end of 1890, after the U. S. Army killed many of the Sioux at the battle of Wounded Knee, the Indians went on a rampage and planned their revenge, including the destruction of the Holy Rosary Mission and the slaughter of the nuns working there. However, Red Cloud uncovered their intentions and although the killing continued elsewhere he sent word that the Indians would protect the staff at the Mission.

Katherine's spiritual advisor, Bishop James O'Connor of Omaha, counseled her against entering religious life, but she rejected his advice and decided to devote her life to God. After a short period of training, in 1891 she founded and later became the superior of her own religious order, the Sisters of the Blessed Sacrament for Indians and Colored People. By 1907 Katherine and the other Drexel women had donated $1,500,000 to the Bureau of Catholic Indian Mission.

Katherine died in 1955 and she was beatified 25 years later. At that ceremony in Saint Peter's Square in Rome the visitors heard some strange sounds. Two foreign men were speaking a language no one understood. Father Stan had met Deacon Victor Bull Bear and they were talking in Ogala Sioux. After another 20 years, the Church declared her a saint in recognition of a lifetime of good work in educating Indian and black children.

Although headquartered at the Stephan Mission Father Stan became so well known throughout the Crow Creek Reservation that some of the Indians thought that he was one of them. He knew that he had won their acceptance after a revealing event one rainy spring evening. While driving from Pierre to Stephan Father Stan saw four Indian children shivering in a ditch. He stopped and put them in the back seat of his car. The kids were nervous and blurted out that they were from "the Indian village," a phrase which alerted the priest immediately. "The Indian village" was an expression that the Indians never used. His passengers apparently wanted him to believe that they lived nearby at Fort Thompson.

Let them talk, Father Stan figured to himself, they will soon trip themselves up. He asked the children to name their teacher and pretty soon they made their mistake. When they answered, "Miss Daggs," Father Stan immediately turned around in his seat and scolded, "You've been telling me a story. Miss Daggs is the teacher back at Pierre Indian School. I'll bet you're from Pierre Indian School, aren't you?" The four youngsters lowered their eyes; they were guilty as charged.

"I'll take you back," Father Stan soothed their fears. The next day the children told the counsellor at Pierre Indian School that after leaving the School they had walked along the river until a man driving a car found them. "Was it a white man?," the counsellor inquired. "No," the children said. "Who was it?," the counsellor continued. "It was Father Stan," they replied.

When the priest heard about the children's answer he considered it the greatest compliment that he had ever received. That wasn't the only time that he was mistaken for an Indian. Sister Rita Barthel invited Father Stan to a discussion about religious vocations. He consented and said that he would bring an Indian panelist. "Oh," she replied. "Aren't you Indian?"

To children Father Stan simply was someone they could trust. To adults of all colors he was a Hoosier priest and that label followed him to Stephan. He was the basketball coach, like it or not, and the intense rivalry with the teams from Marty continued. His teams won all but one of the games which they played at Marty and captured the All Indian Catholic championship at Rapid City, South Dakota. Football and track, however, were different stories. In those sports Father Stan's teams always came up short against Coach Moe Shevlin's squads from Marty.

With those credentials Father Stan was not surprised that he was chosen to referee when the famed Harlem Globetrotters came to Stephan to play an exhibition basketball game. The "referee" laughed as hard as the spectators when the Globetrotters somehow made the ball disappear as he lined up the players for a foul shot.

As he got to know his widespread new parish Father Stan decided that it needed another building for Sunday Masses. With the help of Larry Young Bear, Boots Gregg and Bernie Gregg, he collected everything that was salvageable from a church that had to be razed for the construction of the new Big Bend Dam. Another church building, an old one near Cedar, South Dakota, was not being used, so Father Stan asked the parishioners if he could take it. However, they told him how attached their families were to the church. It was theirs because after all their parents and ancestors had built it, so at first the answer was "No."

A springtime windstorm soon changed their minds; it toppled the chimney and broke open the roof. After water poured in and damaged the plaster, a spokesman for the parish made a suggestion to Father Stan, "If you'll repair the roof and if you'll leave one painting up behind the altar, we'll give you the church." The proposal was satisfactory and Father Stan had his church.

The next step was to relocate the building to a new site, a ten-acre parcel west of Stephan. The local tribe offered a 99-year lease with the condition that the property must be used for religious purposes. The biggest problem was whether the building could be kept intact while it was being moved. Larry Young Bear and Father Stan started by removing the steeple so that the structure would pass under the utility wires along the road, but then the weather complicated the schedule for transporting it across the prairie.

In the mornings when the ground was frozen the moving crew made progress on the highway and across the beds of several dry creeks - until later when the temperature rose, the road surface thawed and changed into mud. The movers reached the bridge at Mac's Corner near the Stephan Road and realized that it was too narrow to cross, so the man driving the tractor that was hauling the building detoured down into an adjacent stream.

That quickly proved to be the wrong decision. All the horsepower of the towing equipment could not pull the load up the slippery bank of the creek. The building was stuck in the mud and Father Stan and his crew had no choice except to wait for colder weather. Two days later the turf hardened, the tractor gripped the ground and the old church was on the road again.

When the building reached its new location Larry Young Bear and Father Stan began to construct a new steeple. They took measurements and prepared diagrams, then cut the wood to size in the basement of Father Stan's house in Pierre. But the church itself was 30 miles to the east. Father Stan's team of movers was worried: Would all the pieces fit together when they reached the site and started to assemble everything?. They did, perfectly, with an eight-foot high aluminum-covered cross on the top. After a furnace was installed and the ladies of the parish painted the building white, Saint Catherine's Church was ready to serve its new congregation.

Father Stan's schedule required him to celebrate Sunday Masses in Big Bend, Pierre and Fort Thompson. The trip to Big Bend was 30 miles and the distance from Pierre to Fort Thompson was 65 miles. The word spread quickly whenever he arrived in town to say Mass and someone rounded up the organist and Bible readers. Still, it became evident that the distances were too far to travel in a single day. After a couple of years Father Stan convinced Father Casimir Kot, O.S.B. to handle services at Fort Thompson.

The teen-agers at Fort Thompson became more interested in attending church after Joe Wounded Knee and Father Stan converted the basement of the building into a youth center. Joe's wife, Julia, helped to run the club which, arranged like the program at Saint Michael's, began each evening with 45 minutes of study hall and then the kids danced and partied until closing time.

With his tiring nighttime trips to Fort Thompson and sometimes traveling between Stephan and Pierre three times in one day, Father Stan realized that he must work out of a more centralized location. Years of experience told him that a priest had to be in touch with his parishioners and he felt that he could be more accessible if he made his home in Pierre, the state capitol. Father Stan's good friend, Dick Harrison, lived there, but it was not until Harrison was murdered that he made the decision to move from the Stephan Mission to Pierre.

Chapter Twelve - A Church Near The City Dump

Dick Harrison and his family lived on Park Street in Pierre. When the abbot at Blue Cloud Abbey assigned Father Stan to establish a new parish in the state capitol and to select a site he picked a location near the city dump. Since it was on Park Street he soon became acquainted with Dick and his wife, Clara.

Dick was one of those countless dedicated Indian lay men and women who were the mainstays of many parishes, performing the nitty-gritty tasks that frequently the pastor cannot do. A bricklayer, a trusted member of the community, the father of sons Donny and Dallas, he became Father Stan's first lay helper at Saint John's Parish in Pierre.

Everyone in the neighborhood knew that Dick always cashed his paycheck on Friday or Saturday evening. He gave all the proceeds to Clara, except for a few dollars that he kept for a beer or two with his friends. One weekend a stranger came to Pierre and watched Dick cash the check, but he didn't know that Dick kept only a small amount for himself.

A few people in the parish were surprised that Dick did not show up for church that Sunday morning. By the afternoon the sheriff announced the shocking reason why Dick had missed Mass - someone had murdered him on the previous night. The police quickly found out what had happened. The perpetrator had followed Dick out of a saloon and into an alley, where he struck him on the head, rifled Dick's pockets and stole his shoes so that he couldn't be followed.

Father Stan heard the sad news on his car radio while driving back from Sioux Falls. His first thought was whether a priest would be available in Pierre to attend the funeral. The sheriff quickly contacted Father Stan and asked him to help catch the killer. "It's got to be a stranger. We all know Dick and we know that he did not carry money. We know exactly how he behaved and how he shared everything with his family," the sheriff said. "So, Father, if you get any news about a stranger in town of any sort, let us know about it."

The policeman's request became a dilemma for Father Stan. He wanted Dick's killer to be brought to justice, but should a priest participate in a manhunt and the interrogation of someone suspected of murder? Stalling seemed the best course of action so Father Stan told the sheriff that he was going to Big Bend to say Mass and he would telephone the police department as soon as he returned.

The call was not necessary; instead the sheriff soon contacted Father Stan and reported, "We have the man. Would you come down and we'll get a confession out of him?" Another quandary for Father Stan. He wanted no part of forcing anyone to confess. That was not a priest's job. Delaying again, he replied, "Well, look, I'm going to get something to eat and I'll be down." He opened a can of food and shortly afterward the telephone rang again. "Father, you need not hurry," the sheriff said. "We've talked to this man and he has confessed."

Such a hasty admission of murder was very troubling. Had the man who was being charged been coerced into admitting the crime? Father Stan needed more details to be assured that the investigation had been conducted correctly. The suspect was indeed a stranger, a man from New Mexico, who was living with a girl from the Standing Rock Reservation. They thought that Dick Harrison had lots of money, but when the man killed Dick he found only 60 cents in his pocket. The murder, however, convinced Father Stan that the folks in Pierre needed a priest to console them in times of trouble and that he should move there.

The people in Pierre whom Father Stan served were poor and many were Indians who had congregated near the municipal dump. There were no roads or street lights or running water or telephone lines beyond that point, yet that was where he chose to live and to establish a home for his congregation. The monks from Blue Cloud bought two lots about a block and a half from the dump and arranged to move a World War II Quonset hut that had done double duty as a dance hall to the site to become the church building.

The church and the house where Father Stan lived were barely habitable, so much that the bishop was in for a shock when he showed up in Pierre to administer confirmation. The drum that the Indians used during Catholic ceremonies was too wide to fit through the doorway into the little church. The entrance, however, was wide enough that a crowd could squeeze into the building. Latecomers had no place to sit except on the steps of the altar and the bishop had to step over them.

Father Stan was hardly embarrassed. His explanation revealed to what extent his ministry had embraced the Native Americans. "Bishop, this is our tradition, us Indians," he said. The usual pomp was missing yet the ceremony impressed a priest who had accompanied the bishop. "I was never at a nice confirmation like that before, because there were people. It wasn't just ceremony. It wasn't just liturgy," he commented.

The new pastor was delighted that his church was not a fancy edifice. Imposing architecture, elaborate vestments and a huge organ could, in his opinion, actually distract people from praying. He was sure that Jesus felt comfortable in simple places of worship and that was what he wanted, too. In fact, there was not even a private place in the building to hear confessions. A friend agreed to build one. "You had to squeeze in sideways and once you were in there was no easy way of getting out, but we had a confessional," Father Stan recalled.

Providing a home for the parish priest proved even more of a challenge. At first Father Augustine Edele, O.S.B. advanced $50 to buy a trailer, but the unstable structure was, in Father Stan's words, "like a floating dish pan," and he got rid of it. A tiny house became available for $100, which was all the money Father Stan owned. It had no windows and the doors were hanging off the hinges, but the structure could be expanded to 20 feet by 20 feet, big enough for a bathroom in one corner and living quarters in the rest of the building.

The material needed for the extension of the house came from the Oahe Dam on the Missouri River, which was under construction at that time. Hundreds of laborers were on the job and plenty of scrap lumber, which they had used for wooden forms to hold the concrete being poured at the Dam, was available for building a house. Father Stan raised another $200 to purchase other materials. With help from the Harrison family the foundation for the house was laid, a water line was brought to the property and a septic system was being planned. The house was about ready to be placed on the foundation when Abbot Gilbert from Blue Cloud Abbey arrived in Pierre.

The Abbot looked over the project and asked Father Stan what he was doing. When the Abbot heard that it was to become Father Stan's residence he ordered him to stop the work. The Abbot decided that the residence was not big enough and his word was final. The two Benedictines walked around the Park Street neighborhood so that the Abbot would understand that the other homes were even smaller. He was reluctant to change his mind, but finally softened his opposition by telling Father Stan that he would supply the lumber to build a larger house.

Father Stan's friends pitched in after a semi-trailer pulled up to the site carrying the pre-cut lumber for the 32 foot by 28 foot building. Jim King, Frank Heenan and Father Stan began construction by borrowing a backhoe from Stephan to dig an excavation. As that phase of the work was ending, some of the monks traveled from Blue Cloud and spent two weeks pouring footings and laying blocks. There were no sewers near Park Street so the men dug a large basin to catch the overflow from the septic tank. The project ended when Albert Bruce helped to install the electric wiring and put the finishing touches on the job.

As the walls were being constructed and everyone noticed the size of the house it became apparent that it would be larger and more comfortable than most of those on the surrounding streets. Some of the neighbors' homes were so shabby that their children could not play on the floors because they were too cold. Father

Stan felt embarrassed about his living quarters and resolved that everyone in the community would have the opportunity to use it at any time. The priest told himself, "The door of this house is never going to be locked. It will always be open." That public-spirited decision led to a problem for Father Stan later.

Finally, in November, 1959, three years after he had been assigned to the Stephan mission, Father Stan moved into his new home in Pierre. As he had anticipated, it quickly became a gathering place for his Indians friends. Father Stan often walked in and discovered a group of kids lying on the living room floor watching television or playing a game.

The house was big enough for four persons to stay overnight and no one, including Father Stan, could guess who might be sleeping there. He returned late one night and found a man asleep on a couch in the living room, two more in another room and when he walked into his room a fourth person was resting in his own bed. A Jesuit priest had not only brought the strangers to Father Stan's home, but also suggested that their host should go to the hospital to spend the night!

The entrance remained open all day long and whenever young men or women knocked on the door and asked, "Father, could I take a shower, please?," he welcomed them inside because he knew that their only alternatives were the washtub in their kitchen sink or no shower at all. Indeed, Father Stan's house was a community resource. It had two spigots on the outside and water was free to anyone who wanted it.

Friends could borrow the tools in the basement and if they needed his station wagon to cart some junk to the dump it was available without charge. Whoever needed to make a telephone call could come to the priest's home, so he was not surprised after returning from a trip to find a penciled note on the kitchen table which read, "Father, I made a call to Eagle Butte. Let me know at the end of the month how much it is." The open-door policy undoubtedly helped to foster his friendship with everyone in the neighborhood.

Families who lived near the dump needed work not merely for the income, but also for the personal fulfillment that results from doing a good job. Father Stan wanted to help and one night while he was praying his attention strayed and suddenly he formed an idea about how his neighbors could earn some money. He remembered that one of his grandmothers had made and sold hooked rugs. His neighbors surely were just as capable.

A group of Indian women obtained the yarn and needles, the wooden frames and the canvas-like material to stretch across the frames. Father Stan chose Indian designs for the rugs and the women picked the colors. He was their unofficial salesman, carrying a supply of the homemade rugs in his car as he traveled on Route 90 back and forth across South Dakota between Sioux Falls and Rapid City. The project employed four women who could earn $10.00 a day, a sizeable sum at that time and place.

Once settled in Pierre, Father Stan began to lend a hand to the rest of the community. The "big church on the hill" needed a basketball coach for its school team so once again he began instructing a group of youngsters. He taught the nurses at Mercy Hospital and the children at Pierre Indian School, served as chaplain to the South Dakota legislature and helped the local police and judges when they asked for assistance. People showed up to arrange a wedding or a funeral and all in all Father Stan, like many missionaries, was so busy that he seldom had an evening to himself.

The people of Pierre repaid Father Stan's counsel and kindness, not very often with money, but more frequently with an occasional cake or loaf of fresh bread dropped off on his kitchen table or a piece of meat left in the refrigerator. The house became the collection point for Christmas gifts for the local children and, because it was never locked, Father Stan came home late one night and sensed that in his absence someone had broken in and things were missing.

He checked the kitchen, the bedroom and his office and found nothing unusual, but when he entered the basement his suspicions were confirmed. The toys were gone. The women in the parish had affixed labels such as "boy - ten years old" and "girl - six years old" so that Santa Claus could distribute the gifts quickly. Nevertheless, all that remained in the basement were three empty cartons and torn wrapping paper scattered around the floor. However, the intruders had left the house.

Should he call the police? After thinking it over Father Stan decided not to investigate. He packed the debris into his pick-up truck and carried it to the dump where he burned it. About four or five days later the mystery was solved. A tall Indian woman knocked on the back door of his house. She stood there crying, but also gripping firmly the hands of her children, a five-and-a-half- year old boy and another about four years old.

"Father, these are the ones who broke into your house and took those toys," the mother said. She was humiliated as she explained that while the kids stole the gifts they only intended to play with them. Father Stan tried to console her, "Well, now please don't be upset. We'll get more. It's only September. We have three months. Please don't punish them."

Christmas presents were not the only things that disappeared from Park Street. Father Stan always parked his car in front of the house, available for anyone to borrow, and usually left the keys in the ignition. About 6 A. M. one morning he was ready to go out the front door on his way to say Mass. His eyes were barely open when he looked outside on the street. The car was not there. He checked behind the house and it was not there either. He couldn't remember where he had left the car or whether a friend had asked to use it. There was no other explanation so Father Stan notified the police that it might have been stolen.

The telephone rang about 9 A. M. and a police officer announced, "Hey, come and get your car. Because it was stolen it's in the middle of the street, sideways, and we want to get it out of there." When he reached the car it wouldn't start. He assumed that there was no gas left in the tank and called a truck to supply some fuel. The driver opened the flap to the gas tank and announced, "You ain't got no gas tank neither."

The thieves apparently had driven over a bump in the road which had ripped the tank loose from the car. Someone found it a couple of blocks away. Later, after the criminals went to jail, they apologized, "Oh, Father, we didn't do no trouble." However, they taught Father Stan a lesson: he stopped leaving his keys in the car.

The neighborhood around the church and priest's house was hardly a peaceful residential area. There was a frequent uproar across the street where the members of a white family drank and fought constantly. One night the priest thought that the worst had happened. Screams of "Murder!, Murder!" filled Father Stan's room and he jumped out of bed to look outside.

The commotion was only his drunken neighbors battling again. One of the sons had been thrown out of the house. He tumbled into a slop bucket, picked himself up and stumbled over to Father Stan's house yelling for him to call the police. The priest, wearing only his pajamas, stood shivering in the doorway, but determined to bar the young man's entry until he calmed him and peace returned to Park Street.

Saints Peter and Paul Church, the so-called "big church on the hill," ministered to many of the Catholics in Pierre, but few of the parishioners were Indians. Father Stan's description of that church told a great deal about the difference between it and Saint John's church, his little building near the city dump. The wealthier citizens of Pierre attended Saints Peter and Paul Parish. The clergy there celebrated four Masses every weekend and operated a parochial school. The white folks headed for the big church on the hill and the Sioux Indians worshipped at Father Stan's Parish. Saint John's nevertheless was a bustling community with three Masses every Sunday. Some were so packed that the floor sagged under the weight of the congregation. A busload of Indian boys came to the earliest Mass on Sunday and Governor Bill Kneip, his wife and seven sons attended occasionally. "It's so nice to pray down here," the Governor told Father Stan. "It's kind of real."

No law or rule of the Church had ordered or even suggested that Indians and other Catholics should worship in separate places, but nevertheless it was apparent in the Catholic churches in Pierre. The public perception of the two parishes revealed a prejudice against the Indians that was barely below the surface. Moreover, a tense relationship had developed between Father Stan and Monsignor McGuire, the pastor of Saints Peter and Paul. A few of the Monsignor's parishioners passed up his church in favor of Saint John's and that annoyed him. He demanded that Father Stan turn away any white worshipers and that he erect a sign in front of Saint John's that would read "For Indians Only."

Instead of rejecting the proposal outright Father Stan offered to make two signs. He would put one reading "For Whites Only" at the entrance to Saints Peter and Paul. "Oh, no," the Monsignor replied, "mine is a Catholic church. It's for everybody." It hardly needed explanation that the little building near the dump was just as much a Catholic church. The idea of the identifying signs never surfaced again and the two priests eventually repaired their working relationship.

Despite Monsignor McGuire's desire to attract all of the white families to the big church on the hill, some of them heard Mass at the little church in the Quonset Hut. Other residents of Pierre who had problems on their mind came to discuss them with Father Stan. Mary Louise Defender, at one time Miss Indian America, was uncomfortable attending Mass at Saints Peter and Paul and finally asked Father Stan if she could come to Saint John's.

"Father, I've tried to go to the big church, but every time I go in there I feel the eyes of people staring me down," she said. "I feel there is something else in their eyes besides that. I don't like to pray when people look at me that way." Father Stan welcomed her to attend Saint John's Church at any time and assured her that she would be praying among friends.

Mike, another Catholic Indian, worked in the drafting division of the highway department and his children studied at Saints Peter and Paul School. "I am with white people all the time," Mike said. "I coach their basketball, I try to be part of the group up there, but I guess I'm different. I just can't pray with them. Can I come and pray with you folk?" He, too, was invited to Father Stan's parish.

Stan Donald "Cheehab" Morin and his wife, Frankie Jeanotte, also were members of Saint John's Parish. He was acquainted with Father Stan, having played on the priest's basketball team that won the All-Indian tournament in 1957. Frankie was the head floor nurse at St. Mary's Hospital in Pierre. Happily married, they invited their pastor to dinner to show off their little apartment.

Barely a week later all their belongings filled their Ford coupe and the couple sat crying in front of Father Stan's house. What happened, he asked? They explained tearfully that they had rented their apartment from a woman whose husband, the owner, was away on a sales trip. When the man returned he saw Frankie leaving the building to go shopping and screamed out the back door, "Who are you? Where did you come from? What are you doing here? Get out of here, you damned Indian!"

The couple explained that they had paid a month's rent in advance and they wanted to stay. Their pleas made no difference. The owner shouted that they must leave within an hour. With no place else to go, they wound up at Father Stan's front doorstep asking for help. He came to their rescue and found the couple another place to live.

The white people who hated Indians often lacked the courage to confront them face to face. A telephone call that an Indian businesswoman received one night was a good example. Mrs. Johnson taught music and operated a small bakery in her home. As soon as word spread that she wanted to expand her business by opening a store in the center of the city, racist hostility revealed itself.

"You're Indian, let me tell you right now that you will never open a shop on Main Street in Pierre," a male caller said. He would not identify himself and hung up the telephone. A little sleuthing disclosed that the bigot-in-hiding was one of the most prominent citizens of the city.

Prejudice could surface anywhere. When an Indian lawyer opened a new office he found that midnight visitors had piled cow guts on his doorstep. Father Stan was a white man who was pro-fairness. He interceded for Indians more than once, including the time when a white tenant refused to pay his landlord, an Indian named Jim Black. An altercation ensued and the authorities charged the Indian with assaulting the white man. Father Stan felt that Black needed support so he went to court and helped to acquit the Indian.

One of the hospitals in Pierre summoned a funeral director to pick up the body of a dead boy. When the man learned that the corpse was Indian he refused to prepare it for burial and instead drove to the Indian school, dropped off the sack containing the body at the door and hurried away. Father Stan was outraged and initiated a program that helped many Indians who were faced with a death in the family.

That incident demonstrated that the Indian people of Pierre needed an inexpensive way to take care of their own funerals. Father Stan arranged such a plan. First he went to the South Dakota Attorney General's office to research the state statute regulating burials. The law simply said that the deceased person had to be buried by the next of kin within a reasonable time and in a decent manner. Neither embalming nor an undertaker was required. Armed with that information, he asked the state lawyers if he could assist in the burial. Don't go into the funeral business, they warned, but caring for the dead was permissible as long as the next of kin consented.

Adding up the price of a coffin, embalming and a hearse, funerals often cost as much as $400, which for some Indian families meant mortgaging their homes or foregoing even the rudiments of a memorial service. Father Stan figured that a dignified burial could be performed for much less money.

Larry Young Bear, the son-in-law of Dick Harrison, and Father Stan bought a table saw and they began building wooden coffins in various sizes. The priest furnished the lumber and Larry did the assembly work. They painted the outside of the box and Larry's wife, Carol, lined the inside with a plain white cloth. When a death occurred the family handled the body, shaving the deceased individual, if it were a man, and combing the hair. For the hearse they used Father Stan's all-purpose station wagon. When the work was finished the total cost to the bereaved family had been reduced to about $90 for deceased adults and $25 for children.

His Indian congregants knew that Father Stan was on their side, not only because of what he did, but also because he kept reminding them that they truly were good persons. Hearing that heartwarming message Sunday after Sunday, one woman remembered, "We looked at each other, wondering if he was really talking about us or somebody else. He kept saying it and finally we began to believe it. That made us feel good and we started to go to communion easily."

By now aware of Father Stan's obvious affection for them, the churchgoers at Saint John's were, to say the least, surprised and dismayed when one Sunday their pastor made an announcement: any family in the parish who wanted a fancy wedding or a big funeral should make arrangements at the big church on the hill.

Didn't he love Saint John's as much as they did? Or perhaps the reason was that their church was being closed. After all, the only time Bishop Lambert A. Hoch visited Saint John's Church he walked around the former dance hall for a few minutes and on his way out grumbled, "Stan, this is the poorest church in the diocese." What was the reason for sending the parishioners away?

No one reacted to Father Stan's pronouncement and after a couple of weeks passed he repeated it. That afternoon Clara Harrison, Dick's wife and the parish organist for ten years, attended a meeting with the priest. She sat smoking a cigarette, watching Father Stan and silently fuming. At last she snapped, "Father, I can see you want to close our church." He denied it with equal vigor. "No, maybe the bishop wants to close our church, then," the woman persisted.

Father Stan told her that he never heard such an idea. "I'm going to write to this bishop and tell him we like our church and we don't want it closed," the still irate Clara declared. She encouraged other members of the parish to protest and the bishop's reply ended the uncertainty. In essence it said, "Mrs. Harrison and my friends, let me say categorically that any time I find people that love their church as much as you love yours, I can promise you that I will never close their place of worship."

Perhaps the Indians thought that Saint John's church would be shut because it was too expensive to maintain it. It was a guess, but close to the truth because, while the monthly expenses ran to about $90 a month, the Sunday collection averaged $8 every Sunday. A weekly bingo game kept the parish afloat financially, but Father Stan tired of it and when summer came he suggested that the game be suspended for a couple of months. "Oh, no, father," the bingo workers said in unison. "We have our birthday parties and everything during the breaks. If you can't be here, we'll make the coffee and take care of everything."

Father Stan had learned how to raise money many years earlier when he and Father Eisenman traveled to Nebraska to examine the successful fund-raising program at Boys Town. Now he put his training into practice by mailing solicitations to people far beyond Pierre. He started by subscribing to seven or eight weekly Catholic papers. They contained wedding announcements with the names and addresses of three families: the couple to be married, the parents of the bride and the parents of the groom. He complied that information into a list of prospective contributors and wrote to them asking for money for the parish.

The struggle to keep the doors of Saint John's Church open was more difficult because of the lack of encouragement from the Bishop and Abbot Gilbert. Ethnicity is the base of any community, Father Stan argued. There are ethnic German parishes, Irish parishes, Polish parishes. If the people want it why shouldn't an American Indian parish stay in business?

Father Stan had worked with the Indians in Pierre for ten years, but the area around the city dump was changing and eventually he and his bishop had to face the hard reality that maybe the church should be closed. Keep the parish going, Father Stan argued, even if a deacon or a sister had to take the place of a priest. It seemed that the handwriting was on the wall when the Abbot at Blue Cloud asked him to leave Pierre and return to Belcourt. The Benedictine community knew that if it were to staff Saint John's Parish they would have to send another priest almost 100 miles each weekend just to say Mass.

That was not a workable solution and the Benedictines announced that after July 1, 1982 they would be unable to provide a priest. The building was sold and the diocese advised its Indian parishioners in Pierre to attend Saints Peter and Paul Parish. Some still felt out of place among the white people at the big church on the hill.

Blessed Kateri Tekakwitha

Chapter Thirteen - The Kateri Tekakwitha Conference

A young Indian woman named Kateri Tekakwitha died in Quebec, Canada in 1680. She lived less than 24 years, yet the legacy of her courage and steadfastness in her Catholic faith spread among all future generations of American Indians and set an example for thousands of priests, sisters and Catholic laypersons. More than two-and-a-half centuries later missionaries, mostly Benedictines, formed an association to assist Catholic Indians in the plains states and within months they honored Kateri Tekakwitha by naming the organization after her.

Her father was a Mohawk Indian chief who lived with her mother, a Christian Indian woman, near Ossernenon, later called Auriesville, in New York State. Kateri was born in 1656, but was not christened at that time. In accordance with the custom of Indian women who converted to the faith their children could only be baptized by a "black-robe", as Catholic priests were called, and black-robes did not reach their village very often.

Kateri's happy childhood ended four years later when a smallpox epidemic swept through Ossernenon, killing a third of the people, including her parents and her only brother. The disease took its toll on Kateri, too, scarring the child's face and leaving her extraordinarily sensitive to light. Sunshine or even the glare of light on newly-fallen snow caused Kateri so much pain that she spent much time in the darkened longhouse in the village.

Despite such impairments she forced herself to leave shelter and go into the daylight to perform her chores. During those periods she protected her eyes and walked slowly throughout the village, feeling her way as she stumbled along. This handicap was Kateri's most noticeable characteristic and when the time came for the elders to decide what to call the child it seemed natural that her name should be "Tekakwitha," which means "She who pushes with her hands."

The girl's uncle, the chief of the Turtle tribe, her foster mother, Anastasia, and some aunts took Kateri under their care and the women began to teach her the skills that she would need to become a wife. She learned to weave corn husks into slippers and to create ribbons from eelskin that she dyed red with sturgeon glue. Although Kateri had the household competence which were necessary for an Indian girl to marry, she had no desire to do so. What the girl desired most was to become a Catholic and she told three Jesuit missionaries who traveled to her village in 1667. However, she was not christened during their visit and there were long intervals between trips by priests to that part of Canada. Nine years passed before another missionary, Father Jacques deLamberville, S. J. baptized her "Kateri" in honor of Saint Catherine of Alexandria.

Kateri's wishes notwithstanding, her adoptive family selected a prospective bridegroom. She rejected the man's attention and when she refused to perform any chores on Sundays other Indians targeted the convert for persecution. Kateri knew the rule: Indians who did not work did not eat. The family deliberately exhausted Kateri with back-breaking chores and the children in the village derisively called her "the Christian."

Although the message to Kateri was clear - stop practicing your Christian beliefs - she remained stalwart in her faith and finally escaped to the Saint Francis Xavier Mission on the Saint Lawrence River near Montreal. Kateri's reputation as a virtuous girl preceded her. Father deLamberville had written to a fellow missionary, "You will soon know what a treasure we have sent you. Guard it well!"

With acts of mortification such as branding her feet as the Indians did to slaves, mixing ashes into her food and round-the-clock prayers on Sundays and religious feast days, Kateri's faith deepened even while her health deteriorated. She was so fervent that she wanted to form her own religious community, but the Church was hesitant to approve it.

The change of scene, however, did not end the harassment of Kateri. A married Indian man made a canoe and needed help to pull it out of the woods. When she innocently offered to assist him the man's wife accused her of engaging in an improper relationship with her husband. Kateri denied the charge, yet suspicions remained amidst the tribe for a long time until her friends realized that she was entirely blameless.

During Lent in 1680 Kateri's health began to fail seriously. The headaches, fever and stomach cramps reached the point where she became bedridden. Kateri realized that life was ebbing away and she called her friend, Marie Therese Tegaiaguanta, to her side. She said, "I am leaving you. I am about to die. Always remember what we have done together since we knew each other; if you change I will accuse you before the tribunal of God. Take courage, despite the discourse of those who have no faith, when they wish to persuade you to marry, listen only to the priests. If you cannot serve God here go to the Lorette mission. I will love you in heaven. I will pray for you. I will assist you."

Kateri died on Wednesday of Holy Week at the Caughnawaga Mission. Her last words were, "Iesos konoronkiwa" which means, "Jesus, I love you." Eyewitnesses were amazed when within 15 minutes of her death the pock-mark scars disappeared and her face glowed with a beautiful smile.

Had Jesuit missionaries not been present at the time of her death and recorded those extraordinary events, Kateri's story might have faded into the recesses of ancient history. Instead, the account of her exemplary life became widely known among the clergy and the Indians. Many believed that Kateri's memory could inspire a miracle. An unexplained event happened after Joseph Kellogg, a 13-year-old boy who had been captured by Indians in 1704 during a raid on Deerfield, Massachusetts, became ill with smallpox. A Jesuit priest, feeling that all other remedies had been exhausted, prayed over him with a relic from Kateri's coffin. Joseph agreed to convert to Catholicism if the sickness passed and when he regained his health he kept his promise.

Kateri's reputation spread not only throughout the United States, but also across the Atlantic Ocean, especially after Pope Pius XII proclaimed her Venerable in 1941, a step toward possible elevation to sainthood. Indians who believed in her sanctity formed Kateri Circles in all parts of the United States. By 1997 about 125 of these Circles were praying for the canonization of Kateri. The movement continues to grow.

A couple of years before the Pope bestowed this honor on Kateri Father Eisenman had an idea. He knew that Bishop Aloysius Muench intended to celebrate the 50th anniversary of the Diocese of Fargo, North Dakota and he suggested that it would be an appropriate occasion to call a meeting of the Benedictine missionaries who worked in the Dakotas and Minnesota.

Bishop Muench, later elevated to Cardinal, agreed and scheduled the first meeting of the Plains States Missionary Conference for the basement of the cathedral in Fargo. Some priests were reluctant to attend. They offered an excuse: the Bureau of Catholic Indian Missions (BCIM) was furnishing money to some of the missionaries and they feared that their presence might suggest some dissatisfaction with BCIM and thus jeopardize their funding. Nevertheless, 24 men assembled in October, 1939, all of them priests except Father Stan, who was then a sub-deacon assigned to the St. Michael's Mission, and three Catholic Indian lay leaders from the Fort Totten Reservation.

Their agenda was far-reaching, for they intended, among other things, to discuss and map out the future of the Catholic schools on the missions, an ambitious schedule for a one-day meeting. Bishop Muench wanted to learn how the missionaries won the confidence of the Indians and he imagined that the Conference would answer his questions. However, the Indian laymen who were there merely listened and did not disclose their side of the story.

Although the meeting the next year remained strictly for the clergy, Father Justin Snyder, O.S.B. took an important step to connect the Conference more closely with the Native Americans. He realized that the heroic life of Kateri Tekakwitha had for centuries inspired many Indians and he recommended that the annual gathering be named in her honor. The other men attending readily agreed.

The agenda of these gatherings continued to be similar for several years: Benedictine priests provided the leadership, a small number of clergy and some nuns attended, but the Indians still did not play a role. Other religious orders, including the Franciscans and the Sacred Heart Fathers, joined the Benedictines as the key participants. But Father Stan realized that some were not taking the planning of the annual event very seriously. He recalled driving to one meeting with Father Timothy Sexton, O.S.B., who was then the Conference chairman, and Father Sexton remarked casually, "What shall we talk about when we get there?"

A revolutionary change in the yearly meeting occurred at the Sacred Heart Monastery in Yankton, South Dakota in 1979. For one thing the crowd was larger; four bishops sat at the head table and about 300 invited guests from the reservations were in the crowd. In the rear of the room Bea Swanson stood near Father Stan. She was a shy woman, but Father Stan saw that she was determined. Finally he asked, "Grandma, what's the matter?" Bea replied, "Can I say something sometime?" For an Indian woman to address the assembled clergy would be a major departure from past practices, but Father Stan nevertheless passed the request on to Bishop Paul Dudley.

"Oh, come on, grandma, come on down here," the smiling Bishop said, welcoming Bea to come forward. When she reached the front of the room, the little Indian woman turned toward the bishops and declared, "Oh, you bishops are so nice." They nodded and smiled amid appreciative laughter. "You say such nice things," Bea continued and the smiles became bigger and the expectations of the audience became grander.

Having captured the attention of her audience, Bea got to the point immediately. As the hierarchy sat awaiting more praise she changed the tone and surprised them: "But you say them all the same way. There's nothing new after all these years." The minutes of the meeting do not record any more smiles and laughter. She became bolder: "Can we Indians talk to you by ourselves? You say you are our pastors. Can we just be alone? Can the priests and the sisters go out? We have something to say to you."

Uncertain where the discussion was headed, but certain that they had been trapped into listening, the bishops sat silently and heard a series of complaints and recommendations. Priests often were not available for wakes, home visits and gatherings of Native Americans, Bea and other Indian spokespersons charged, and they urged that more of their own people be ordained to the priesthood. The Indians obviously prepared well for their first opportunity to make their case before the leaders of the Church. They checked off a host of other concerns, among them a stronger role for Indian women in the Church, encouraging religious orders to send native sisters to live among their own people, the possible use of married clergy, and a plea not to assign priests to the reservations if they didn't want to work among the Native Americans. After all, they reminded the audience, the Indian people had accumulated centuries of wisdom and the Church should make good use of it.

That meeting was the turning point for the fledgling organization. With the Conference now bearing the name of an Indian heroine, representatives of various tribes had an even better reason to participate and they did, their numbers soaring into the thousands. It was no longer just a plains states event. Instead the Conference convened in such diverse locations as Spokane, Washington; Orono, Maine; Albuquerque, New Mexico; Potsdam, New York and the Blue Cloud Abbey in South Dakota.

Approximately 15,000 men, women and children from reservations all over North America assembled in Phoenix in 1987 to pray with Pope John Paul II. Two years later, Francis Cardinal Arinze of Nigeria spoke at the 50th anniversary convention of the Conference at Fargo, where it all began. As the years passed Father Stan became the only survivor of the group that had attended the original meeting.

The Tekakwitha Conference continued to play an important role throughout Father Stan's life. He served as chairman in 1971, the first time anyone other than priests were invited. A different opportunity seemed available in 1978. The Bureau of Catholic Indian Missions informed Father Stan that he had been nominated to become permanent executive director of the Conference. It was just the kind of leadership assignment that he wanted. The offer sounded good enough to inquire about the salary, but ultimately he didn't get the job.

The Diocese of Sioux Falls scheduled its own celebration of Kateri Tekakwitha Day for July 10, 1983 and Bishop Dudley assigned Father Stan to coordinate the event. An unforeseen problem arose immediately because Abbot Alan of Blue Cloud told Father Stan that he should not accept the appointment. After a number of telephone conversations with the Bishop the Abbot agreed to change his mind.

The next year ten Indian convicts from the South Dakota state penitentiary were invited to participate in the celebration of Kateri Tekakwitha Day festivities at St. Joseph Cathedral in Sioux Falls. The men were singers and drummers and the warden agreed to let them attend. Still, some people worried about their guests, particularly because one of them had been convicted of breaking into St. Isaac Jogues Chapel in an incident in which one priest died of a heart attack and another was shot in the leg.

Father Stan said the principal Mass and one of the prisoners was his altar server. The sermon and the Mass itself were said in the Indian language and afterward the convicts sang a song in honor of Kateri as the worshipers filed out of the Cathedral. None of the prisoners caused any trouble and the entire program went off peacefully.

Kateri Tekakwitha Day became an annual event in Sioux Falls and convicts continued to participate. Father Stan booked The Freedom Singers to come in 1988. They too were prisoners from the state penitentiary and five of the men came along with the wives of two of them. The following year two inmates who were serving life sentences were chosen to sing, but a few days before the ceremony was scheduled another convict tried to escape and the warden ordered that all prisoners remain locked in their cells. Deacon Ed Zephier, an Indian himself, saved the day by arranging for the Rising Hail Drumrners and the Rising Hail Singers to fill in for the convicts.

Chapter Fourteen - The Medicine Men

"Wakantanka, Tunkasila, Great God, Grandfather, look on me today. I am old like you. We old people know everything. We know what the young people are looking for. We know, because we were that way once, and we learned. We lived under the great blue sky, and we learned. We lived with your wide prairies, and we learned.

"We lived with the two legged and the four legged, and we learned. We watched them all, and they taught us during the warm days of summer and during the long nights of winter. We learned that being nice is better than being right. We learned that being generous is better than being greedy. We learned that forgiving is better than getting even.

"Now we see a new world and we pray for its happiness. In this world no one listens, so we show them how to be quiet. No one takes time, so we are patient. No one works carefully, so we look closely. Grandfather, do not let our knowledge disappear. Help us to share it with our relatives. They are our family. You took time to teach us. We are happy in our lives because we learned what the sun and the sky and the earth and the animals had to say to us. We learned that we are all related. What happens to any one of us happened to all of us. What we do that is good for one is good for everyone. No one is alone.

"Grandfather, keep our family together. Help us Elders to reach out and bring your love to every land and stream. If you ask us we will do it. He hecetu!"

The daughter of an 80-year old Indian woman asked Father Stan to compose a prayer for her mother. His thoughts, written above, were a blend of traditional Christian ethics and ancient Indian beliefs, expressed in simple and direct words so that both white persons and Native Americans could understand them.

In the beginning God was a very distant creature for both the early Judeo-Christian community and the Native American. The Dakota people called him "Wakan," the "Other," a mysterious, holy being, "anything that was hard to understand".

The word "Wakan" was combined with other words to form expressions which when translated are comparable to terms that are familiar to Catholics. "Yutapi wakan," which means holy food, reminds Catholics of the Holy Eucharist. "Tipi wakan," which in Lakota Sioux described a sacred place, were the words for a church building. The Indian God became an individual with the name "Taku Wakan" and later took on a personality with an awesome greatness and a different name, "Wakantanka," the opening word in Father Stan's prayer at the beginning of this chapter.

In the lore of the Dakota Sioux, one of several groups of the Sioux Indians, "Wakantanka" was never born and could never die. Although their God was still the Great Mysterious, the Dakotas began to see in him attributes such as wisdom, age, benevolence and love. These were the characteristics of a grandfather and so they called God by another name, "Tunkasila," or sometimes Great Grandfather, "Tunkasila Wakan Tanka."

As Catholics ask the Blessed Mother and the saints to petition God on their behalf, the Dakota Indians also have their intercessor, "Wakinyan." A combination of two words which mean "he who speaks holy," Wakinyan's might is demonstrated by the English-language title: "The Thunderer." The Indians consider Wakinyan a combination of mediator, judge and guide who presents their problems to God and who in turn tells them God's answer.

Wakinyan often is depicted as an eagle. The Indians find attributes in eagles, other birds and animals that white persons do not appreciate. So it was in the death and burial of Elijah Eagle, who for many years had been a mainstay at the annual summer conference of several hundred Catholic Sioux. Elijah earned the reputation of being dedicated to his friends. He proved his mettle on one occasion when a man who had visited him in the hospital died in a head-on collision on the drive home. When the news reached Elijah he left his hospital bed without a second thought and went to help at his friend's funeral.

As the date grew near for the annual summer gathering of the Sioux, Elijah was hospitalized again with a heart condition. He worried who would feed all the guests at the conference. "I'm going to be there," he said to Father Stan. "All these people have been nice to me all my life and now they are coming to our reservation. I have to take care of them." By the third morning of the conference, the odor of fresh coffee reached all corners of the camp and, true to his word, Elijah was on the job, cheerfully carrying fry bread and syrup from table to table.

Elijah had just welcomed a group of Ogala Sioux and turned to greet more friends when suddenly he became pale and slumped to the ground. By the time Elijah drew a hand to his chest a heart attack had killed him. Clara, his wife, wanted the funeral services at a tiny chapel that her husband had helped to build. However, so many persons were eager to attend that the building clearly could not hold them. The second church chosen also was too small. Finally the family moved the ceremony to a white church in Sisseton, South Dakota and still it was barely large enough to accommodate the mourners and many stood in the aisles.

At the cemetery the deep pounding of the buffalo skin drum echoed among the crowd. The military veterans rendered a final salute and the Traditional Men of the tribe brought their sweet grass to the graveside. As the Indian pipe was being passed among the crowd, Father Stan noticed that more and more of the men and women were looking upward. About 1,500 feet in the sky, three eagles could be seen against the cumulus clouds, wheeling slowly in intertwining circles above Elijah's final resting place.

"Look, Father," Hiram Owen nudged Father Stan. "They say other creatures don't know anything. Those eagles know what Elijah did with his life. He spent it, Father. And that's all you can do with your life. Give it to others." Everyone gazed upward in awe and when they walked away silently, they heard Hiram say, "That should say something about the power of Indian prayer." Father

Stan left the graveyard thinking of his own name, Eagle Man, which an old Indian woman and her friends had conferred on him.

Hiram Owen's comments demonstrate how strongly the Indians feel the presence of God in all things and in all places in their lives. Their dead are seen as intermediaries to the spiritual realm, spirits who can be transformed into rain clouds or who appear in dreams to provide direction.

Another story, about Bob Clifford's missing son, Donald, combined a Catholic family's belief in God's mercy and its reluctant appeal to an Indian holy man for help in finding the boy. Bob Clifford was the basketball coach at Holy Rosary Mission and a gentleman in both victory and defeat. If Father Stan's team triumphed, Bob was the first person to cross the court, his hand outstretched, with words of congratulations. "Father, your boys were in great shape. Nobody could have beat them tonight. You really taught them well." Sometimes it was Bob's team that won and he was equally quick to greet the priest with a good word. "Well, Father, the ball bounces in our favor once in a while. Sometimes the breaks come our way. Your boys played a real good game, but this was our lucky night."

There were several children in the Clifford family. One was a nun and a son, Donald, attended the School of Mines in Rapid City, South Dakota. He came home for the Christmas vacation and soon left with his .22 caliber rifle to go hunting in one of the canyons nearby. The boy did not return that night, or the following day. At first Donald's absence did not concern his parents. The Cliffords were a large family with grandparents, cousins and uncles spread throughout the area and the young man might have decided to spend some time with any one or more of them.

When several more days passed and no one had seen or heard anything everyone began to worry. Donald's brothers searched the canyons and didn't find a clue to his whereabouts. For several weeks the family prayed and arranged for a Mass to ask God to bring the boy home safely. Bob Clifford's father was staying with the family during that period, but offered no comment about his grandson's fate. His silence was typical of elderly Indians who possess the wisdom of their years, but hold back from expressing themselves. Father Stan summarized their attitude: "That you be not forward, that you be not brash, that you not push yourself, but you wait until you are asked for advice." Finally, Bob asked his father what he should do.

The advice - go see Frank Fool's Crow, the Indian medicine man - troubled the Cliffords. Catholic priests had told them for years that these medicine men practiced witchcraft and they were evil. Yet Fool's Crow was one of the most revered of the Sioux shamans or holy men, the wicasa wakan. For several days Donald's mother agonized over her father-in-law's suggestion and finally made her decision. "I want my son," she told her husband.

Would it be wrong just to speak to Fool's Crow? Fretful yet desperate for an answer, the couple drove to the old Indian's home and found him sitting on the doorstep. Near the house was a prayer hut lodge, a round low structure made of bent twigs and covered with leaves. It was there that the old man took his pipe, his drum and his flute when he wanted to be alone with God.

The Cliffords sat next to Fool's Crow, a heavy, elderly and wise man. No one said anything, observing the Indian custom that there is no need for conversation when sharing another person's company. The silence ran its course and Bob asked Fool's Crow if he could help find their son. "Yes, I will help you," he replied. "Come back tomorrow and I will tell you."

The parents returned with groceries and some tobacco for the shaman and sat beside him again. Fool's Crow held out four fingers and said, "Your son is dead. He is shot. He is under a tree. The animals have not disturbed his body." The holy man then named the canyon where the corpse was located. Distraught, but thankful for the information, the Cliffords hurried home.

The boy's brothers saddled their horses immediately and raced off to the canyon. A ride from one end of the canyon to the other revealed nothing. Turning around provided a different perspective of the shadows on the earth and they detected traces indicating that some object had slid down the wall of the canyon. On reaching the floor the search party found about a dozen .22 caliber shells. Someone had tumbled down the wall and at the bottom had fired a rifle repeatedly, no doubt trying to attract attention. The boys widened their search and beneath the low, spreading branches of an evergreen tree they discovered the body of their dead brother.

People soon pieced the facts together and reconstructed what had happened: As Donald fell down the side of the canyon his rifle discharged accidently. A bullet struck him in the groin. He removed his shirt and tried to make a tourniquet, but he was too weak to apply enough pressure to halt the flow of blood.

One by one the boy fired his bullets into the air, hoping that another hunter would hear the sound and rescue him. At last, with his ammunition exhausted and his strength ebbing, he pulled himself under the protective bough of the evergreen. Donald pressed his shirt against the wound, but it was too severe and he slowly bled to death. Fool's Crow had been correct; even though drops of blood surrounded the body, the animals had not touched it.

Fool's Crow had once described the powers of the medicine man: "One gives tobacco and food to the departed spirits of friends and relatives, to the grandfathers who go to Heaven with Jesus our Father, to the grandmothers who lay in the ground until they are remarried in the future. I can communicate with spirits and tell what they say." In the spiritual rituals of the Sioux, it was the holy man who led the hanbleceyapi, known in English as the "vision quest," and the Sun Dance.

Some of the medicine men were practicing Catholics who saw no inconsistency in following both Indian spiritual customs and Catholic practices. One was a catechist at his church. A monk at Blue Cloud Abbey remembered that his grandfather had been a medicine man who said Lakota Sioux prayers in the morning and the rosary with his family in the evening.

Not all were that religious. Some were charlatans bent on making money by ceremonies and accouterments that were intended to deceive their own people. In fact, one medicine man, Dog Ghost, confided to Father Florentine Digmann, S. J. that when treating a sick Indian he concealed flesh or blood in his mouth and then faked sucking it out of the body of his patient.

Charles Kills Enemy was a Catholic prayer leader, but he had not always been a scrupulous advisor. "When I was young people came to me to ask me to pray for them," he said. "If they gave me a present I prayed for whatever they wanted. Sometimes they asked for bad things. I prayed anyway. I lost three kids that way. That wasn't fair to God. He said that he would answer prayer and

He did. And the bad things I prayed for always came back to me."
The early missionaries and the medicine men often clashed over
spiritual practices. Even so, the missionaries recognized that these
Indians could perform a valuable service because of what they knew
about herbs and roots that were beneficial to the body, especially in
treating wounds and ailments in the stomach. The twin aspects of
the medicine man's role were discussed by Father Digmann:

One day...I was approached by Black Thunderbird, a medicine
man. He shook hands with me and asked, "Did you baptize my
children?" "Yes," I answered, "they are all baptized now. You are
the only black crow in the family. When will you come around?"
He answered, "You know that I am a medicine man, and by my
practices I get many blankets, ponies and money. But I know before
you pour the water on me, you will forbid me my practice. I am not yet
prepared for that"... "You may continue to give medicine," I told him,
"but you must give up all superstitions and pagan ceremonies."

One of the functions of the medicine man was to introduce an
adolescent male Indian to the ritual of his hanbleceya, meaning
"crying for a vision" of the direction of his life. A hanbleceya began
when a shaman escorted a boy into a sweat lodge in order to purify
his body. To Father Stan the ritual of dropping cold water on the hot
rocks to generate steam was a ceremony akin to pouring water in a
Christian baptismal ritual, although the Catholic Church did not admit
that the benefit of the Indian ceremony was at all comparable.

In hanbleceya, the Indian lad then goes immediately to the top
of a hill where he remains for up to four days without any food.
Alone, naked except for a breechcloth and his buffalo robe, his hair
unbraided and his sacred pipe in hand, he stands facing east and
lifting his hands toward Wakan he prays all through the night. Over
and over the boy repeats words such as, "I am nothing. I am empty.
Fill me. Teach me the way I should go. Show me what you want me
to do." This is his vision quest.

The holy man remains in the vicinity, but it is up to the boy
to detect a sign, perhaps a sound or the appearance of a bird, to
indicate that Wakan has given him special knowledge to help him
perform his duty during life. If the sign appears he is required to
accept it. Sometimes there is no signal and the disappointed boy
must come down from the hill knowing that he must try again. To

Father Stan the vision quest is like a Catholic retreat, although the quest can be a more severe test of faith and more demanding both physically and emotionally.

Chapter Fifteen - Death Without End

Instruments such as the pipe and the drum, which the Indians use in their rituals, are different from religious symbols and relics which are familiar to traditional Catholics. Father Stan learned how important they are when he visited Pat Gourneau's home. The Indian man clearly had something on his mind. After a pause Pat said, "Father, I want to show you something I never did show to no priest before."

He reached into his pocket and pulled out a little piece of deer skin. Unwrapping it, he revealed his prayer bone, a small section of a deer's horn. On one face of the bone there was a red painting of the sun and other parts were decorated with a cross, a sacred pipe and a thunderbird. "Father, every morning when I get up I turn and say hello to God and I ask Him to take care of all of us, all me and my kids, and take care of my family and everything, so everything goes good," the Indian told his visitor.

Pat stated that people need something in their hands when they pray. Father Stan's response was to pull out his rosary beads and show them to Pat, saying, "You know I think your prayer bone is better than this." Then he explained the difference; it was God who had made the prayer bone. It had been part of the body of a deer which also provided meat that was used as food, while the rosary beads were only a combination of beans and wire which might have been assembled together somewhere in Asia.

Father Stan planned to lead a religious service the next Sunday on the pow-wow grounds at the Turtle Mountain Reservation and he thought that he should display the prayer bone in front of the crowd. Could he borrow it? Pat hesitated, afraid that the priest would not return the little talisman, but finally he agreed, "I'll let you do that, but remember I need that every day. Every day."

The prayer bone was a reminder of a major difference between the Sioux and white people concerning how they think about death. For some white persons their last breath is the end, a frightful and sad occasion. Catholics, of course, are comforted by the hope of reaching heaven. However, for the Sioux nothing is final; life and death are part of an ongoing circle. As the Indians understand it, at the beginning of life human beings are swept from God's hands to earth and at death they are carried back into His hands.

Attending a wake means something special for Indians. They want the bereaved relatives to know that the place that has been vacated by death will be filled by others who love the family. In the two or three days after someone dies friends offer prayers and reminisce about the deceased person to assure the survivors that their friends intend to remain in contact and to help them deal with the loss of a loved one.

The passing of Frank Davis, therefore, was not a time to mourn. Father Stan had just pulled the school bus into the garage when Sister Vita rushed over and announced, "Hurry! Frank Davis is dying." The priest grabbed the black bag containing the holy oils and his vestments and began driving out on Jackrabbit Trail toward the Davis house.

Donald Bruce was walking along the road near Batosh Houle hill as Father Stan's car was passing. The priest mentioned the news and asked whether he wanted a ride to Frank's home. Donald replied enthusiastically, "Oh, yes! I don't want to miss his death. I want to go."

Frank Davis was a tribal judge and he and his family lived in one of the first wooden homes that the federal government had constructed for the Indians. Father Stan entered through the kitchen door and saw that, in accordance with the Indian custom at the approach of death, Frank's wife, Angelique, and Mary Jane Davis were standing at the stove and stirring two large kettles of soup for the family and friends who would be arriving soon. Frank was sitting in a rocking chair in the next room, waiting for the priest. It was apparent that his time had not yet come so Father Stan sat beside him and they talked.

"Frank, you don't feel so good," the priest began the conversation. Frank answered in a matter-of-fact tone that he expected to die and he instructed Father Stan, "You better give me the works." By the time the Sacrament of the Sick had been administered and supper had been served, wagons, horses and Model A cars already surrounded the three-room house. Almost 30 persons had crowded inside and more were en route. Frank welcomed each of the visitors and after a while told a hushed and expectant crowd, "I'll be ready after a while."

Father Stan tried to pay attention, but he was distracted and kept looking down at his watch. Finally he had to mention that the first of two basketball games between an Indian squad from Belcourt and a white team from Bisbee, North Dakota was already underway and he had agreed to referee both of them. He could miss the preliminary contest, but everyone was counting on him for the feature game. "That's alright," Frank said. "I'm glad you came. Now you make sure we win tonight." Later Father Stan wrote about how typical Frank's remarks were for an Indian at the hour of death, a sense of joy that would turn into a lighthearted moment.

Belcourt did defeat the Bisbee team and despite the excitement after the game the priest was able to return for a while. There wasn't much conversation among the relatives and friends and the littlest children were wide-eyed at the sacredness of an approaching death. "Grandpa, are you going to Jesus?," one of his granddaughters asked. "Yes, me girl, I'll be there pretty soon. Stay here till I go," Frank replied. However, some of the family had not yet arrived and the old man hung on to life.

Late in the evening another of his sons appeared and all of the family assembled. Frank placed his hands on the arm of the chair and looked at his wife. "Cheri, help me," he said in Mitef. Frank was ready. The family accompanied the old Indian into his room and he went to bed. A candle was lighted and the lamp was turned down. It was quiet. Everyone watched carefully.

Father Stan learned the remaining details the next morning while he was parking the school bus. Two of the Davis sons drove up in a Model A Ford. He asked whether Frank had survived the night and they reported that he had passed away. At what time? One of the young men said, "Well, the bus from Minot was late, and Fred was on the bus and his wife and kids and Daddy was waiting for them. So maybe 9:30 P. M. because Fred got there and Daddy could give everyone his blessing."

Among Indians time is not measured by the moving hands of a clock, but instead by a state of mind that expresses the feelings of the moment. It was time to pray when the priest arrived at the church to say Mass, not because the service had been scheduled for a fixed hour, but simply because at that moment everything was in readiness. In Frank's life, he was ready when he saw everyone in his family gathered around.

A meal and gift-giving are important parts of the rituals associated with the death of an Indian in the Dakotas. Father Stan recalled the memorial service for Irene Tyona. Her mother prepared 20 star quilts to be distributed among the mourners and altogether there were close to 70 gifts for the guests. A hearty dinner, a vase of flowers at each place setting and words of friendship helped to demonstrate that the days after death are not a time for tears but instead a period to sustain the survivors. An Indian custom called "watecha" required that any food that remained after the funeral meal should be distributed to needy people, so when Ishmael Shepard died the leftovers were given to the elderly folks in Sisseton.

To ignore the tribal customs brought severe consequences. The Indians told a tale about the selfishness of an Indian woman whose husband died. In accordance with custom she was obliged to give away, "wichpeyapi", all of his property, his tipi, even his dogs to show how good a life he had lived. However, the widow liked one of the man's horses and hid the animal in the bush in order to save it for herself. After the Indian funeral rites, the Indian god Wakinyan told her, "Listen, old lady, you still have not given everything. You are dishonoring your husband." She still refused to turn over the horse and, reminiscent of Lot's wife in the Old Testament, the story said that she was turned into a pile of bones.

By no means, however, was the distribution of the Indian's property meant to diminish the worthy qualities of that individual. Each aspect of the burial was intended to portray some honorable characteristic of the deceased person. For example, in the case of a man, his spear showed that he provided meat for the tribe, his headdress indicated that he was upstanding and his prayer pouch proved that he was prayerful. Placing the body on a platform or scaffold demonstrated that he was the protector of his people. His family believed that when the man's soul reached the place where the good people live he would need transportation to run and play with his friends and therefore they tied his horse close to the platform. An empty place at the dinner table preserved the memory of the decedent during the months thereafter until at last, on the first anniversary of death, a final meal was held.

Many years working in the Dakotas led Father Stan to understand why many Indians look forward to death so serenely and die so happily. Their idea of an afterlife appealed to Father Stan. He decided that he would like to spend the first 100 years after his death at the Grand Canyon or Glacier National Park, depending on whether it was summer or winter. During the next century he wanted to be recognized as "the best darn surfer" in Hawaii.

Chief Crazy Horse once expressed what many Native Americans believed: that people live in a shadow world on earth and the real world awaits them only after they die. Some Indians felt that their burial with feathers and soaring eagles was simpler than a Christian ritual and one of them told a priest, "Gee, you white guys, your religion is up here, in your head; big words and big things. It should be in your heart." They understood their way and preferred it.

Chapter Sixteen - The When and Why of an Indian Name

"Maji Kenewash!," an Indian saying that means something that flutters over the people and blesses them. Blessing Eagle!

Charlie Cree, an old friend of Father Stan, came to visit him on the Turtle Mountain Reservation one day in 1966. "Father, I'd like to have a ceremony for you next Sunday. Is that okay?," Charlie said. "Come to the powwow after you get back from your Masses." The Ojibwa tribe had decided to award a special name to their beloved priest.

Although the crowd at the powwow grounds prayed and danced, it was a puzzling ceremony for Father Stan. He didn't understand the Ojibwa or Cree languages and Charlie had trouble speaking English. The priest couldn't comprehend very much about the ritual except the words "Maji Kenewash." He wanted to remember "Maji Kenewash" so he asked Charlie to repeat the words over and over again. However, no one explained the significance of the Indian expression.

Several weeks later Father Stan and Sister Susan Scheet, O.S.B. were driving around the reservation and calling on their friends. Sister said, "Let's go visit Mr.and Mrs. Cree." The Indian couple lived in a two room log home about a mile off the highway leading from North Dakota into Canada and they were delighted to receive a pair of guests.

With typical Indian hospitality Charlie's wife immediately put the coffee pot on the stove, set the bread, butter and jam in front of their visitors and everyone gathered around the table. The old Indian man clearly was uncomfortable with arthritis, but everyone talked for a while. Then Charlie grew silent and his wife lowered her head. Father Stan knew the ways of the Indian elders well enough to sense that Charlie was about to say something significant - why he had decided to call the priest "Maji Kenewash".

"Father Stan, Sister Susan, I want to tell you something that I didn't tell to anybody before. When I was a little boy I got that sickness we got from the white people. Whenever we got that sickness we always died. I was chilly and I was hot. I was shivering and I was sweating and I was begging and crying to my mother to let me go where the good people are, because they always told me where the good people are there are lots of children to play with, lots of choke cherries, lots of pecans, lots of horses to ride, lots of lakes to swim in, lots of things to do," Charlie said.

"I begged and I cried and she cried," Charlie explained. "She said. `No, my boy, don't go, don't go. Wait now, wait. Don't go.' But I begged her. `No, first let me go get Auntie,' " she said. People who knew Auntie believed that she could cure anything. The Indian woman arrived to find Charlie lying on the floor of the house, alternating between flashes of hot and cold. "I looked in her face and she looked in mine," Charlie said. "She got down on the floor with me and made me take my shirt off. Then she began to rub my chest and my back."

Charlie repeated Auntie's words, "`My boy, you are going to get well. You are going to live a long time and you will be a Prayer Man.' She rubbed and she rubbed and then she began to sing, `I come from the south. It is warm. I'm flying high. I see far. My name is Maji Kenewash. I'm a blessing for my people. You will now get better. I am a leader of my people.'

"`Since you are a leader of the people there are four things that you must remember. First, you must be silent. It is only when you are silent that you can hear the voice of God when He is talking to you in the clouds, in the rain, in the wind, in the snow, in the animals, in the seasons.'

"'Next, you must be humble,'" Charlie continued Auntie's prayer. "'It is only when you are humble that you know what it means that God is telling you. The proud man does not understand or learn anything.'

"'Next, you must be forgiving. Never try to get even. When you try to get even you get down and that is not good.'

"'Next, you must be generous. If you can't give it away, that's a sign that it is not yours.'

"'Remember these four things. Be silent. Be humble. Be forgiving. Always share. Then you will be a good Prayer Leader. There's one more thing, though. You will live a long life. You will bless many people. But one day you will die. But that name should not die. Your name is a powerful name. It should not die. Don't let it die. Give it to someone else who will carry it the way I have said to you.'" Auntie instructed the Indian boy: when he was old and felt his strength waning he must conduct a ceremony and pass the name on to a worthy successor.

The story was finished. Charlie was relieved; a burden had been lifted from his mind. He spoke again, "Lately I don't feel so good and I told my wife that I might die. She said, `Well, old man, you know what you are supposed to do. If you die, don't let that name die. Give your name to Father Stan.'"

Turning to his priest-friend, Charlie said, "Now you are Maji Kenewash. Your name means a feathered creature that is fluttering in blessing over the people. So be silent and listen. Pray long. Give your love. Be patient. Do everything right the way my Auntie told me." Father Stan replied, "I'm trying to be that way." Two months later Charlie died. Consistent with Indian tradition, his name did not die, but the title, "Eagle That Blesses," instead was passed on to a younger person, a Benedictine missionary.

Ironically, it was a blessing from heaven administered by Father Stan some time earlier that changed the life of Charlie Cree's daughter. The story began one steamy September day when a telephone call from the local hospital alerted the priest, "There's a young lady here with pneumonia. She's dying. You'd better come soon."

Father Stan found the patient alone in the hospital bedroom. The girl's mouth was open wide as she gasped for air and struggled for every breath. Her clothing and the bed sheets were soaked from perspiration. Her parents, Charlie and his wife, were nearby, distressed but unable to help. As Father Stan bent over the bed, the girl gave him a frightened, pleading look. He administered the Sacraments of the Church and stayed near her while the light in the room faded and she fell asleep.

Later that evening Charlie's daughter awoke and summoned strength to whisper, "Father, what do you think? Before I die could I get married?" The surprised priest hardly had time to answer when she continued, "There he is, over there." A young man crouched in the corner of the darkened room, hidden there through many tense moments, but once discovered he quickly hurried to the bed and kissed the girl's hand.

"Let me talk to your father and mother," Father Stan cautioned the anxious girl. He saw Charlie and his wife in the corridor and explained the situation. The parents didn't hesitate, "Oh! Father, if they want to get married that would be good. They've been going together now for three months and he's a very nice boy," the parents agreed. Paperwork and formalities were brushed aside and Father Stan decided to marry the youngsters. Their church was the hospital room, their witnesses were the girl's parents, and their audience was a group of tearful nurses. It was a happy, but sad moment. Father Stan prayed that God would bless the newlyweds.

He returned to the hospital early the next morning and the doctor met him at the door. "What in the hell did you do to that girl! She's going to be OK," he said. The pneumonia had disappeared! Father Stan hurried to the girl's room and saw the boy asleep at the foot of the bed. The bride's appearance amazed him. She was wide awake and her face looked cool and dry. Someone had combed and braided her hair and arranged the bedclothes neatly. The girl greeted him cheerily, "Hello, Father. How are you?"

The happy couple left the hospital a few days later, before Father Stan realized that he had overlook the legal requirement of a marriage license. When he located them he said, "Hey, kids! We've got a problem, an easy one to take care of (to himself: `I hope'). But don't tell anybody. Go to the courthouse and ask to get a blood test (again to himself, `I hope you pass'). Then get a license and bring it to me. I'll sign it, your folks will sign it, we'll all be in the clear." Everything went according to plan and no one was the wiser.

An eagle feather is especially meaningful among the Indians. Father Stan knew something important was involved when Estelle Hamely, a friend in Belcourt, confided in him, "I got something here that's sacred, that's holy. It was given to me by my grandpa and he told me to keep it." Estelle then reached into a trunk and brought out an eagle feather about eight inches long. "Father, you know and I know that this is sacred," she continued. "Can you use it in a sacred way?" "Estelle, this is just the thing," Father Stan answered. "My name in Sioux is Eagle Man and I will use this on my `wahookeza'," which he explained was the Dakota word for the staff that he carried sometimes as a symbol of his position as Catholic Vicar to the Indians.

Among the Dakota Sioux, Chaske is the name given to a newborn Indian boy whose traits are not yet revealed. A baby girl is named Winona. The tribe regards a newborn as a revelation of the face of God. Friends and family will watch the infant carefully for characteristics that might signify a name. Perhaps at three years old they may notice that a boy follows his father rapidly around the camp. His uncle might see that the child is fast on his feet so one day he leans over and calls him the Indian words for "Swift Walker." The young Indian begins to know something about himself, about what's unique in his makeup. Meanwhile, the tribe focused on the personality or spirit of the youngster, similar to the way in which Kateri Tekakwitha received her name, and those traits cannot be determined in a month or two.

At about 13 years old the young man walked to the hilltop for his hanbleceya. When he returned he might announce that he intended to be a storyteller or a prayer leader or he might tell his mother, "I'm to be the hunter. That's my life - to feed the poor." In that case she would supply him with jerked meat and whatever else he needed to sustain himself on a hunt. Suppose a young man killed a couple of deer and brought them back to his family. Having thus demonstrated the qualities that would identify his life, from then on he would be known as "Nunpa Kte," meaning "Killed Two."

The tribe observed a young boy or girl until the Wakan, or spirit, of the child became apparent. Then it was time for the tribal Elder to convene a happy ceremony and announce what the child should be called. A song that recalled the deeds associated with the name accompanied the ceremonial drum and the honored young person paraded throughout the camp.

When the Sioux picked names for missionaries they chose words that were specifically descriptive about the particular priest or sister. The names often were colorful and the very act of naming suggested that the tribe accepted the missionary, an important step in the process of bringing the faith to the Indians.

Like Father Stan, Father Eisenman, O.S.B., was restless being tied to a desk or confined to a classroom. A good organizer, he kept on the move around the reservation and acquired an descriptive name - "Tikdisni" or "Never at Home." Father Eisenman's mother, Elizabeth, who helped her son at Marty Mission, earned a title whose meaning is obvious: "The Woman Whose Soup Is Good," in the Sioux tongue "Wahanpi Waste Win."

The Indians called Father Timothy Sexton, O.S.B. "Ihanktowan Hoksina" or "Yankton Boy." A lighthearted, energetic man who played golf with one club, he spoke Dakota well. Father Timothy had a youthful outlook on life even though in his old age he was handicapped by a detached retina, which forced him to stay indoors most of the time,

Unci White Tallow named not only Father Stan, but also Father Daniel Madlon, O.S.B., one of the Benedictines who attended the first Tekakwitha Conference. He was a man of many skills: an expert photographer, an excellent swimmer, a carpenter and a scholar who compiled a Dakota hymnal.

Called "Zica Tamaheca," meaning "Thin Squirrel," Father Dan surprised Unci one day near the water tower at Marty. The old woman was hunched over and shuffling along when she heard a puzzling noise above her. She looked up to see Father Dan slowly descending from the top of the tower. Only a squirrel could have climbed that high. Father Dan became so well known in Catholic organizations that the missionaries awarded him a whimsical title, "Dan, Dan, the Congress Man."

"Iron Hem Woman" or "Unpi Maza Win" was Sister Irene Demarris. She collected tin cans from men who used snuff, bent the cans and attached them to her skirt - all for a purpose. When the Indians heard the cans clinking they knew that Sister Irene was walking about. Father Jerome Hunt's name was equally revealing. Called "Iron Eyes" or "Ista Maza," he wore glasses with metal rims and although the Indians had seen other missionaries who wore metal-rimmed eyeglasses he was the first such person to live among them. Eyeglasses also distinguished Father Justin Snyder, O.S.B. from other monks so his title was "Ista Topa" or "Four Eyes."

As an adult matured he or she might develop additional characteristics that justified a second name. Even more names could be added until all of the dominant qualities of that individual were described in several titles. Father Thomas Rosnowski, O.S.B. answered to three names. The Indians on the Yankton Reservation knew him as "Wambdi Numpa" or "Two Eagle," but among others he also answered to "Wi Hinape" or "Rising Sun." On the Crow Creek Reservation his name was "Hoskina Waste," which means "Good Boy."

None of his Indian names saved Father Tom from being attacked by a drunken man wielding a knife. It was after midnight when his assailant knocked on the door of the rectory at Marty and asked for food and alcohol. Dissatisfied with the answer, he forced Father Tom into his car and when the priest tried to flee the attacker slashed him across the face and side of his body. Three teenagers found the battered priest and took him to the hospital. He recovered, but the shock of the assault depressed him for a long time.

Sister Susan Scheet, O.S.B., a tiny and lovely woman who had been a teacher when Father Stan was the principal at St. Ann's School, had two names. The Cree tribe gave her an almost unpronounceable title, "Esh-peck cape-me-sat-equa," which when translated meant "The Little Lady Who Is Flying Over Us". Her happy manner inspired another name, "Ista Haya" or "Laughing Eyes".

Although Abbot Ignatius Esser, O.S.B. visited the reservations only once a year he was sufficiently important to earn a name, "Wicanhpi Iyoyamwicaya" or "The Star That Lightens Them." His Indian friends called Brother Phillip Ketterer, O.S.B. "Poge Tanka" or "Big Nose" in memory of a famous Indian horseman, Chief Big Nose. Sister Charles Palm, O.S.B. helped to prepare 11 catechetical books based on the Seven Rites of the Sioux and acquired an enviable title, "The Good Woman" or "Wiyan Waste".

Father Augustine Edele, O.S.B. suffered from tuberculosis when he came to the prairie states in the 1930s. Even so his Benedictine superiors assigned him to rebuild the Mission at Stephan. Father Augustine did such an outstanding job that his Indian name "Ticage Waste" or "Good Builder" aptly described his work. A builder on a smaller scale was Brother Felix Haug, O.S.B. He spent years repairing St. Michael's mission in North Dakota and was known as "Yuzakahapi" or "We Take Hold of Him." Even Bishop Marty acquired a name, "Ite Tamaheca" or "Thin Face," perhaps because he showed the strain of many years of hard work in the missions.

"Tokaheya Mani" was the Sioux name that the Seven Dolors Catholic Community at Fort Totten awarded to Abbot Denis Quinkert, O.S.B. It was the first parish to be supervised by a Benedictine abbot and the first to combine Catholic rituals with Indian drums and singing and dancing groups. The Abbot served seven years at Seven Dolors and his parishioners remembered him for his peace pipe and his Indian war bonnet.

A murder occurred in the Seven Dolors Community in 1984 and during the period of grieving the parishioners asked Father Stan to perform the ceremony of giving a name to their pastor, Abbot Denis. The title that they selected, "Walks First," was appropriate because the Abbot led the way in integrating several religious customs of the Indians with conventional Catholic practices.

On the Crow Creek Reservation, Father Mattingly was known in the Sioux language as "Hoksina Pesto" and in English as "Sharp Boy.". He was blessed with an Irish wit and his favorite activity was attending a picnic for the children from the Marty Mission. Unfortunately, he suffered from poor health, which was made worse when he fell down a flight of stairs. He became ill while telling stories to a group of children and although friends rushed him to the hospital at Yankton, it was too late for the beloved "Sharp Boy."

Father Stan earned the second of his Indian names during the winter of 1952 while he was the Superior of St. Michael's Mission.

He was running along an icy path to the post office. Frank Grey Horn and two other Indians were watching. The missionary recalled, "I hit the cross path and attempted to stop. My feet went high into the air. While I lay helpless the three men bent over roaring in laughter. Instantly the words "Nasdad Mani" came from Frank. `You are a graceful walker,' he said." That one humorous event led to a new name, "Graceful Walker," and word spread quickly around the reservation.

The people on the Crow Creek Reservation decided that they too should choose a title for Father Stan. Joe Wounded Knee organized a ceremony and an Indian holy man began by blessing everyone. Then, with a shout of "Hiyu po," Joe summoned Father Stan to the place of honor.

When the crowd heard the name which had been chosen for their guest, some of the young women covered their mouths with their hands and Father Stan noticed that they were giggling. Joe explained why; when people on the Reservation went to the Mission and asked for the priest they were often told, "Well, we don't know where Father Stan is."

If someone else inquired at a different house, the answer could be, "He left here this morning." A knock on another door might lead to a conversation which ended, "Well, if you know where he is tell us because he's not here." Hence the Crow Creek name - "Tikdisni" or "Never at Home." The Indians realized that the tribe already had given that name to Father Eisenman, yet they wanted Father Stan to use it too because what it said about him - "Never at Home" - was true.

Some names were practically identical because the Indians recognized the same characteristics in different missionaries. Father Stan's "Never at Home" was close to the description that the Sioux gave to Father Snyder, "Doesn't Live Anywhere" or "Tuktena Ti Sui." Both men spent time traveling to raise money for the missions. Hence, the similar names.

In 1976 the Blackfeet tribe gave Father Stan the last of his five Indian names. The process started after Mary Spotted Wolf, the chief judge of the tribe, contacted Father Stan and asked him to travel about 1,000 westward to their Reservation and speak about Indian spirituality. He protested that he didn't know anything about the Blackfeet language or ceremonies or sacred places, but Mary persisted and the missionary spent 10 days living with the tribe and instructing them.

Two years later Mary telephoned Father Stan and said, "Some of us have forgotten some of the things you said and we've been talking to the Elders. We want you to come again and talk once more." He returned and, after preaching to the Blackfeet for a week, he was ready to leave for the railroad station and the train ride back to Blue Cloud when Mary stood up and approached the front of the room. "When Grandmas stand up at a meeting it is important," Father Stan recalled.

"Father, this was a very good week. No one ever talked like this to us before. No one ever said there was a sacredness in our land or in our prayers or in our ceremonies," Mary said. The tribe wanted him to remain for a ceremony on Sunday, but he protested that his ticket on the Amtrak train could only be used on the following day, Saturday. "I can take care of that," Mary announced as she confiscated the ticket and so he stayed. The tribe staged the ceremony on the parade ground and afterwards as Mary and Father Stan sat in her kitchen she explained the history of the priest's final Indian name, "Yellow Medicine."

"Years ago when it was cold and the winters were long we prayed a lot," Mary said. "We were running out of wood and the meat was almost gone. We had to tell God about it. We did and He listened.

"We prayed and we prayed and all at once there came a little bird, a little yellow bird. It was only this big (holding her thumb near her forefinger to show its size), but its medicine was very strong. When it came it was a good sign. It brought behind it a clear sky with big warm clouds, and the wind came from the south.

"When the wind came it touched the ice and the ice melted. It warmed the earth and the earth opened. The grass turned green and the animals could take off their coats. The warm wind called the little animals out of the ground and the flowers started to bloom. It made all our hearts feel good.

"Now, Father, that's the way you made us feel when you said our spirits are good. You are like the Yellow Strength, Yellow Medicine, Yellow Bird because behind you and with you, you brought warmth and goodness and flowers and love and an openness. You brought joy. You are Yellow Bird for us. Now the springtime has come and we are happy."

Father Stan reminded his friends later that among the Blackfeet the word "medicine" in this final Indian name did not refer to a chemical compound. Its meaning is deeper and more spiritual. In that tribe "medicine" is "a force that is mysterious and powerful." The missionary priest readily admitted later that his Blackfeet name and in fact each of his five Indian identities was more important to him than Stanislaus, the name he adopted when be became a Benedictine monk.

The Indians sometimes assigned an undesirable name to an individual who was so obnoxious that no one was able to get along with him. They referred to that unfortunate person as "Toka," meaning an outsider or someone who is apart from the tribal society. Everyone quietly closed into a circle which excluded the ostracized man and his family. They were left to the mercies of the elements, wild animals and their enemies. The tribe was no longer concerned with their welfare. It was as much an excommunication as the similar exclusion procedure in the Catholic church.

No one ever called Father Stan "Toka." He was not only a friend, but also a spiritual leader to the Indians and after more than half a century of work among them, he felt qualified to comment about their way of life. "The reservation world is a different world from the world of academia, the world of chanceries, the world of the epicurean. The reservations are a world of humility, of cooperation with the Creator and one of constant prayer and talk with Him. Indian people wonder at, they are aghast at, the wars, the killings that people have done over their prayers and their theology," he wrote in his diary.

Chapter Seventeen - Indians Take Over the Schools

The Indian tradition for passing knowledge from generation to generation did not depend on blackboards and textbooks, nor on computers. It relied on the elders to tell stories about their ancestors and lead ceremonies and rituals which instructed their children. An example was the legend about the beginning of the Dakota people.

The story started with two evil gods, one named Waziya, Old Man, and his wife, Wakanka, known as Witch. They lived beneath the earth with their daughter, Ite, an extraordinarily beautiful girl. Ite married Tate, an associate god who controlled the seasons, and their union produced four sons - the North, West, East and South Winds. However, Tate took the place of one of the sons and the rambunctious West Wind moved to first in the order of the Winds.

Enter Iktomi, an evil god who was called Trickster for his eagerness to spread discontent. He asked Old Man, his wife and their daughter to help him ridicule others in exchange for making Ite even prettier and granting new powers to her parents.

It was a treacherous bargain because Ite's increased beauty pleased her so much that she devoted less and less attention to her four offspring. The god Wi, called Sun, became attracted to Ite and invited her to take the place of his wife, Hanwi, named Moon, at the feast of the gods. Trickster had planned everything, for his scheme humiliated Moon who hid her face while everyone else laughed at her plight.

Justice eventually prevailed. Skan, the judge of all the gods, announced that Sun, who had displaced his wife, thereafter would dominate all only during daylight. Moon, forevermore in shame, would cover her face and rule in the dark. Skan gave Ite a new name, Anung-ite, the Double-faced Woman, because only half of her remained beautiful and the other half became so ugly that people feared looking at her.

Trickster got what he deserved. The judge banished him to the edge of the world where he would be friendless for all eternity. Old Man and Witch received lighter sentences; they were exiled until they learned to do good for old people and children. Four Winds emerged unscathed by the judge's decision and with Yumi, called Whirlwind, they traveled everywhere. Upon returning home they learned that their father, Tate, had decided to treat another beautiful girl, Whope, whose title was Great Mediator, as his daughter and had admitted her to their lodge.

Each of the Four Winds wanted Great Mediator as his woman and they competed for her attention. Eventually the gods came to a feast where she revealed her choice. Standing next to Okaga, named South Wind, she spoke, "I want a tipi for Okaga and myself, a place for him and his brothers." Her decision pleased the gods and, according to the legend, as a present for the newlyweds they made the world and all there is in it. However, the tale does not end there.

The repentant Double-faced Woman wanted to assist her people, to teach them about clothing and tipis and to show them how to enjoy meat. She persuaded Trickster to cooperate and he encouraged wolves to drive moose and deer toward Double-faced Woman's tipi as an inducement to the people. A wolf was chosen to carry a package of selected items to the entrance of the cave which opened into the outer world.

Once there the wolf encountered a young man, Takohe or First One, whom the story credits with leading the Dakota Indians on to the earth. First One, his wife and their friends were impressed when they tasted the meat and wore the clothes that the wolf gave them. Others wondered where this bounty came from. Was First One telling the truth about the wolf?

A search party of First One and three companions traveled through the cave into the strange other place. There they met Trickster and Double-faced Woman, now a seemingly handsome young couple. They really were very old, Trickster said, but by eating earthly things they remained attractive and energetic. Double-faced Woman made the world seem more appealing when she offered gifts of fine clothing to these visitors from beyond the cave.

First One and his party returned through the cave back to their own people. Their stories excited everyone. Some were suspicious, yet others wanted to make the trip to this new world immediately. Their chief cautioned that anyone who tried to make his way through the cave to the earth might become lost and be unable to retrace his steps to the world below.

Six brave men, their wives and their children decided to follow First One on the trek back to earth. However, upon arrival they experienced only weariness, hunger and fear. The bad became worse when Double-faced Woman reappeared in all her ugliness. Trickster laughed at their discomfort. First One was ashamed. It looked as though they had been deceived.

Old Man and Witch appeared and brought a happy ending to the story. Having learned a lesson from their past errors, the formerly evil pair greeted the newcomers with tenderness and mercy, food and drink. They brought First Man's party safely to the world of the ghosts and showed them how to live happily as men and women do. The myth says that First Man and his followers were the first persons on earth and the earliest of the Dakota people.

Stories such as the foregoing were the foundation of Indian education. Much of what the boys and girls learned required not just memorization, but also comprehending the five mysteries of life. "Who am I?" was the first unknown. Perhaps a boy found that he was good at working with his hands or a girl realized that she was skillful with a needle. Another child was given a task and emerged as a leader. Or, sadly, a youth proved to be vain and selfish. In thinking about "Who am I?" a personality emerged and the young Indian began to see his or her place in the tribe and the world.

Other questions followed that caused Indian children to think beyond themselves. When they discussed "Who is my brother?" and "To whom do I belong and who belongs to me?" the children learned that as human beings grew into adults they needed someone to whom they could be joined. When a girl married and moved to live with her husband's new family, at the beginning of the relationship the tribe called her "Toka" which meant "she doesn't belong to us." As the girl learned her husband's language and could speak and work with her new family the community accepted her. At a "making of relatives ceremony" at last everyone recognized that the girl belonged to the family and she received her own distinctive name.

The third set of questions was at the core of Indian education: "What is happiness?" and "What am I searching for?" The elders sat among the boys and girls and explained the change in seasons, the ways of the animals and birds, how the earth was formed and how these phenomena related to each other. Happiness, they told the children, followed from understanding these relationships.

After being taught about the sun, the moon and the world around them, the Indians asked instinctively, "Who is in charge?" Everything they had learned pointed to an acceptance of one supreme being, whom the Sioux called "Wakan." The fifth and final mystery was "What is coming afterward?" Some persons do not believe in an afterlife, but the Indians taught an explanation that Catholics understand - that the death of the body is not an absolute end, but instead merely the continuation of an ongoing circle. Their art and cultural ceremonies of Native Americans confirmed that this was a fundamental belief.

The Elders had to pass on many practical skills for their future generations to survive. At the same time they taught their young to strive for wisdom rather than merely the application of what they had learned. From Father Stan's perspective the Indian way of education reflected the difference between an instructor who teaches "how," such as how to drive a car. and one who stresses the more important "why," which requires more introspective thinking. The earliest missionaries to reach the American plains began preaching Catholicism to whatever Indians they encountered, but it was the financial support of Saint Katherine Drexel that gave a real boost to structured Catholic education in that region. During her lifetime she established and funded 60 schools. One of them was the Immaculate Conception School at Stephan, whose name was chosen by the sainted educator in honor of her mother.

The history of that school illustrates the conditions at some of the missions from the latter part of the 19th century onward. A building for 20 boys and 17 girls opened in 1887 under the leadership of Father Pius Boehm, O.S.B., who was beginning 44 years of service at Stephan. A tragedy the following winter revealed how fragile life was at a mission school. Sister Wilhelmina Kaufman, O.S.B., who was walking barely 100 feet from the laundry to the dining room, lost her way during a blizzard and froze to death. People today would consider that even in the beginning of the 20th century life on the mission stations was primitive. The children carried their drinking water from artisan wells and creeks served as their bathtubs. At Stephan, the teachers and students grew their own barley and corn on a 125-acre farm. The Mission had no fire protection equipment and a blaze in 1916 that destroyed the dormitories forced the children and the staff out into conditions of 35 degrees below zero. The superintendent of a nearby government school responded immediately with blankets, bedding and other help.

Disaster struck again in 1924 when a tornado destroyed the Immaculate Conception Church and damaged most of the buildings. More fires and another tornado wreaked havoc in future years, but the missionaries didn't abandon their work and modern facilities were constructed in the 1950s and 1960s.

Financing a Catholic education was a problem from the beginning. Indian parents whose children attended the Catholic schools were requested to fill out applications asking for federal money for tuition, but some were lackadaisical about filing the forms. If they failed to file the papers or submitted them late, the family was penalized five dollars per month.

Even where the paperwork was done correctly the amounts that the government paid was not enough to keep the missions schools open. Although federal support increased substantially, for example, to $450 per pupil at the Holy Rosary School in the 1960s, it was not sufficient because by then the annual cost of educating a child at that mission had risen to $1,037. The Benedictines, Jesuits and other religious orders solicited contributions from throughout the country to make up the difference in the cost of operating their schools, but depending on contributions created another problem.

Banks were reluctant to lend funds to the missions because they relied on voluntary donations to pay their bills. The schools had no predictable source of income to cover a loan. A good example was the situation that faced Father Augustine Edele O.S.B. when he wanted to borrow $200,000 to pay for building a school at Stephan. The Mission controlled land, cattle and cash worth close to $1,000,000, but the bank nevertheless considered the school a credit risk and rejected its application for a loan.

After Father Stan relinquished the pastor's job at St. John's Church in Pierre during 1966 he became a schoolmaster again for a short period. The Abbot at Blue Cloud, Father Gilbert Hess, O.S.B. instructed him to supervise St. Ann's School in Belcourt. That assignment put him back in the company of Father Elliott, who had remained in charge of St. Ann's parish.

Father Stan discovered immediately that the classes were much too large; for instance, 62 children were jammed into a second grade class. To make matters worse the nuns were trying to teach with whatever hand-me-down books that had been discarded by the local public schools. There was a mixed collection of history textbooks and the same was true for the written material for arithmetic and other subjects. Father Stan decided that the problem had to be solved so he made a unilateral decision to purchase $2,000 worth of brand new books.

When an attack of influenza swept through the School and Father Stan learned that three of the sisters had been hospitalized and other sick nuns were struggling to teach, he recommended to Father Elliott that the Mission tell everyone at Sunday Mass that classes would be suspended until the parents heard an announcement on the radio that the School was re-opening. However, the pastor rejected that idea and directed Father Stan to walk the children from the school buses into the gym and play with them all day.

Father Stan pulled out his letter of appointment from Abbot Gilbert, which authorized him to take control of the School, and announced that he would leave the Mission unless his suggestion was implemented. A discussion followed with Father Elliott who in the end accepted that Father Stan would make all the decisions concerning education in St. Ann's Parish and the School closed temporarily.

The Benedictine monks at Blue Cloud Abbey supervised four of the mission schools, not only the one at St. Ann's. but also those at Stephan, Marty and Fort Totten. The nuns who taught and cared for the students were collectively both loving and strict. Sister Afra Nisch, O.S.B. was the principal cook at the Stephan School and she knew the universal complaints of children when it came to food: they did not like vegetables, they refused to eat mush, the kids did not like this, they would not eat that!

The youngsters, however, enjoyed bread and ate plenty of it. At the Stephan Mission Sister Mark knew what children needed and how to provide it. Sister followed a routine every night: She arose between 2 and 3 A. M. and went to the bakery. Then she shook yesterday's ashes from the oven, put in the special coal that was used for baking, lighted the fire and returned to sleep. Awake again at 5 A. M. the nun began to supervise the Indian girls who were kneading and baking the bread. Her motto was "a pound of bread per kid per day" and by the end of the school year each child had consumed up to 230 loaves of freshly-baked bread.

On Saturday nights the girls who boarded at the Stephan school would plead with Sister Andrew, "Sister, there is a radio show. Could we please listen to it?" She knew how much the girls loved music and she didn't want to disappoint them. Still, the nuns arose at 5 A. M. and staying awake until midnight would be well beyond her usual bedtime. Finally Sister Andrew proposed a compromise: If Father Stan would sit up with the girls during the evening hours, then they could hear their program. How could he say "No?" and he didn't!

A sister's working day was not only long, but also constant, a full seven days a week. Most had no place to relax and little privacy, with only a sheet between each woman's bed. At Stephan they lived in a dormitory for up to 20 women. For such a stressful life all that each sister received was room, board and $100 per year.

At least the nuns were not obliged to learn or teach the Sioux language. Since the federal government was paying the tuition it insisted that the students speak English, and only English while in school. Some children slipped sometimes and reverted to their native tongue. Mostly, however, little by little the Indian boys and girls became less and less familiar with the rituals and customs of their ancestors.

There was another reason why some Indians were losing touch with their culture. More and more were leaving the reservations for what they hoped was a better and more modern life elsewhere. A consequence of this uprooting of the population was that more seats in the public schools became vacant and were filled with children who previously had attended the mission schools.

The decline in attendance in the Catholic schools reached the point where the federal agency cancelled its contract to provide food and clothing for the children at the Stephan Mission. For a time, the government officials wavered, first reinstating the contract and then cancelling it again. Sister Katherine Drexel finally stabilized the situation by providing the money that kept the school doors open.

In the early 1970s the Benedictines at Blue Cloud began to discuss what was then a revolutionary concept for administering schools for Indian children. The monks considered turning over to the Indians not only the ownership, but also the responsibility for running all four of their schools, at the Turtle Mountain and Fort Totten Reservations in North Dakota and the Crow Creek and Yankton sites in South Dakota, together with the buildings at those locations.

Many individuals in the plains states, both Native Americans and white, were suspicious of the monks' motives and openly opposed the suggestion. Father Stan recorded some of their comments. Local politicians told the Benedictines in a nutshell: "Give us the money that you are spending to teach the Indians and we'll educate them." The message from their white neighbors was blunt: "What are you pulling off now? Are you out of money? Can't you hack it any more?" Tim Giago, a newspaper editor, charged that the priests were willing to give up ownership of the land only because the Indian Education and Self Determination Act of 1974 required it. The proposal confounded the Indians. "You mean you're going to dump this on us and leave us flounder,?" some inquired. They reminded everyone that they had no training or experience in administering schools.

Some also feared that the Benedictines would offer no help, but would simply walk away from the institutions which they had founded and retreat behind the walls of the Blue Cloud Abbey. The positive side of the idea was that assuming control would enable the parents of the students to establish the curriculum, hire and fire the teachers and operate the schools as they thought best. That was attractive enough to spark the Indians' interest in the plan. But could they do it alone?

From the outset the Benedictines tried to reassure the people on the reservations that they would work hand-in-hand with them as long as the Indians needed them before the transfer would take place. The monks' message, in the words of Abbot Alan Berndt, O.S.B. was "We recognize the present desire among Indians for self-determination. We also are aware of your natural right and acquired ability to determine your own affairs."

The overall plan was to deliver all of the cattle and give deeds for all of the land and buildings, except for the churches and a few places where the missionaries lived. Everything would be passed on debt-free at a modest cost, perhaps only a dollar and the cost of recording deeds. In all the monks planned to give away about $16,000,000 worth of assets. If it took a year or more to work out the legal wrinkles, so be it!

For two years residents of the nearby communities refused to believe that the Benedictines would voluntarily surrender anything to the Indians. It took some convincing to change the public's perception of the program. Father Stan appeared on television twice to assure the local citizens that the monks had made the decision for their own pastoral motives instead of any economic advantages. There were two reasons, he said, for giving up their schools; first, the missionaries were ordained to work as priests and not as controllers and managers of institutions. Second, and equally persuasive, the land truly belonged to the Indians and it was imperative that they design the education for their own society.

The first transfer took place in 1973 when control of St. Michael's School passed to the Indians. In earlier years during Father Stan's administration he had persuaded the parents to become involved in activities at the School. If they wanted a report card for their son or daughter, the parents had to visit the school and meet with the teachers to discuss how their child was progressing. Personal contacts such as that helped to prepare the Indian community for the turnover. Such hands-on experience proved beneficial when they took charge of their children's education.

When the time came to deliver control the Indians received not only 1,400 acres, but also buses, boilers and other equipment which they checked carefully before accepting it. They expanded their operations to the point that when a new building was needed at St. Michael's the Indians constructed it with their own architects and craftsmen. At the Turtle Mountain School there was a $60,000 debt that the Benedictines paid off in two years before transferring that property.

The federal government proved to be a major obstacle to the turnover of the facilities at Marty. The problem was funding from Washington and Father Stan described it in his diary in 1978: "Now we are struggling with the Bureau of Indian Affairs, which is on the Yankton Reservation. We have given the land and everything to the tribe, but unfortunately the same thing has happened which has happened so repeatedly.

"The solemn word of the Bureau of Indian Affairs somehow or other got desolemnized by the time it got here to the Dakotas. So the funding that had been guaranteed simply did not come through. So up to now we have been giving the Indian people the money. They have been administering it, but hopefully by next September they will have impressed B.I.A. and H.E.W. that they are indeed capable of running a school for themselves."

The Indians finally became responsible for operating all four of the schools. The pupils reacted favorably, even while the new Native American administration made major changes and a few mistakes along the way. In the past if a teacher were silenced or a child were expelled the monks handled the problem without much fanfare. However, after the Indians took charge what happened in the schools became public knowledge and every action had to be explained and justified to the families on the reservations. At last the Indians could say that these were "their" schools. The difference from administration under the Benedictines was evident in the way they treated anyone who was absent from classes. Father Stan recalled his time as the superintendent of the mission school at Fort

Totten. If a child did not attend school, a priest would be dispatched to find the student. "Of course, the child would run like heck because this white guy is after him," Father Stan said, adding "Now, grandma goes out and says,`This is our school, my boy. Come on, my baby, you're going to school now.'"

Chapter Eighteen - Hardly a Typical Day

At 8:30 A. M. on August 18, 1987 the sirens sounded on the Fort Totten Reservation. Worried residents watched emergency vehicles speeding to the scene of a fire. An hour later Father Stan began a stressful day when a police officer telephoned and said, "Please, Father, go to a house in the Crow Hill District. There has been a fire and there are four bodies."

When the priest and Brother Roman reached the scene they discovered that the dead persons were Carrie Price, age 23, and her children, who were two, three and five years old. All of them apparently had suffocated from the smoke and heat of a blaze that had started in the furniture. Three adult members of the family, who were working, were away from the house and escaped the catastrophe. Father Stan did not know whether the dead persons in the house were Catholic, but he anointed their bodies anyway.

Moments later more bad news frightened everyone - a young man who tried to identify the victims reported that there was another victim, a baby. The firemen quickly re-entered the smoldering building and continued searching. Their efforts proved unnecessary when a woman showed up and told the rescuers, "No, you're mistaken. The girl had another baby, but it died. We remember."

Father Stan did not return home, but instead drove straight to the hospital. A nun had telephoned to say that Carletta Walking Eagle had delivered her baby. In almost 50 years of working in hospitals the priest had never seen an infant that was so badly deformed. The child was expected to die and he prayed that if it were to happen it would happen quickly.

Carletta and her boyfriend, the baby's father, were in shock and tears. When the girl's father showed up at the maternity ward a tense situation became worse. The man showed no sympathy and brutally told his daughter that he hated her because she had become pregnant without being married. It was a moment when a skillful priest was needed, not only to comfort Carletta but also to persuade her to ask her father for forgiveness.

Among the other hospital patients was 45-year-old Tim McKay, a devoted father of six children. After counseling Carletta and her family, Father Stan went to visit Tim, who was suffering from cancer. Everyone expected him to die soon, yet his spirits lifted when the priest administered the last rites of the Church. A happier event broke the spell of tragedy that day when Father Stan visited the home of Deacon Tony McDonald, where a party was underway celebrating his son's departure for college.

One day of distressing news was not over. From the McDonald house Father Stan went to the wake of Alvina Jetty. A 33-year-old member of St. Michael's Parish and the mother of four children, Alvina had died of cirrhosis of the liver. Word of still another tragedy reached Father Stan that evening. Paul Peltier had hanged himself and a religious service was being held that night in the basement of Paul's home, the place where he had died. A caller asked: Could Father Stan come and join in the prayers?

Looking back over such a range of misfortune, all within a span of 16 hours, Father Stan mused about the role that the priest played in these circumstances. Some clergy think that they must say magic words and transform the tears of the family into smiles. However, Father Stan disagreed with those ideas; he believed that the mere presence of the priest among the mourners brings the image of Christ into the grief-stricken surroundings. In his opinion, the most important contribution that a priest can offer at such a stressful time is just sitting with the family and friends of the dying or dead person as often and as long as is needed.

After a head-on collision near Belcourt killed a man and injured his wife Father Stan hurried to the hospital to comfort their three children. It was typical of other fatalities that the priest had known and he summed up his feelings: "This is the kind of evening that we fear, but an evening in which we are glad that we can be there, in some small way to ease the pain of persons hurting like this."

It was not just the man or woman who was about to die or the family of a dead Indian who needed the reassurance that a priest could bring. Many individuals who lived alone on the reservations or outside the small towns had no one to whom they could turn for comfort. An old friend telephoned Father Stan one time and said what became a familiar plea, "Please, Father, come to see me. I am so lonesome I could die."

August 18, 1987 was hardly a typical day in the life of Father Stan nor probably in the life of any missionary. Yet the events depicted the variety of people and the range of problems which confronted a priest who worked among the Indians. Unfortunately, many such problems involved deaths and some of those were the result of murder or suicide.

A triple homicide happened on the reservation near Belcourt in 1993. Melinda LaFountain, age 49, her daughter, Angela LaFountain Travis, age 21 and their neighbor, Lewis D. Houle, age 79, all died of gunshot wounds. Another victim was shot and was expected to lose a leg. The tragedy occurred when a rapist surprised Angela and then killed her, her mother and their friend. The slayings enraged Father Stan and his sermon at the 10 A. M. Mass on the next Sunday revealed how upset he was. He told the congregation that the murders were a manifestation of an evil atmosphere that existed on the Turtle Mountain Reservation. Brutality, drugs and alcohol had degraded their community and, according to Father Stan, that was why the white population did not respect the Indians.

Violence and death were especially painful for Father Stan when they involved individuals whom the priest knew well. He was visiting a parish rectory one spring day when the telephone rang at 6:30 A.M. No one picked it up so he answered the call. The voice at the other end of the line was Ivan Bercier, who years before had played on one of the priest's basketball teams.

"Father, I got a call from the FBI. They found my sister's body," Ivan stated. "Monica has been missing since the first part of April. Over two months she'd been gone. They found her body in the

James River south and west of Aberdeen. Could you please come with me and go tell my dad, John, and my mother?"

Sudden tragedies usually required the priest to come and help right away. Father Stan didn't even wait to wash his face; he dressed hastily and was ready when Ivan's car arrived to bring him to Monica's parents. He intended to stay and console them while the Bercier family and friends gathered for the funeral.

Like the Bercier girl, Art Primeau, who worshiped at Saint Michael's Church, also died suddenly. He had gone there to sing at the funeral of a friend who had perished in a railroad accident. The Mass was in Latin and the congregation listened to Art's beautiful voice in the words of Miseremimi Mei, in English "Have Mercy on Me."

The last note faded and silence followed. From the altar Father Stan heard a sigh, then the full range of sounds from the organ as a hand raced from one end of the keyboard to the other.

A heavy thud signaled that a body had fallen. There was scurrying and commotion for a moment until from somewhere in the church Sister LaVergne called in French, "Fadder! Come! Mr. Primeau has died." The sister asked for a quick blessing, but Father Stan felt otherwise. "Art needed no blessing. He was himself a blessing," he said.

The suicide of a 14-year-old child was equally disturbing. Father Stan was visiting in Minnesota and did not know the boy, but the story of his death began to unfold while the priest was in church. A woman dropped her head and sobbed so loudly throughout Mass that when it ended Father Stan and a sister found her and asked if she needed their help.

Looking up through her tears the woman said, "Just before Mass my friend called me on the phone and her voice was strange. She said, `Lucy, my Timmy can't help you any more.'" Lucy became apprehensive and asked "What are you saying?"

"Lucy, Timmy is dead. Please tell everybody not to be mad at him. We were getting late for church, and I called him, and he didn't answer. I called him again and there wasn't any sound. I got afraid. And, Lucy, I went up to his room. And, Lucy, there he was, wet with his blood in his bed, dead, next to him was a .22. My Timmy is dead, Lucy, and he won't be able to help you any more," the crying woman said.

Father Stan drove to the morgue immediately. Timmy's body was there and an employee at the morgue had washed away the blood from the gunshot wound. As Father Stan blessed the frail body he was determined to get more information about the boy's life. What he learned was heartbreaking.

Timmy's father had gone away when the youngster was five years old. He had no brothers or sisters. A thin child, he won no medals in any sports. Timmy was not cute or handsome and the teenaged girls did not give him a second look. In school he was considered a slow student. Words such as "sinner, failure, hell," which he heard from the pulpit on Sundays, only confirmed Timmy's belief that he was worthless. Each disappointment chipped away at the boy's little reserve of self-confidence. So he pulled the trigger and ended his suffering.

When Father Stan learned about the accusations that had cascaded down upon Timmy as he attended Mass he felt that it was not the boy, but priests such as himself who had failed. Speaking collectively, Father Stan wrote, "I had not said the real words loud enough." Preachers should have told Timmy that he was "blessed and good and secure and saved and free" and Father Stan promised himself that those were the words he would use with children when he was preparing them to receive the sacraments of the Church. Despair, Father Stan believed, was not the reason for suicide. Instead, it was caused by some desperate hope for something better to take the place of life.

Sometimes as death nears a priest can do nothing more than advise from a distance. Will Brown was in Montana when he telephoned Father Stan and sought guidance. "Tonight I'm to have a ceremony for a man who is dying of Agent Orange," Will said. "He's a Blackfeet and he wants me to have some kind of ceremony to bless him and I don't know what to do."

Will had stayed at Blue Cloud Abbey for six months and the priest knew him well. Still, the question puzzled Father Stan. As a starting point Father Stan decided to find out if Will had the ingredients to lead an Indian prayer service. "Will, do you have any cedar?" he asked. "Ya, I have some flat leaf cedar," Will replied. "Do you have a pipe?" "Ya." "Do you have tobacco?" "Ya." "Do you have a candle?" "Ya." Will apparently had the right tools for the job.

Father Stan told Will that the Benedictine monks at the Abbey would form a circle at 8 P. M. that evening and pray for the sick man. It was a reminder of a ritual on Holy Saturday around the baptismal font and the paschal candle. The priest emphasized that the prayers that Will would say would be linked with the ceremony being held simultaneously at Blue Cloud and he should remind the dying man that all people are related as brothers and sisters.

"Will, remember that there are seven directions in our prayers, the four directions - east, west, north, and south - and down to the Mother and up to the Father," Father Stan instructed. "Touch him with the pipe so that he will know that the seventh direction is in his spirit. That's where the spirit lives. That's where his strength is. Let him know that direction is a sacred direction and the spirit of God is with him."

Father Stan's work crossed the lives of thousands of people, either personally or through his fund-raising solicitations for the missions. Reports of his work carried around the world. In one day in 1995, he received letters from England, Austria, Germany, Missouri and New York. An Indian imprisoned in Tennessee wrote, "I am smaller than an ant and there's not much I can do for people any more. But I pray. But I really don't know how. Can you find somebody that could come here and help us?"

At one time or another his path crossed those of Presidential candidate and Senator George McGovern, South Dakota governor and World War II flying ace Joe Foss, Senator James Abdnor, Francis Cardinal Spellman of New York and, perhaps the best known, Lyndon Johnson.

Johnson was Vice President when he and his wife came to South Dakota for the beginning of the construction of the Big Bend Dam. Father Stan had been invited to recite a prayer at the beginning of the ceremony. He wrote one in the Dakota language and when he showed the Vice President a copy, Johnson snapped, "What's this?" Father Stan replied, "It's just an Indian prayer."

The Vice President was surly and irritated while he was waiting out of view of the crowd, but when he mounted the speakers' platform it was as though a hidden hand had flipped a switch - with a big smile he turned on his Texas accent and dazzled the audience with his political charms.

Perhaps it was best that the Vice President could not understand Father Stan's invocation, which when translated into English read, "O good God, here come these white guys again. They take the buffalo, they take the prairies, they dammed up this whole river, but if they need the water, well, God bless it."

Chapter Nineteen - Women Such as Mary LaVerdure

Father Stan called Mary LaVerdure his grandma. He also regarded Rosemary Brossart, Sweetheart Thomas, Rose Crissler, Viola Shepherd and Annabelle Hall as "grandma," a term he used loosely to describe older women who had been his friends and advisors. Not to overlook the earlier influence of maternal grandmother Hester and paternal grandmother Maudlin, but it was Grandma LaVerdure and her family who occupied a special place in the missionary's heart.

He frequently asked God to assign someone to guide and correct him. Mary LaVerdure proved to be the answer to his prayer. She and her husband were living in a two-room log house on the Turtle Mountain Reservation when Father Stan met them for the first time early in the 1940s. Going to church required a good walk, two and one-half miles from their home, and St. Ann's Mission where Mary worked was the same distance away, but in another direction. Mary was not only an active Catholic, but also a good friend whose home was a refuge from the priest's regular schedule, a place where he could count on some rest and a good meal.

Not long after Father Stan became friendly with Mary he learned that this was one lordly, loving and straight-talking Indian woman. She sized up the almost brand-new priest and said, "You're pretty young. You don't know much. Listen to me and you'll learn." He didn't flinch from Mary's strong words and instead they developed a friendship that lasted almost 50 years until she died in 1987. She truly treated Father Stan like a grandson. He was so at ease with her that after a day of sleigh riding with a bunch of happy boys and girls he didn't hesitate to lead them to Mary's house for a meal of boiled bush rabbit with salt pork.

Mary's parents lived far out in the bush and Father Stan brought Holy Communion to them on the first Friday of every month. On one occasion Mary put a dollar bill into his hand. It immediately triggered another instruction that he had received when training for the priesthood at Saint Meinrad's: "Never accept payment for sick calls. It might make someone not call you because they don't have money." As he tried to force the cash back into Mary's hand her eyes flashed and she snapped, "You take this whenever I give it to you. I'm not dumb enough to think that I'm paying for communion."

Grandma LaVerdure and her young protege remained in close contact even after the Benedictines transferred him away from St. Ann's to work at Devil's Lake and later at Immaculate Conception Mission. Mary continued to express herself bluntly and clearly. Later in life, on the eve of a major operation she told her doctor, "I know you are trying to do your best. I know this is dangerous so if you don't have good luck with me, don't feel bad. I know you are doing what's right. If you have bad luck and I die, that's all right; I don't want you to blame yourself."

In the event the operation failed, she prepared a detailed list of instructions for the funeral, even naming the participants, but when she passed away some time later only Father Stan and two of the pallbearers had survived her. However, it was after Mary died that she seemed to exert the most profound effect on his life. He prayed to her every time he preached at Mass, asking her to give him the tone of voice, energy and whatever else was necessary to tell the good news of Christ most effectively to the congregation.

"Into her hands I put everything, without question, letting her open the path before me," Father Stan said in his diary. No problem was too small to seek Mary's assistance, whether it was chest pains, a squeaking fan belt in his car or a decision whether to make an unscheduled visit to a parishioner. A tick-tick-tick in the engine one day suggested a problem under the hood. It was the mechanic's day off at the local service station, but after a quick prayer alerted

Mary, the man appeared and performed the necessary repairs. "So every time I get into the car it's an adventure, but it's also another time for me to take Mary along with me and lean back, confident that whatever happens she'll have the cure for it," the priest reminisced.

Whenever Father Stan lost something he prayed to Mary to find it. His camera disappeared and he looked under the seat of his car and even telephoned the pawn shop in Rolla, North Dakota, but the camera was gone. So he prayed, "Mary, I'm going to relax about this. I'm not going to be concerned about the camera or about the photos that were in the camera or even about the person who took it. I'm going to let you find that person and make them somehow or other return that camera to me."

Two days later Father Stan picked up a couple of heavy gray sacks of mail at the post office and dragged them into the kitchen at St. Ann's Mission. After emptying one bag he stretched his hand deep into the other. Something was down at the bottom, a heavy lump covered with deerskin and tied up in twine. It reminded him of the wrapping around the camera and when he opened the package he knew that his prayers had been answered.

"A man brought it in," the clerk at the post office informed Father Stan," and said `this camera belongs to the priest up at the Mission.'" Father Stan's request to Mary had been answered. That was enough and he told the postal clerk, "Don't tell me who it was. It's all right. I got my camera back. That's all I want to know." Nevertheless, he decided that from then on he would lock his car whenever he was carrying anything valuable, particularly his tape recorder.

"I never make a decision without asking her to control it. I never go anywhere without asking her to make the going a success," the priest said. "I never say a prayer or a Mass without asking her to stand beside me and put the proper words into my mouth." Sometimes the right phrases and emotions seemed spontaneous. Father Augustine heard him preach at a funeral service and commented, "Stan sent that woman directly to heaven." Not everyone agreed. After listening to Father Stan one time, another priest remarked, "Oh, he's just a bullshitter."

His relationship to Mary was like having a guardian angel constantly sitting on his shoulder and reminding him of something he overlooked. Father Stan might be driving away from the Blue Cloud Abbey to a new assignment when perhaps half a mile down the road an inner voice would alert him, "Look, you forgot this." Sometimes it was merely a reminder to take three or four apples so that he could enjoy them in the car.

In a silent yet friendly reprimand to Mary, Father Stan sometimes said, "How come you didn't tell me about this when we were back at Blue Cloud?" It just proved that his now deceased good friend was still looking after him. He prayed to her continually, asking that he be buried near her grave in Belcourt so he could be sure that they would pursue their work together in heaven.

The long friendship between Father Stan and Grandma LaVerdure led to an equally strong relationship with Grandma's daughter, Frances LaVerdure, and Frances' husband, Alfred "Bud" Jetty. They knew Father Stan when he was working at St. Ann's in Belcourt and when the Abbot transferred him to Stephan, Frances and Bud moved there, too.

The priest proved to be a good friend when Frances, not yet 30 years old, developed a serious heart ailment. The problem could be treated, but an operation would cost up to $8,000 and the Jettys could not afford it. They turned to Father Stan who thought that Senator William Langer of South Dakota might be willing to help. So he put Frances and Bud in touch with the Senator, who made arrangements for the federal government to pay their expenses to the Mayo Clinic.

The operation relieved Frances' problem and the Mayo doctor added some good news: a prediction that within a year she would become pregnant with her first baby. Anna Marie Jetty was born 14 months later, but by the time the child was five years old she had become withdrawn and stopped speaking. It became obvious that the little girl would need specialized care for a long time.

The distraught Jettys reached out to their Benedictine friend once again. One health-care facility proved unsatisfactory and then Father Stan recommended an institution at Redfield, South Dakota. But there was a problem: a long waiting list for admission. Father Stan didn't give up; instead he went directly to the medical facility at Redfield and convinced the superintendent to admit Anna Marie within a couple of months.

His prayers to Grandma Mary assisted Father Stan in coping with his own health problems, including kidney ailments and high blood pressure. Among the most serious was Meniere's disease which afflicted him frequently during his adult years. When Meniere's attacked him, he couldn't hold on to a chair, take a step or even control any of the movements of his body - reminders of his suffering in Rome years earlier.

One of the worst attacks occurred when he returned to Indianapolis, Indiana to celebrate the 50th anniversary of his ordination to the priesthood. The night before the big celebration Father Stan awoke with severe symptoms - dizziness, nausea and vomiting. He struggled alone to the bathroom and prayed to Grandma Mary for help to overcome the attack. However, the pain persisted and finally he called out for assistance. Father Stan's sister, known in the convent as Sister Marie Kathleen, O.S.F., was staying with him, having returned to Indianapolis to join in the anniversary festivities, and she telephoned for an ambulance. By that time he realized that he was so weakened that all of the family's plans for the 50th jubilee would have to be cancelled.

After a few days recuperating in the hospital Father Stan figured out what had brought on the attack. He had been sleeping near an air conditioner and the noise had irritated his inner ear, a part of the body where the Meniere syndrome begins to disturb persons. The unhappy incident taught him a lesson. "Other times my grandma has given me signs of her acute interest and attentive care, but this last episode of missing my 50th jubilee is unequalled," he wrote later. "It's unimaginable, but I'm so intensely grateful that she used this way of impressing on me that never, never do I get concerned or upset about anything.

"How wonderful it is that we can call on these friends of ours like Mary LaVerdure or go back to our parents and lay at their tombstone the life which they gave us. Laying our life at their feet ensures, absolutely ensures, the successful attainment of those things for which God has made us. So it's simply a matter of surrendering to the energy that our parents put into us and that God empowered within us."

A calmness enveloped Father Stan after he felt stronger and recognized how the spirits of Grandma Mary and his own parents were available to guide him. This newfound acceptance was tested shortly after he left Indianapolis to drive back to Blue Cloud Abbey. His car hit a curb and blew a tire. It was 8 A.M. and he waited a long time for help. It was a test of his patience, but he resolved that from then on little things would not upset him.

Father Stan had not completed his return trip to the Abbey when another attack of Meniere's disease forced him into bed at a motel. The disease began to sap his energy and as the motel room seemed to whirl around him, he became concerned that Meniere's disease eventually might immobilize him and prevent him from practicing his ministry. It was a completely helpless feeling, yet Father Stan was convinced that the answer was neither whining nor becoming a burden on other people. In his mind Jesus appeared to be saying, "Well, my son, I'm just letting you experience a test. See how you can work through this."

Women, from Grandma Hester to Unci to Sister Susan Scheet, had helped Father Stan deal with many tests and projects and he formed opinions about their collective strengths and weaknesses. Women, he said, are "wakan" people; they are crisis-oriented and inspire others, yet they are practical and effective at building personal relationships. A community of religious sisters is a permanent presence in the place where they live. By contrast, some priests and religious brothers serve God well without a lasting commitment to a specific institution or location. There are exceptions to the rule: The veteran Benedictine's record of more than 60 years in the Dakotas obviously is one.

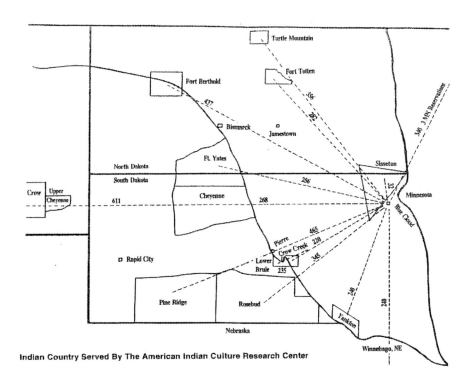

Indian Country Served By The American Indian Culture Research Center

Chapter Twenty - American Indian Culture Research Center

Some persons think about vocal prayer as a conversation between God and a man or woman. That's true, but spoken words are not the only way to communicate. Father Stan understood the distinction when he noticed a man who attended early Mass every day. He sat in the same seat in the rear of the church and never moved, yet his smile revealed that he was happy.

"Sir, I see you here every day in the same place and I don't see you do anything. Everybody else is praying or singing or walking around, but you're not doing anything," the priest said. "Tell me what are you doing here anyway?"

The question did not upset the man. He realized that others might have wondered why he was alone and silent, but no one had asked. "Father, I come here every day and I sit in the same place so God can find me easy. I look at Him and He just looks at me," he answered.

Unlike the patient man in the back pew, many Catholics rush through their conversations with God. In Father Stan's opinion, "They just don't give God time to talk. I think He's saying to Himself, `For God's sake, I wish he or she'd shut up. I've got something important to say, but I can't get a word in edgewise.'"

No single act of praying satisfies everyone. A woman who lived in a center for the elderly told Father Stan that she was unhappy about the way Indians prayed. "Don't they know any better? They pray with everyone. They go to all the religious services and they sing everywhere," she complained. "You ought to tell them that they are Catholics and they should stop that kind of praying." When Father Stan offered a prayer he often asked God to give him a person to whom he could pour out his soul, someone who would energize his flagging strength, an individual with whom he could share his innermost thoughts. "I have often said that I have prayed fervently and frequently for God and Jesus to give me a partner. Someone who would understand what I say when I open up my own soul," referring no doubt to some of the close friends he had made on the reservations.

"But I have nothing except this tape recorder so I have no one to correct my faulty expressions of my ideals and concerns," he added. But no person ever completely filled that special role. Annoyed because he felt God wasn't listening to his prayers, Father Stan held an unconventional soliloquy in which he recorded his monologue with God.

In his own words, he "leveled with Jesus on a long prayerful trip yesterday. Jesus is Jewish so he has been dallying with me. Jews love to bargain, to barter even. They love to haggle and a simple sale is obnoxious, I suppose. So Jesus has been acting out of his culture, leaving me unfulfilled and very angry. During my trip yesterday I leveled with him and told Him that the time had come for me to call His bluff."

Recalling Jesus' promise that the Father would grant whatever was asked in His Son's name, Father Stan continued, "But Jesus has held off, no doubt laughing up his sleeve, offering us a sign of a deal and then withholding, offering straightforward terms and then changing them. So, as I said, yesterday very clearly I called His bluff.

"I said I promise to do absolutely anything You ask, if You now promise to keep your promise. Now it's up to You. If you don't answer then I go to Your Father and ask Him to correct You. You are an unfaithful son. I recognize that what is happening may indeed be nothing more than a culture clash, a clash between the Jewish world view and the Gentile world view.

"But I felt it was time to call a halt to these years of His tactics. He was having all the pleasure and we were having none of the joy of the opportunity at hand. As I arrived at Blue Cloud last night that's the way it stood. I am going to give Jesus 24 to 48 hours before I go to a higher authority."

Nothing happened right away. Father Stan's thoughts drifted off to other topics, including wondering whether he could live at St. Michael's Mission and still fulfill his duties as Vicar to the Indians in the Diocese of Sioux Falls. His conjecture was interrupted during the monks' prayer vigil at Blue Cloud when Father Julius dropped his head onto his hands and then collapsed in his choir stall.

As they rushed Father Julius off to the Abbey's infirmary and anointed him in preparation for death, Abbot Denis sidled over to Father Stan and whispered, "You go to St. Michael's on Thursday and take over." This, Father Stan believed, was God's answer to his promise to do whatever God asked of him. However, the deal had not closed. "I made my offer. Jesus has taken me up on it," he wrote. "Now I will see how he handles His side of the bargain."

Sure that Jesus was his intercessor, Father Stan wondered why God took so long to answer some requests and why some never seemed to be granted. After giving it much thought. he concluded that there were delays because God was working overtime to combat the powers of the devil. As for why some prayers were not heard, that happened, Father Stan explained, because Jesus is Jewish and while many Jewish people are talented, self-assured and generous, they can be stubborn, too. In view of that, he decided that Jesus didn't like granting the petitions of a whimpering individual.

Prayer is expressed in different ways and customs, such as the Irish way that Father Stan knew during his childhood, the German way, the Italian way and the Indian way with its drum, sacred pipe and mantra of pleas that are repeated more fervently each time. For an Indian dancing can be a prayer and that thought provoked a discussion when he was training a group of Lutheran ministers.

"Father, what do you think about dancing, because a lot of churches say that dancing is sinful?" one of the students asked.

He replied, "The Indian people say to me, `Hey, you white guys, your religion is up here, in your brain. Religion should be here in your heart. When you guys pray, you pray like this (demonstrating with bowed head and folded hands).'

"`This is the way you should pray (showing open arms and lifted face), open to Our Father, God. Second, if your head is praying, your shoulders say, `I would like to pray a little bit, too.' Next, your hips say, `Let me get in the act as well.' Then your knees and your feet and then everything is praying."

Father Stan declared that many people in the world dance during their prayers and dancing is part of the exuberance of life in the Catholic churches on the reservations. "If I love somebody I want to dance with that person. I want to be in harmony with that person in every possible way," he stated.

While he did enjoy the help of his secretary at Blue Cloud, Colleen Heminger, Sister Susan Scheet and other women with whom he worked, Father Stan never mentioned that he had achieved the personal relationship that he desired. In the absence of a life-long friend to whom he could unload his innermost ideas and aspirations he began to tell them to a recording machine.

Father Stan started dictating while he was riding through Indiana in May, 1971. He was on the way to visit his father, who was hospitalized in an intensive care unit. His thoughts had wandered back to 11 P. M. the previous evening when he had paid 60 cents for a meal at a waffle house and he wasn't paying attention to the road.

"Doggone it, I wasn't watching there and I took a wrong turn. Well, I suppose…I'm on a freeway now. I guess I'll have to go 50 miles to get off this crazy thing in the wrong direction," he said. "Well, there it says Exit, Route 46, seven miles, Standard station, too. Well, maybe I'll get off there. I'm talking into this microphone rather than watching the road, I guess."

He continued talking to his dictating machine for many years. The biggest benefit of the oral diary, according to Father Stan, was that it made him remember his past. It also became a sounding board by which he expressed ideas to himself. On religion, for example, his first tape said, "Religion is attitude; it is not culture. Religion is fundamental; it is not peripheral. Religion is pervasive. It can live with anything. Just as Christ can fit into anything. It is not necessary that our rights, our regulations, our customs, our feasts, our laws have to be universal. I think in the movement of making these things universal we destroy the universality of Christ. He is all things to all men."

The transcript of his oral diary revealed how Father Stan aspired to move toward a leadership role in Church activities. As a first step he offered himself as an assistant to Father John Tennelly, the longtime head of the Bureau of Catholic Indian Missions. The BCIM acted as an advocate for the Indians in political and economic affairs and as an intermediary to help make the Native Americans understandable to non-Indians.

A new and different opportunity arose in 1968 when Abbot Gilbert urged Father Stan to form an organization which the monks at Blue Cloud Abbey had been discussing for several years. It would be called the American Indian Culture Research Center (AICRC), a not-for-profit corporation that was intended to serve as a pastoral facility to work with the Indians. The Abbot transferred Father Stan from his work on the Turtle Mountain Reservation back to Blue Cloud to get the project underway.

The Benedictines established two goals for AICRC: first, to support emerging Indian leaders as they attempted to rebuild institutions and concepts that had been damaged, such as the family, church, education, law and order and the economy, and second, through this new ministry to persuade non-Indians to respect the spirituality, philosophy and culture of the Indians. These ideas foreshadowed a major change in the relationship between the Indians and white people, especially Catholic clergy. The plan called for Indian leaders to lead meetings that included whites and sometimes clergy, instead of the past practice of white speakers addressing an all-Indian audience. In time the type of meeting which Father Stan envisioned really happened.

AICRC organized a board of directors under the chairmanship of Ishmael Shepherd, an Episcopalian man who led the Brotherhood of Christian Unity on the Sisseton Reservation. The board was sufficiently diversified for Father Stan to comment, "On the reservation, of course, we're all one church. We don't go too much for denominational differences. We look for denominational likenesses."

As time passed, AICRC's mission expanded. It was decidedly a pastoral program devoted to the spiritual well-being of the Indians.

Father Stan reminded everyone that AICRC was not an academic center or a welfare agency and it did not solve economic problems. Nevertheless, word spread that he could and would help people and requests began to stream across his desk. They needed nurses at the Pine Ridge Hospital; did Father Stan know anyone who might be available? The schools at Marty and Stephan had openings for teachers; could Father Stan find some qualified persons? On that point, AICRC lobbied the South Dakota legislature and convinced the members to pass a law requiring that anyone who wanted to teach in primary or high schools must complete six credit hours of education in Indian subjects.

AICRC had its financial ups and downs. Money was in short supply and at times Father Stan worried about whether he could afford to pay his small staff. Yet at another point AICRC received a much-needed bounty, a $100,000 infusion of cash from a grant that was arranged through the Sisseton Reservation.

Eventually AICRC became the vehicle through which Father Stan broadcast Catholicism over radio and television. He hadn't thought of preaching on the airwaves until one day in 1980 when he was traveling from Sioux Falls to Blue Cloud. His car didn't have a radio, (but he made sure that his next used car was properly equipped.) As he drove along he looked out at the houses alongside the road and wondered about the best way to tell the families who lived there about the Catholic faith. A radio program was the answer, but Father Stan had no training in broadcasting. He decided to pursue the idea anyway and started by testing Brother Nicholas' recording machine. The results were satisfactory and a new phase in his priestly life got underway.

In the beginning the local radio stations gave Father Stan air time free of charge. The Turtle Mountain Reservation was the first in the area to broadcast and later four more Indian stations carried his program. His weekly show attracted a wide audience and the director of the station in Milbank agreed to put him on the air every day to deliver a one-minute message.

Father Stan became a familiar voice to listeners in the area and his renown on the radio was helpful when he ran out of gas on a back road one night. He knocked on the door of a darkened farmhouse nearby and called, "Please, ma'am, I'm up the road a ways." No one opened the door, but the woman inside, who heard his Saturday morning broadcasts, called out, "You're Father Stan."

There were many listeners on the reservations and he recognized that broadcasting was a valuable opportunity to teach the Indians, Catholic and otherwise, about Catholicism. He knew that his talks had to be interesting, so he varied the subjects, ranging from the Gospels to AIDS to simple homey stories. In one 11-minute interview he not only explained who were the Benedictines at Blue Cloud Abbey, but also spoke about the life of Kateri Tekakwitha and his own role as Vicar to the Indians for the Diocese of Sioux Falls.

The station in Mobridge, South Dakota told Father Stan later that he would have to pay for his radio time. When the station manager suggested a price of $1.00 per minute, he made a counter offer of $10.00 for 15 minutes and they made a deal at that price. Father Stan was never shy about requesting money for good causes. This was indeed a good cause so he went on the air and explained that he needed help to pay for the quarter hour of air time. The station agreed to announce the names of the contributors and say, for example, that they had contributed in honor of someone's birthday or in thanksgiving for a gift that they had received. A local department store, the Knights of Columbus and the Catholic Daughters also donated part of the cost.

Father Stan believed that Sunday should be a day of good news so he called the Sunday morning radio show "Bible Upbeat" and tried to make the program joyful and positive. The weekly program also gave him a forum in which to draw some comparisons between the accounts in the Bible and the lives and ways of the old Indian people. "Bible Upbeat," however, was not the only religious program that was available to the Indians. "Sioux for Christ," which featured Indian music and songs, carried from nine stations into seven states and three of the provinces in Canada.

AICRC broadened its outreach activities and began to produce both television programs and videos. However, Father Stan's first experience at televising a Sunday Mass was less than professional; the program didn't run long enough and there was dead air time at the end. But he improved and began to work on a video about traditional Indian ceremonies which he intended to show to prison inmates.

One Palm Sunday Father Stan received a telephone call that gave him an opportunity to lift his radio and TV work to a higher professional level. Sister Judith Fischer, O.S.B. reported that a course at the National Catholic Center for Television and Radio Production in London would begin soon. There was room for 17 students and 15 seats already were taken. Father Stan was working on three radio programs and Sister Judith felt that the course would help him. Was he interested in attending?

Father Stan almost shouted "Yes!" and suggested that Sister Jeanne Giese, O.S.B. should be the 17th and final student. But first a couple of hurdles had to be cleared. The Abbot often turned down an idea the first time he heard it so Father Stan was prepared for a disappointment when he requested permission to travel to Great Britain. However, after a little thought "no" sometimes became "maybe" and when the Abbot heard that Father Stan would learn how to use TV to instruct not only the people on the reservations, but also the priests and brothers at Blue Cloud he approved the trip.

Once the Abbot consented Father Stan still needed a passport and the money to pay for the trip. The cost was $680 for airfare, room, board and tuition so he asked Father Damien Kraus, O.S.B. who supervised the finances at Blue Cloud, for the funds. If Father Stan could raise $200, Father Kraus agreed that the Abbey would provide the balance. A friend, Carol Davis, assured them that a bingo game would bring in Father Stan's share of the expense, and it did.

The departure date was three weeks away and Father Stan realized that he needed his birth certificate in order to obtain a passport. He wrote to Indianapolis requesting a copy and after ten days found that his letter had not arrived. A telephone call disclosed that it had been mailed to the wrong address and might not reach the proper office for another week.

The clerk at the county office asked how much money Father Stan had sent to pay the fee for his birth certificate. Two dollars, he replied. Sorry, she said, the fee is $3 and we cannot process the application until we receive another dollar." Time was getting short, but Father Stan's brother, Xavier, saved the day. He and his wife lived in Indianapolis and they paid the extra dollar so that the birth certificate would be delivered in time.

The flight from Winnipeg, Canada to London was booked for May 3. Just moments before Father Stan was to depart for the airport, Adeline LaJimodiere telephoned him and said that she must see him immediately. He told her that he was preparing to leave to catch a plane. But how could he turn down a friend of 40 years, so he hurried to the retirement home where she lived. Upon arriving there Father Stan realized that he had made the right decision - Adeline unfolded a gift for his trip, a beautiful handmade sweater with a face and headdress of an Indian on the back.

Upon reaching London, Father Stan was assigned to live in the home of Mr. and Mrs. Harold Carter, about three blocks from the National Catholic Center. He discovered that 15 of the students would live in heated rooms and that he was one of two with unheated quarters. The first night, which he spent sleeping under several blankets and a feather comforter, ended at 7:30 A. M. with a tap on his bedroom door.

"It is I," said the lady of the house, "may I come in?" "I'm in bed," Father Stan said. "That's all right," the woman replied and entered anyway, bearing a tray with a huge pot of tea and crumpets. Hot tea in bed every morning hardly compensated for sleeping in a frigid room. After a week he had developed a bad cold and arranged for heated lodgings in the National Catholic Center.

What might have been a leisurely visit to London turned into a demanding three-week course about how to produce television and radio programs and advertisements. The staff at the British Broadcasting Corporation (BBC) arrived at the Center every weekday at 8:30 A.M. and instructed their students all day long until 10 P.M. Father Stan's team, one of three among the group from the United States, was assigned to create a three-minute TV spot. They learned that three minutes means not a second more, or less. The BBC people criticized the ineptitude of their Americans students with, in the priest's words "much more harumphing in waddled English throats."

The intensity of the all-day schooling frayed everyone's nerves, especially when the group began to produce a four-minute television segment, with all of the necessary writing, music, lighting, rehearsal, etc. Tempers were short and, when a cameraman intruded into directing the production, Father Stan passed the limit of his patience and took command. "From now on no one speaks here in the studio except me," he shouted. "No one, absolutely no one, gives directions except the floor manager. No one so much as moves without my hand signaling in which direction he should move."

The group completed its practice program and Father Stan looked forward to the weekends to enjoy London. The Indian-head sweater that Adeline had given to him attracted amused stares and comments wherever he traveled in London, such as the typical comment from a passerby, "Look at that bloke!" If Father Stan entered a store wearing the sweater the customers looked him over and began to whisper. He smiled and invariably someone would ask, "I say, chap, are you from North America?" He identified himself, "Yes, I am from the Turtle Mountain Reservation. My name is Eagle Man."

The Londoners occasionally were arrogant, but more often helpful, especially when they found Eagle Man in the underground with a subway map in his hands and a puzzled expression on his face. Father Stan walked often around the Hatch End district where he lived and many people began to recognize him. He was friendly to all the strangers; just the right attitude because he had decided to take photographs for a slide show and the grocer and two old ladies pushing a pram proved more than willing to pose for their visitor from North America. Classes finished, leaving Father Stan and Sister Jeanne one final week in Great Britain, time enough to visit and photograph their Benedictine confreres throughout the country.

Although they were all well fed, Father Stan and his classmates yearned for a truly American meal. Their wish came true after one of their hosts asked a student to describe a "fun meal." When he answered "cookout", the word puzzled their British friends. The Americans bought everything that they needed, steak, charcoal, tossed salad, beer and wine and asked the staff from the BBC to enjoy it with them.

As the festivities began Father Stan noticed a change in his crowd. "Get a touch of wine in some of these staid English ladies and their tongues loosen dramatically and their personality takes on a new color," he wrote later. Some of the guests joined in throwing frisbees and darts. As the evening was winding down Jerry Teague and his fiancée helped Father Stan wash the dishes. He noticed Jerry's white Irish knitted sweater and remarked how much he admired it. Jerry had been wondering what would be his parting gift to Eagle Man. He knew immediately and gave his priest friend an identical sweater.

The surprises were not over, even though the students didn't know it, when they were driven to Heathrow Airport for the return flight to North America. Their bus passed a magnificent hotel and Father Stan thought to himself how anyone would feel comfortable living in such opulence. He would find out soon enough. The jet was airborne only 15 minutes when the captain announced, "Ladies and gentlemen, we have a little problem. It is my decision to return the aircraft to Heathrow. There is no danger, but I apologize for the delay."

The seal around the cargo door of the plane was not holding the air pressure. Repairs were made and two hours later the plane raced down the runway again. Twenty minutes into the flight, the passengers heard a familiar voice. "What can I say, folks!" the pilot announced. "We didn't solve the problem and it's my decision to go back again. I apologize profusely."

The delay this time was eight hours long. The airline gave each person one British pound to buy food and finally transported everyone to a fine hotel - the same one that Father Stan had admired several hours earlier. It lived up to his expectations. He enjoyed a steak dinner and received a key to a room with a king-sized bed and instructions to be prepared for departure at 6:30 A.M. the next day. From then on the trip back to Blue Cloud Abbey was happily uneventful.

Sister Jeanne and Father Stan had already decided how to make the best use of the training they had been given in London. They planned a 30-minute slide show to support the efforts of the Indians to attract new industries to the Turtle Mountain Reservation. Another project was scheduled to demonstrate the cooperative work of the monks at Blue Cloud with the Benedictine sisters at the Harmony Hill Monastery.

Father Stan also had a personal dream: in union with AICRC to build and operate a radio studio as modern as the BBC facilities. His long-term objective was to spread the Lord's word in several ways: through prayer, radio and TV programs and by teaching lectors to read from the Bible in Catholic churches. The project could be expanded, Father Stan thought, by showing parish priests and Protestant ministers how to use the radio pulpit to reach their congregations.

Did the energetic Benedictine realize his dream? Decades of hard work passed in several media and Father Stan's secretary, Colleen Heminger, was still reminding him about their next project: "Father, it's time for us to make another radio tape. I'm going up to the studio. You can come in a few minutes."

Father Stan seemed naturally to aspire toward leadership roles, especially in programs that were designed to benefit his Indian followers. He requested the authority to confirm Catholics at the three parishes, two schools and two penitentiaries that were under his care - something that a bishop ordinarily would do - and he was given the power to confer that sacrament.

His vision extended beyond North and South Dakota. He urged the Church to appoint a vicar for Indians all over the United States. He hoped that he would get that assignment, but he settled for a more local appointment. In 1982, Clarence Skye of the United Sioux Tribes, Edward Red Owl, Father Webster Two Hawk and Father Stan met with Bishop Paul Dudley of the Diocese of Sioux Falls and asked him to name Father Stan a vicar for the Diocese with special responsibility for the Indians. Just before Christmas in the following year he learned that after months of negotiation with Abbot Alan the Bishop had given him the job. He agreed to become Vicar on two conditions: first, that it must not be a strictly bureaucratic post and second, that either he or the Bishop could terminate the arrangement at any time.

Father Stan wanted everyone to know that Vicar was not just an honorary title, but it meant that he was the Church's representative to the Indians of the Diocese. He would demonstrate his role with a wahookeza, a rod similar to a bishop's staff. It had to be genuine, so he checked on the dimensions for a wahookeza while visiting the former home of Sitting Bull. At the top of the staff was a cross and in the middle was a beaded God's Eye.

Colleen Heminger attended to the decorations, placing a large eagle feather in the middle of the God's Eye and attaching ribbons on the arms of the cross to display the meaningful four colors of the Indians. More color was added when Colleen draped red flannel on the back and black flannel at the bottom. After she had braided some of her hair and hung it on the cross, Father Stan's wahukesa was ready for any ceremonial occasion.

Typically, the new Vicar used his status to organize and head leadership programs for Native Americans, including the annual Tekakwitha Day celebrations at the cathedral in Sioux Falls.

He was the third person to be honored as vicar to the Indians, the first being the beloved Abbot Martin Marty, and he represented the Church when a delegation of Belgian officials and citizens traveled to the United States to honor Father DeSmet, the revered native of Belgium.

A disagreement at St. Joseph's Indian School called for the intervention of Father Stan. Some of the teachers couldn't accept a program about the Indian perceptions of Catholic doctrine. Stepping into the dispute in his role as Vicar, Father Stan moved toward a solution by hiring Rosalie Jones and Tony Shearer to dance and sing and, through that medium, to explain to the staff the significance of the traditional Indian ideas of creation, obedience and prayer.

Meniere's syndrome continued to interfere with Father Stan's ability to perform his priestly duties. Poor health finally forced him to submit his resignation as Vicar in 1992 after nine years of service. Once again the disease tested his faith, but the outcome was not all bad because the Bishop chose Father Stan's good friends, Alfred and Frances Jetty, to succeed him as the diocesan representatives to the Indians.

Chapter Twenty-One - Adventures Behind the Wheel!

Had Father Stan been assigned to work in metropolitan area churches and had he traveled by public transit he might never have dictated some of the source material for this book. He drove long distances, often alone, around the reservations in North and South Dakota and had plenty of quiet time on the road to express his thoughts into a recording machine.

Traveling at night along the country roads could be an exhilarating, but tiring, experience. An antelope or a deer might suddenly leap out from a ditch into his path. With no one alongside him to keep up a conversation he could become distracted and drowsy. The fuel line in the car might freeze. One time it did, and Father Stan went looking for help and knocked on the door of the first house he could find. He called out, but an old woman inside did not recognize the voice of the radio priest and yelled out, "Go away, go away, I can't help you." No one else was available to solve the problem. On such occasions he had to be his own mechanic and that time he managed to restart his car.

During some long trips Father Stan's thoughts sometimes wandered back to memories of his deceased father. He prayed to his dad one evening - please don't let me run out of fuel before I reach Wagner, South Dakota. His plea was answered; the car coasted into the gas station five minutes before it closed. "So I have great trust in my dad traveling with me in a car," he said.

Weather could be another reason to worry. The snow was swirling one night as Father Stan drove from Pierre to Stephan. Alongside the road it was piled several feet high. Two headlights were barely visible ahead of him, but when Father Stan stopped to investigate he spotted a car in the ditch and a man standing near it.

"Come on, get into the car! Bring your suitcases and you can travel with me," the priest shouted into the darkness. "Which way are you going?" the traveler asked. "I'm going to Stephan, where you just came from," Father Stan replied. To the priest's surprise, the man turned around and began to put the suitcases back into his car, at the same time saying, "I'm not going over that road again." He had driven out of Stephan in weather conditions that were so frightening that he refused to return.

Father Stan decided that it would be more prudent to turn around and head back to Pierre. He dropped his passenger off at a motel and then took shelter at a home for the elderly. They assigned him a bed near the entrance to a bathroom and when the bathroom door opened out came an old lady. No one had told Father Stan that his roommate was a woman. She approached his bed, bent down, looked him in the face and said, "You're a funny-looking woman." Then she turned around and returned to the bathroom.

Snowdrifts three feet deep clogged the road when Father Stan drove toward the reservation on another night to pick up the relatives of a woman who was dying. They had traveled from California and Chicago, but the snow and heavy winds stopped them from continuing to the hospital in Belcourt, South Dakota. No one else volunteered to try to reach them, so the priest headed toward Rolla where they had been staying. He couldn't see over one snowdrift, but headlights revealed that a car was bringing people in his direction. However, the snow stopped it well short of reaching him.

Three women, the family of the dying lady, emerged from the other vehicle and stumbled half a mile through the snow until they approached Father Stan's car. He wondered: Could he turn the car around and break through the drifts or would they be stranded on the road all night? The trip ended happily because the three passengers added enough weight to his car to enable it to plow through the snow and continue on to the hospital.

It was not only blizzards that threatened his travel plans. Hailstones that seemed as big as baseballs shattered Father Stan's windshield in the wildest storm that he ever encountered. As his passenger, Father Paul McHarness, O.S.B., cringed, Father Stan managed to drive within 20 yards of a house and could see the woman inside peering out at them. But the barrage of hailstones was too severe for the two priests to run for shelter. Twenty minutes later, when the storm had abated and they drove away, they saw that for miles the storm had destroyed the crops alongside the road.

Father Stan blacked out once while driving just outside Belcourt. He was returning to the Mission after visiting a young man who had tried to commit suicide. The last thing that he remembered was seeing three little red flags that surveyors had placed in the road and hearing some rattling as the car slid off into a ditch.

As he struggled to regain his senses a pickup truck roared up behind him and the driver got out. "Oh, it's you, Father. I thought it was some damn drunk," the man said. "What happened?" the priest asked. "When you went off to your left side I had to go way down in the ditch to miss you," the man continued.

"I'm a policeman," the driver declared. "I get a lot of practice in driving, but look at my wife. She's scared to death." Father Stan saw the couple's baby, happy and gurgling, and understood why the woman was afraid. He decided that Mary LaVerdure and Jesus were at his side that day.

The police officer left without issuing a traffic summons, but at another time Father Stan had to talk his way out of a speeding ticket. He was rolling along, passing all the other cars, at what he believed was close to the speed limit. However, within minutes flashing red lights in the rear view mirror warned him that something was wrong.

When the policeman said that he had clocked Father Stan traveling 80 miles an hour, the priest retorted, "Impossible!" "I'll prove that I'm right," the officer told him. The two cars drove side by side and, when the police officer's speedometer reached 70 miles per hour, Father Stan's showed 62. Like any other motorist caught driving over the limit, the priest had an explanation. He had put oversized snow tires on his used car and they had distorted the true speed of the vehicle.

Cars and freezing weather in the Dakotas were a tricky mix. Father Stan learned a lesson about winter the first time he saw a fire underneath a parked car. Driving along one cold day around 1940 he noticed smoke and flames at a vehicle alongside the road. His car skidded to a halt and he ran to the closest house to sound a warning. Once inside he yelled, "There's a fire under your car."

No one rushed outside. Finally one of the occupants looked up and asked in a leisurely tone, "Is it burning pretty good, Father?" The priest replied quickly, "Yes, it's burning," but when someone else said, "Oh, fine!," it dawned on Father Stan that the fire had been set deliberately and these people understood why.

Everyone on the Turtle Mountain Reservation knew that during cold weather they should take burning coals from their stove and place them under the front of their car. The heat would warm the entire engine and keep the oil and the water lines from freezing. The anti-freeze in use then wasn't reliable, which was the reason why Father Stan often had to bundle up and depend on a horse-drawn sleigh to carry him out on a nighttime sick call. Besides that, if he had to cross the frozen Missouri River, it might not be solid enough for a car to drive across.

Joe Jerome and most of the Indians had other ways of protecting their cars from the cold. Joe knew what to do when the thermometer dropped, yet one day he waved to Father Stan and called, "Father, can you give me a lift? I can't get my car started." The priest agreed and pushed Joe's car on to the road, expecting to hear the engine turn over at any moment.

The two men drove down a hill and nothing happened. They turned west on to Jackrabbit Trail and Joe's car did not respond. When they reached the cemetery, they turned around and headed east to Dahlstrom's pool hall, where Father Stan stopped his car. "Good gosh, Joe, what are we going to do? Nothing seems to happen," he said. "I don't know, Father. It ran good yesterday," his friend answered.

They walked to the front of Joe's car and Father Stan said, "Let's take a look." As they lifted the hood, both men burst into laughter. The battery was gone. Joe explained sheepishly that he had wanted to keep the battery warm the previous night so he had taken it inside his house and forgotten to install it again in the morning.

Almost two-and-a-half feet of snow covered the road the time that Father Stan had an accident on the Turtle Mountain Reservation. It happened because Ernest Keplin needed transportation to basketball practice with the St. Ann's Eagles. He had been promised a ride to and from the gym. The priest and his passenger were en route one Sunday afternoon, but the driving was tough. Only one lane of roadway was passable and Father Stan's car entered it at the same time that another vehicle approached from the opposite direction.

Would the other driver veer away first? Father Stan could only guess so at the last minute he turned sharply to avoid a collision. Too sharply, for his car slid off to the right side of the road and tipped slowly on to its roof. Metal crunched, glass broke and Ernest's basketball gear tumbled around him.

Perhaps Father Stan's father or Mary LaVerdure was praying hard because he pulled the boy out of the car, unhurt, and sent him to look for help. Almost providentially, Tommy Parisien drove up with his truck, chains, ropes and three helpers, who righted Father Stan's car even before Ernest reached the nearest house.

Other accidents proved to be more serious. Father Stan always wanted to be prepared for the worst so he carried the holy oils in a decorated deerskin pouch in the glove compartment of his car. Not all of the injured were Catholic, but the priest felt that when a crash happened everyone would appreciate a consoling word or two.

Twice Father Stan anointed persons who died in accidents on the road. The most heartbreaking tragedy involved a car carrying six boys and girls. It smashed into a stopped freight train and all of the children died. The priest experienced some close calls of his own. Sometimes he drove long after he should have stopped to rest and once, in a drowsy state, he barely missed striking a herd of black Angus cattle.

Father Stan wore his clerical collar when traveling so that everyone would recognize that he was a priest. A crowd at a Baptist church saw that he was a clergyman and invited him to join in the baptism of eight of the parishioners. He made some new friends at the ceremony and told them that he must be at the local airport early the following day, but had no transportation. He needn't have worried because they arranged for a van to pick him up the next morning.

The sight of the stiff white collar encouraged some passengers to talk freely and unload their stories on Father Stan. He once offered a ride to a hitchhiker who called himself Christopher. The man said that he was 29 years old, part Cherokee and headed for Sioux Falls to enter a school that taught truck driving.

As Christopher entered the car he said, "You look like a monsignor." Father Stan asked how he knew the word and his passenger mentioned that he had done gardening work for a priest in Georgia who was indeed a monsignor. "You're just a priest, huh?" Christopher continued. "Yes, I'm just a priest," Father Stan answered.

As they drove along a tragic story unfolded. Christopher related that his mother had abandoned him at age nine and he became a male prostitute. A wayward life led to drugs and alcohol, but he said that he had shed all of his addictions several years earlier and now he was looking for God to forgive him.

Father Stan sensed that he could help his rider. When he told Christopher that his name means "Christ-bearer," the young man's eyes brightened and he asked, "Could I be that?" Then he started to cry as Father Stan answered, "Well, someone gave you that name hoping that you would be a Christ-bearer. You thought that you could not. I tell you now that you can be and will be a Christ-bearer."

For many years Father Stan never drove a new car. After all he was a missionary and he felt awkward if he sat behind the wheel of something so shiny and expensive-looking. So it was with his first used car, a Cadillac that came from an elderly couple in Philadelphia. They owned two Cadillacs, one for church on Sunday and one to tour around the block once in a while. Their son persuaded his parents to donate one of the cars to Father Stan. He accepted it, but was uncomfortable at the wheel. "All alone in the huge machine I'd look behind myself once in a while to see the long green monster still following," he recalled.

Years later the same uncomfortable feelings returned when Father Stan borrowed an Oldsmobile from another priest. To Father

Stan it was a luxury car that was not fitting for a Benedictine monk and he was ashamed being seen driving it around the Ft. Totten Reservation. He thought about switching to his Ford station wagon, which had no air conditioning, but he shelved his concerns when he realized how quickly he would become worn out if he had to drive around in the heat of summer.

Unlike the gift of the long green Cadillac, Father Stan had to bargain for his other automobiles. Bill and Bob Kneip, who were automobile dealers in Arlington, South Dakota, made him a novel offer. They would exchange a used car for plywood coffins. He accepted the barter because he knew that Father Casimir would help him to build the coffins at Blue Cloud Abbey. Another time the Kneip dealership provided a 14-year-old Ford LTD station wagon. It included just what Father Stan wanted - a big storage area where he could throw his winter gear and some apples that he often carried on long trips.

While driving through Sioux Falls, South Dakota he passed Billion Dollar Motors and noticed a display of used cars. His 1965 Ford showed over 100,000 miles on the odometer and it seemed like time for a swap. He introduced himself to the owner and said, "I'm Father Stan from American Indian Culture Research Center and you fellows have a lot of cars out there. I'd love one of them. You can have my car. We'll just make an even-up trade."

"Father, we've got a JetStar out there with only 60,000 miles on it. Is that okay?" the man asked. Father Stan accepted the deal and drove off with his JetStar and new snow tires, to boot. He liked the way Billion Dollar Motors did business and made a mental note to return there the next time that he was in the market for a second-hand car.

His travels ran the odometer on one vehicle from 81,000 up to 191,000 miles during a four year period. When he began a seven-night trip to Indian communities near Fargo, North Dakota and Red Wing, Minnesota his old car already had recorded 137,394 miles. It could be a grueling test of car and driver, but he had a different outlook: "This is my work. So I'm happy to do whatever will further the work of building bridges between communities."

Old cars break down, especially in hot weather, and Father Stan's journal contained notations about several occasions when his friends kidded him while they made repairs. He was driving a 1965 Oldsmobile on a warm day early in the 1990s. It had no air conditioning and the car crawled up to the priests' garage at St. Ann's Church on the Turtle Mountain Reservation. Father Stan was worn out and as he struggled out of the front seat he pressed his foot on the floor board. It fell out onto the ground.

Louis Bercier and some of his friends were watching and burst into laughter. "Father, we can see it's an old car, but you don't have to drag your foot to stop," one of the men said. "We think it's got a brake somewhere. You've got to learn how to use it." Ducky LaRocque approached with a piece of aluminum and said, "Go easy with this, Father. If you don't push on it too hard, it'll keep the dust out. . .maybe."

Another time, amid a clatter and clang of metals, the muffler broke loose on his car. The family in the next farmhouse didn't recognize Father Stan, but they repaired the muffler anyway and their kindness started a friendship that continued long afterwards. The rear view mirror dropped into his hands when he reached up to adjust it one day. Father Stan wasn't sure whether Jerry Azure, a gas station owner who was suffering from cancer, would be able to repair it, but he asked him anyway and Jerry restored the mirror in a few minutes. Mokie Martin, who worked at another service station, was worried when Father Stan drove up leaving a trail of gasoline. Maybe the old car would blow up. Mokie checked it and found that the car needed a new gas tank. He located an old one, installed it, and put Father Stan and his car back on the road.

To the Benedictine monk there was a common theme to all of these stories - how human beings help each other and specifically how people he knew and sometimes strangers came to his aid. Father Stan tied the events together in the following paraphrase of Chapter 25 of the Gospel of St. Matthew:

As each of Father Stan's friends approached heaven, Jesus said, "I've got to return your favor." "What favor?" each man asked. "You've got a short memory, partner," the Lord answered. "Remember when I broke down and you worked on my car. Remember when it was a blizzard and you saw that I got home. Remember when my rear view mirror fell off and you glued it back on. I've got a big bill to pay to you, friend. Come on in! There are lots of guys like you in here. You'll love it. Just keep it quiet. I don't let everybody in."

Chapter Twenty-Two - The Rule of Benedict and the Abbey

Listen carefully, my child, to my instructions, and attend to them with the ear of your heart. This is advice from one who loves you; welcome it and faithfully put it into practice. The labor of obedience will bring you back to God from whom you have drifted through the sloth of disobedience.....First of all, every time you begin a good work, you must pray to God most earnestly to bring it to perfection.

Those opening words of the Rule of Benedict have guided the conduct of life in Benedictine monasteries since the sixth century. The unique element of the Benedictine way is community, where each monk or sister is knit to the others by the place where they work and live, by the group they form, and by the ideals of the group. It is through such association, these men and women believe, that the monastics discover their own identities and purpose in life.

Democracy and communism are said to exist side by side in a Benedictine community. Monks and sisters express their personalities by speaking their mind to the group, yet surrender their individuality to the collective will of all. St. Benedict anticipated that there would be wrinkles in how the men cooperated with each other and how they followed the leadership of their abbot. His worries remained valid centuries later because some viewed the brothers merely as workers for the priests and that led to tensions within the Blue Cloud community.

To establish a pattern for the conduct of the monks' lives St. Benedict wrote a set of 73 interrelated rules that still apply not only in Blue Cloud and other abbeys of Benedictine monks, but also in monasteries of Benedictine sisters. They are based on collegiality and an openness to what each monk and sister had to say. Collectively the precepts which St. Benedict wrote are called the Rule of Benedict.

Chapter 53 of the Rule. "All guests who present themselves are to be welcomed as Christ, who said: `I was a stranger and you welcomed me.' (Matt. 25:35). Proper honor must be shown...to all, especially to those who share our faith (Gal. 6:10) and to pilgrims...

"Great care and concern are to be shown in receiving poor people and pilgrims, because in them more particularly Christ is received; our very awe of the rich guarantees them special respect."

"Garbage collectors of the world" - that's what Father Stan called the Benedictines who worked at Blue Cloud Abbey. "We are the men and the place where the refuse of society can find shelter, hospitality and healing," he wrote. Many guests came to Blue Cloud, some invited, some strangers, some familiar faces, some returning unexpectedly. They included drunkards, individuals with family problems and others just searching for spiritual respite. More and more Indians accepted Christianity and word spread that the Abbey was a place where others shared their religious feelings. For everyone Blue Cloud was a place to enjoy silence and study. All guests, no matter how long they stayed, became a part of the community. They ate with the monks, prayed with them, and slept overnight in the same quarters as their hosts. A few visitors, such as the men from the Oblates of Mary Immaculate religious order, drove to the Abbey just to pick up a truckload of fresh tomatoes from the Abbey's farm.

More often the guests came looking for religious direction. A visitor named David was the divorced father of a seven-year-old boy, but he also was a man with credentials - a well-educated former Anglican priest, who for four years had administered the Hare School on the Rosebud Reservation.

The monks welcomed David and assigned him to work in the library at Blue Cloud. However, filing library cards was a discouraging task for a man with a degree in theology. One day he threw up his hands in despair and gave up the job. Walking along the corridor in the Abbey he encountered Father Stan. David mentioned his frustration and asked the priest whether he could help in some other, perhaps more challenging way.

Father Stan had the answer; he was collecting material for Bishop Paul Dudley to use in a local session of the Tekakwitha Conference and he asked David to complete the job. The former clergyman enjoyed the new project and took on such diverse assignments as organizing papers on the sociology of the Dakota people and the future of the Catholic Church in the Dakotas.

Instead of helping the monks, other visitors needed help themselves. Few required assistance more than two young men who arrived unannounced at the door of the Abbey during the summer of 1981. Their heads were shaven, they were shoeless and each of them was wearing a dirty sheet. When Father Cletus, O. S. B., the guest master, fed them their ravenous appetites revealed that they had not eaten well in a long time.

"We do have a laundry room here. If you'd like me to, I'll wash that sheet for you," the priest said to each of the youths. "That's all we've got on," one of them replied. Father Cletus solved the problem - or so he thought - when he asked them to stay in a closet while he cleaned the sheets. But the cloths disintegrated when they were put into the washing machine and new togas had to be created from a set of bed coverings.

The monks at Blue Cloud received many such young men who roamed about searching for a hospitable community, but never settled anywhere. Some visitors, according to Father Stan, simply were looking for a group of men to act as their mother and that kind of person was not encouraged to stay. Among them were so many alcoholics that the monks finally organized three or four-day sessions for persons with drinking problems. On these occasions as many as 20 men and women went to the Abbey for a meal with the monks and the Fifth Step in the Alcoholic Anonymous program.

The monks had to balance discipline and kindness when dealing with alcoholic guests. One visitor decided to needle his hosts, some of whom he knew from their teaching days on the reservations. Smiling a toothless grin, he said, "You priests and sisters made me everything I am today." Another man, an ex-convict, came to Blue Cloud for three months after he was released from the penitentiary. He returned to drinking later and wrote a book that criticized the Benedictines for being too understanding. The man offered some advice about handling alcoholics: "You have to be rough with us."

Jerry Sully arrived often for early morning coffee with Father Francis, but the priest knew Jerry well and was sure that he had his eye on the refrigerator, where the beer was kept for guests and the monks' social hour on Thursday nights. While Father Francis could be impatient sometimes, many who knew him felt that he guaranteed all visitors a welcome to the Abbey. In 1985, for the first time in many years, the monks invited about 150 of their neighbors in Marvin and the surrounding farms to come to the Abbey for a picnic, a tour of the buildings, and a slide show that Father Stan had arranged.

Some guests, while not Catholic, were active Christian ministers. A Lutheran pastor from Madison, Minnesota brought a class of children to Blue Cloud to prepare them for confirmation. He had planned every 20-minute segment of the curriculum, but Father Stan suggested a more relaxed schedule that would allow more opportunity for the kids to unwind and enjoy themselves. The pastor agreed and at the end of the visit told Father Stan, "My gosh, these kids said it was a beautiful time here."

Kwen Sanderson was another Lutheran minister who was the pastor of two churches. Unmarried at age 35, he wondered whether he was being called to missionary work and so he asked the monks at Blue Cloud if he could live there while he mulled over his future. They accepted Kwen for six months and Bishop Dudley authorized him to receive holy communion once a week.

Kwen was a round-the-clock Christian. Even at breakfast he radiated the love of God, so much so that one of the monks might plead, "Don't talk about God early in the morning. I want my corn flakes." Another visitor, Father Warren Murman, and Kwen became friends quickly. Father Murman was on a sabbatical from teaching at the St. Vincent Archabbey in Pennsylvania. Like the Lutheran minister, Father Murman came to Blue Cloud for a specific purpose

-to brush up on his liturgical practices. The two men prayed and traveled together and went through the ancient Sioux purification rite at a sweat lodge.

Some men who had withdrawn from the Benedictines retained an allegiance to the Abbey and returned to visit. Dr. John Bryde, a former priest who had been the principal at Holy Rosary High School, traveled to Blue Cloud a couple of times a year. Roger Dieckhaus had held the position of prior at Blue Cloud, but later he decided to marry and left the monastery and the religious order. However, he kept in touch with the monks and returned with his wife and children every year to celebrate the Fourth of July. The kids put St. Benedict's rule about hospitality to the test when they touched off firecrackers outside the chapel during evening prayers. Dieckhaus had an ongoing affection for Blue Cloud. He asked if he could be buried in the cemetery there and the monks agreed.

Occasionally a visitor caused a problem at the Abbey, such as the time when an unruly visitor disrupted the spiritual readings. A man from the Yankton Reservation, he started shouting during supper and all eyes turned toward Father Stan. The other monks counted on him to police any kind of disturbance. Big enough and sturdy enough to handle most emergencies, he was not comfortable that evening because he was recovering from an operation just a few days earlier.

Father Stan knew that somehow he had to eject the drunken man. He ushered him toward an exit and simultaneously told him that his misconduct was giving a bad name to the Indians. The conciliatory tone didn't calm the man. The visitor wanted to fight, and Father Stan realized that he was too weak to control someone who was so upset. The incision in his stomach was still healing and he worried that his wound would be reopened in a scuffle.

Still, Father Stan kept pushing the visitor toward the door. At last, as he maneuvered him outside the man stumbled and Father Stan fell with him. They separated without any punches being thrown, but as the man shuffled away from the Abbey Father Stan feared that he would circle back and try again to interrupt the monks who were now praying in the church. However, the disturbance was over and Father Stan's reminder of the incident was a sharp pain where the operation had been performed.

Chapter 6 of the Rule. "Let us follow the prophet's counsel: `I said I have resolved to keep watch over my ways that I may never sin with my tongue. I was silent and humbled and refrained even from good words.'" (Ps.39: 2-3).

Silence isn't easy and sometimes when the dam is broken the wrong words spill out. Father Stan noticed that sometimes the priests and brothers disagreed so vocally about the leadership of the abbot that an atmosphere of frustration descended over the monastery. One generation of monks often complained about another, a problem which Father Madlon noted: "It is saddening to note an occasional tendency to consider the old missionaries as a group of outlaws. All these old missionaries were experienced, did field work and lived with the Indians in their home surroundings, sometime or other."

Chapter 58 of the Rule. "Do not grant newcomers to the monastic life an easy entry, but, as the apostle says, `Test the spirits to see if they are from God' (1 John 4:1). Therefore, if someone comes and keeps knocking at the door, and if at the end of four or five days has shown patience in bearing harsh treatment and difficulty of entry, and has persisted in the request, then that one should be allowed to enter and stay in the guest quarters for a few days....

"If they promise perseverance in stability, then after two months have elapsed let this rule be read straight through to them, and let them be told, `This is the law under which you are choosing to serve. If you can keep it, come in. If not, feel free to leave.'"

Some men who came to the Abbey found contentment, accepted the Rule of Benedict and stayed there. Yet even when they became monks they retained their individual personalities and interests. That was evident one evening when several of them gathered in their recreation area. Some chose a movie about colonization, others listened to an opera and a third group looked at a TV show about psychiatry. Several were creative and at another time they presented a play, a spoof entitled "Spoiled Monks," about a group of monks who wanted to build an indoor swimming pool in spite of declining numbers in their community.

A number of guests remained for a lifetime and others departed after a while. One became a priest, but left after five years to work for a manufacturing company writing manuals about how to operate heavy equipment. Edward Red Owl also spent five years as a monk and explained why he withdrew from the Abbey, "I simply cannot erase my Indianess. My skin is Indian and that's all there is to it. I cannot be white."

David left under different circumstances. An observer found that it was difficult for him to acquiesce in casual decisions and perhaps worse the former Anglican priest held strong opinions about religion. In true democratic fashion the community at Blue Cloud decided to cast ballots about whether he should stay. The vote went against David and he had to leave.

The monks at Blue Cloud supported themselves and therefore it was important after the arrival of each candidate to determine whether and how he could contribute to daily life at the Abbey. Could he work on a vegetable farm or care for animals? Did he have the skills of a carpenter or a mechanic who knew enough to service the Abbey's cars and trucks? Had he any experience as a teacher? Father Stan got to the point with two very personal questions to newcomers: "Why did you come here? What do you have to offer us when you come?"

Such inquiries were important in order to weed out someone who came to the Abbey thinking it would be a warm haven from society. Anyone interested in joining the Benedictine order had to understand that the monks were committed to a daily regimen of prayer, work and study. Anyone who aspired to become a monk had to know that a Benedictine monastery was not a place to become wealthy. Father Stan received no salary; if he wanted to purchase something for AICRC he had to ask the abbot for the money to buy it.

Blue Cloud offered a program for men between 19 and 50 years old who were thinking about their future. They could live there for up to two months and, if Abbey life appealed to them, then they could apply to join the order. If they remained the Rule of Benedict authorized four more months to consider whether they wanted to stay. These time periods also gave the Benedictine community an opportunity to evaluate these prospects and to decide whether they should be allowed to remain.

The welcoming atmosphere at Blue Cloud attracted people with problems. One crippled man who had trouble speaking applied to enter the Benedictine order and was not accepted. A group of four men in their 30s asked to join, but three who were alcoholics were rejected. For some who passed the initial screening and became monks, alcohol eventually forced them out of the community.

Brother Robert Sterner O.S.B. first visited the Abbey when he was about 50 years old. He had cared for his parents on their farm in New Germany, Minnesota and, one day after both had died, he and his sister drove to the Abbey. "I wonder if I could live here. I'm hardly any good any more," Robert told the monk who greeted him.

"The only requirement to join this monastery is if a person seeks God. That's all. Whether he's poor or rich or short or fat or tall or thin or whatever makes no difference," the monk reassured him. "Well, I can work," Robert said. For years Brother Robert cut the stones that were used to build the Abbey. A heart condition slowed him, but he continued to contribute by doing repair work on the buildings.

Chapter 3 of the Rule. "As often as anything important is to be done in the monastery, the prioress or abbot shall call the whole community together and explain what the business is; and after hearing the advice of the members, let them ponder it and follow what they judge the wiser course. The reason why we have said all should be called for counsel is that the Spirit often reveals what is better to the younger.

"The community members, for their part, are to express their opinions with all humility, and not presume to defend their own views obstinately. The decision is rather the prioress's or the abbot's to make, so that when the abbot or prioress of the community has determined what is prudent, all must obey. Nevertheless, just as it is proper for disciples to obey their teachers, so it is becoming for the teacher to settle everything with foresight and fairness."

Most of the monks at Blue Cloud were born in the United States and the democratic culture in which they grew up had prepared them to speak their minds. Although each man had promised to follow the will of God and the leadership of his abbot, he still was an independent-thinking citizen. So when an issue had to be decided that affected the entire community the discussions sometimes became lively. Younger men were encouraged to express themselves, so much so that at one time the elder monks who weighed their comments carefully before speaking protested that they could not break into the lively discussions.

Some monks were absolutely against debating any changes. One man announced, "I will not agree to anything that has not been practiced for at least 30 years in the monastery." Nevertheless, there were different points of view and long deliberations on critical topics such as whether to continue the fund-raising activities that had raised millions of dollars for work on the reservations and whether to turn the administration of the Benedictine-operated Catholic schools over to the Indian parents of the students.

Many subjects were substantive, but others ranged from complaints about the noise of ringing telephones to smoking in the recreation areas to accusations that a couple of the monks were lazy. The Rule of Benedict not only allowed each man to express himself that way, but also compelled him to announce his own mistakes. The monks met once a week in the chapel to tell publicly of their impatience and discontent with others and to ask for forgiveness.

Brother Dominic recommended at one meeting that the Abbey should purchase 160 acres where the monks had been working and which were located nearby. An important subject like that occasionally resulted in countless questions. Abbot Denis, who was presiding over his first meeting as the head of the community, guided the discussion by saying, "I picked rocks on that land. I helped haul the hay from that land. I think we should include it in our holdings. What do you think?" Any subjects of that importance required the approval of everyone living in the Abbey and the monks, following their Abbot's lead, passed a motion to buy the land.

Father Stan felt that some community meetings could be more productive and he offered a suggestion to Abbot Denis. Although the Abbot did not favor long-winded discussions, Father Stan felt that the monks should be encouraged to be more forthright in their deliberations. So he suggested that the Abbot relinquish the chairmanship of the meeting and simply sit in the audience as an observer. The Abbot accepted the idea, but he also made sure that the other monks heard his opinion on the subject.

Some places in the Abbey were more conducive to an exchange of ideas than others and a warm, comfortable meeting place could effect the outcome of the discourse. Father Stan had that in mind when he agreed to moderate a discussion on liturgy and prayer service. The dining room was a cheerful place that was likely to encourage conversations so he called the meeting there instead of the auditorium where the monks normally talked about business matters, such as how much it cost to heat the Abbey.

Chapter 2 of the Rule. "To be worthy of the task of governing a monastery, the prioress or abbot must always remember what the title signifies and act accordingly. They are believed to hold the place of Christ in the monastery. Therefore a prioress or abbot must never teach or decree or command anything that would deviate from God's instructions. On the contrary, everything they teach and command should, like the leaven of divine justice, permeate the minds of the community...

"The prioress and abbot must always remember what they are and what they are called, aware that more will be expected of one to whom more has been entrusted. They must know what a difficult and demanding burden they have undertaken: directing souls and serving a variety of temperaments, coaxing, reproving, and encouraging them as appropriate. They must so accommodate themselves to each one's character that they will not only keep the flock entrusted to their care from dwindling, but will rejoice in the increase of a good flock."

Some of St. Benedict's instructions sound harsh today. However, he was aware of the responsibility placed on the abbot or prioress to lead those in their care and the possible penalties for failing to do so. Chapter 2 of the Rule offers further explanation:

"...They should not gloss over the sins of those who err, but cut them out while they can, as soon as they begin to sprout, remembering the fate of Eli, priest of Shiloh (1 Sam. 2:11-4:18). For the upright and perceptive, the first and second warnings should be verbal, but those who are evil or stubborn, arrogant or disobedient, can be curbed only by blows or some other physical punishment at the first offense…

"…The prioress and abbot must know that anyone undertaking the charge of souls must be ready to account for them. Whatever the number of members they have in their care, let them realize that on judgment day they will surely have to submit a reckoning to God for all their souls - and indeed for their own as well…"

What an awesome responsibility - the abbot would "hold the place of Christ" in the Benedictine community. It was a challenge for any man who accepted the assignment.

For a time in the 1980s Abbot Alan was the chief administrator at Blue Cloud. In Father Stan's words, an abbot's responsibility was to provide hope for the present and a plan for the future of the Benedictine community. Abbot Alan had been a monk for many years and was well prepared for the job; his experience in the order eventually reached 50 years. The other monks found him to be a cautious leader; he would not begin a project unless he felt assured of a sufficient return. As his term ended some of the men at Blue Cloud insisted that no one among them had the credibility to assume the mantle of the abbot.

Nevertheless, the traditional election process began and the field of candidates was narrowed through six ballots until the monks voted for Denis Quinkert to become their Abbot. He was an unpretentious, down-to-earth man, if occasionally forgetful. When informed about his election, he asked for half an hour to pray and think about it before accepting the assignment. The new Abbot told the other monks that they must evaluate his work and decide how well he performed and if, after six years, the men were dissatisfied they should vote him out of office.

Abbot Denis brought a varied background to the task, having served 17 years as a religious brother before he was ordained to the priesthood. Benedictine tradition held that the installation of a new abbot normally occurs on a fixed date when the local bishop is invited to bless him. That would have delayed the ritual, but Abbot Denis signaled a change in how things would be done - he asked Bishop Dudley to come to the Abbey that same afternoon so that the ceremonial aspect of the event could be minimized and completed quickly.

The Benedictine method of choosing an abbot could seem like a crowded primary election for the presidency of the United States. On one occasion when the priests and brothers were choosing a new abbot they first prayed for five days before they assembled and learned that 11 among them had been proposed for the position. Each candidate's qualifications were posted and studied for a day.

Three of the nominees said that they couldn't serve. The list narrowed down to three candidates, who were asked to leave the room while the remaining priests and brothers deliberated. The Benedictine style is consensus, meaning that even though a monk favored a particular nominee he would support the decision of the whole assembly. From this process emerged a new Abbot, Thomas Hillenbrand, who Father Stan found open to ideas and determined to carry out those which the group most favored.

Chapter 33 of the Rule. "Above all, this evil practice [of private ownership] must be uprooted and removed from the monastery. We mean that without an order from the prioress or abbot, no member may presume to give, receive, or retain anything as their own, nothing at all - not a book, writing tablets, or stylus - in short, not a single item, especially since monastics may not have the free disposal of their own bodies and wills."

No one thought of gifts of computers or cell phones when St. Benedict wrote the Rule. However, such a phone could be vital to an elderly man who drove long distances alone and who while on the road at night might need help in case of an emergency. Father Stan's family had all that in mind when they assembled for his birthday party. There was a ringing sound somewhere near the priest. "Answer it," someone shouted, "It's a gift - a cell phone, your birthday present." The phone proved its worth when on more than one occasion he spotted trouble on the road ahead and pressed 911 to ask for assistance.

Chapter 72 of the Rule. "Just as there is a wicked zeal of bitterness which separates from God and leads to hell, so there is a good zeal which separates from evil and leads to everlasting life...No monastics are to pursue what they judge better for themselves, but instead what they judge better for someone else."

The principles and goals that St. Benedict described in the ancient Rule were a fundamental guide to Father Stan and he mentioned them often in his writings. Summarizing how the missionaries spend their lives, he said, "The Benedictine order is supported by three foundations: prayer, work and study. When any of these foundations is allowed to crumble, the whole begins to collapse.

Chapter Twenty-Three - Thinking Out Loud

A missionary's random thoughts were spoken into a dictating machine while driving through rural country or sitting at his desk in the Abbey. They could start with musings as natural as "Well, anyway, I've had my shower now and I'm going down to listen to the news. Today was the testing of the space shuttle and I want to see that. So I'll put my pants on now and go down to see what has happened in the news today."

The journal entries ranged from geography to history to Almighty God, as, for example…"Just now as I talk I am approaching Wasta. That's the English spelling of the Dakota word `Wash-te.' It's the name of this town on the Cheyenne River. As I go down the hill into Wasta, I'm again overwhelmed by the creative majesty that can take earth and rock and weather it and carve it and move it into grandeur. This kind of valley with the undying stream shows how inexorable is the creative presence of the Creator. Nothing can withstand his conserving, creating power. Humans with shovels and hoes and scrapers try to move the earth, but once they have turned their backs on their work the Creator begins to rearrange what they have disturbed…"

The ideas in Father Stan's journal were often disconnected, occasionally speculative, and lacked a central theme. Yet his words also were candid, far-ranging and an historical record of life as a missionary among the Indians in the 20th century. He accepted the limitations on his efforts: "The thoughts on these tapes will be fragmentary as each day I bring a new bit of understanding. These thoughts may be chaotic because in a search one must of necessity range back and forth, far and wide. One must of necessity discover the trail is a dead one. One must of necessity have to retrace oneself and reorient oneself."

The imperfections notwithstanding, the chance to let his ruminations flow freely was too good to pass up. "I don't know what I would do if I didn't have tapes like this unto which I could express my feelings and thoughts. I'm not a writer so it would be impossible for me to put onto paper a logical essay. But unto a tape I simply let the thoughts follow the stream of consciousness," he spoke into his recorder.

Some of the tapes were so homespun that while at the beginning the stories seemed factual they ended as fictional. A boy named Farrell Crissler had an intelligent dog named Buck, but his family did not have a car so Father Stan had to pick up Farrell and drive him to basketball games. He arrived at Farrell's house and the boy was not ready to leave. Edward Frederick, one of the players, had brought his guitar so he and the other boys amused themselves in Father Stan's car while Farrell's mom urged her son to hurry.

"Buck, go get my shoes. They're under the bed," Farrell instructed the dog. Buck twisted his head and looked up at Farrell. "Go ahead, Buck. Don't fool around," the boy said, swallowing his lunch as he spoke. Another order followed, "Please get me a shirt. Don't bother looking around. Just get whatever is on top." Buck trotted into the next room and Father Stan wondered how the dog could find the shirt in the dark.

"I'm waiting for my shirt. We're going to Cando and we have to look nice," Farrell explained to his nervous parents. In the meantime the priest peered into the other room and saw that the light had been turned on. Buck had the shirt, all right, but a button was missing. The dog was next to the lamp squinting. The light was dim, perhaps not bright enough for Father Stan to see clearly, but he could have sworn that Buck was trying to thread a needle.

The dictating machine recorded how Father Stan had a dream about climbing a ladder into heaven. An angel stood at the pearly gates and handed a big piece of chalk to each newcomer. He said to each person, "Take this and go over to the next ladder. It'll be a big ladder and you'll have to climb it. On every step take your chalk and make a mark. Every mark is for one of your sins. When you finish marking you'll be in heaven."

Up the ladder into the clouds went Father Stan, marking, climbing, huffing and puffing. He was engulfed in a mist and at last he tired and sat for a moment. Then there were noises and legs and arms, moving frantically, came closer in the mist. It was Ray "Flab" LaVerdure, descending the ladder rapidly.

The surprised priest greeted his friend, but all Flab said was, "Don't talk now, Father, I can't stop." As Flab sank into the mist and disappeared, Father Stan heard him shout, "I used some rough words once and now I have to go down and get some more of that damn chalk." Then, faintly, "Damn! Maybe that's another mark."

At times Father Stan felt depressed, especially about his health and the future of AICRC. For five months in 1987-88 he was so afraid that he had become negative about the Church and the Benedictines that he didn't dictate anything. He explained later that "...revealing our feelings, attitudes, sentiments about any organization may lay us open to hurting that organization or leave us open to being hurt by the organization. Maybe that's why some people die with their thoughts left silent."

Yet even during a period of personal malaise Father Stan felt compelled to express his thoughts, both good and bad. "A story is not true if a darker part of it is hidden," he wrote. With that as his standard, the tapes sometimes revealed his dissatisfaction with the people around him. "Maybe once in a while in my storytelling I will express an opinion. I think we need to express opinions, but they should be identified as opinions and not taken as incontrovertible fact," he said in his journal. His opinions and recollections covered a wide range of subjects.

Women - They are crisis-oriented and once they see a problem, start immediately to solve it. The assistance of women, Father Stan observed, is as important today to the success of a missionary's work as the women who accompanied Jesus on the way to Calvary were a part of His ministry. In particular, religious sisters bring stability to a mission whereas priests come and go without any long-term commitment. He was unstinting in his praise of the dozens of nuns who had assisted him for many years. "Priests who do not have sisters as their partners in ministry are crippled," he wrote.

One day a year was not enough for Father Stan to celebrate his affection for the women, Indian and white, family and friends, who had influenced his life. "I wish it were Mother's Week," he said. "I could never in one day express my feelings for the mothers I have known."

His long-time secretary, Colleen Heminger, understood the special role that women had played in the priest's life. When he was preparing a sermon for Mother's Day she didn't hesitate to recommend that the theme should be, "An ounce of mother is worth a pound of clergy."

Wisdom - "I think wisdom simply means shutting up and letting the other persons develop their own thoughts quietly, pour out their hearts and applauding what they are saying. They feel that this is my wisdom and it certainly is not. It's their own being finally put into words and surprising them as the words take shape and the sentences mount.

"Finally they say, `Gee, you really told me a lot.' I didn't tell them a thing. It is they, who in the presence of Jesus, heard His words to them. They responded to it and they resonated with it to their own surprise. It's a delightful, tremendous feeling to see people develop like this."

Christians - "A person has to be out-directed, selfless rather than selfish. He has to think of others rather than himself. He has to die for others rather than himself. He has to work for others rather than himself. He has to serve others. That's his calling. That's his ordination in baptism."

Faith - The oral diary told how John Warren died after suffering horrible burns. It happened one evening after John and his family returned home from visiting friends. His wife and children remained in the wagon while he entered the house to put kerosene in a lighted lamp. It was dark and John mistakenly poured gasoline which exploded all over his body. Everything burned except his belt and his shoes.

Father Stan hurried to the hospital in Belcourt and saw his friend's charred body lying on a huge rubber sheet filled with cooling oil. "John, it doesn't look good," the priest said. "Well, you better give me the works, then, Father," John declared. "There's one thing I regret now." The nurses, who had been in tears, held their breath and awaited the confession of a dying man. The year was 1946, during Joe Louis' time as heavyweight boxing champion, and through his unimaginable pain, John spoke, "Father, Joe Louis can be happy. I always thought I had a pretty good left-right combination, but I guess now I won't ever get into the ring and show it to old Joe."

The next day John's spirits remained strong and loving, although the burned flesh had hardened all over his body. He could barely move his lips and was nearing death, yet he summoned Father Stan and his wife, Delia, to his bedside and said, "I can't talk much now, Father. But, Delia, let me hear the rosary again."

The Elderly - "Look on the faces of old people, people whose mouths crinkle in a smile easily. They've discovered who they are. They've watched God through many years and discovered what they are. They have prayed and talked to God much; they know what He is and so they're at peace with the world and with God. Nobody can hurt them anymore. They're great people to be imitated."

Anger - People can handle anger in one of three ways: deny it, express it, or forgive the person who caused it. The story of the murder of Candace Rough Surface showed that the right choice is forgiveness. Police caught the alleged killer and held him for trial. Candace's mother and the daughter's Indian friends walked from Kenel, North Dakota to Selby, South Dakota to attend the hearing, praying all along the route for a just verdict.

The group arrived at the court only to learn that the accused man had admitted the crime. When Candace's mother was told, it was evident that a spirit of forgiveness had prevailed over a thirst for revenge. "He confessed. That's all. I am at peace," she said.

Losing...and winning - Billy Mills, a Native American runner who represented the United States in the Olympics in Tokyo, occasionally shared a speakers' platform with Father Stan. "You never learn anything from winning," Mills told an audience. When he won a race, the runner-up usually said that he would beat him the next time. "I, too, every time I lost a race, hurried to congratulate the victor, but warned him that I had learned and I would beat him the next time. If you are successful you never change. When you lose you change in order to win."

Mills won the 10,000 meter race and that evening telephoned his sister in Pierre. His young niece was calm when she answered the telephone. "Aren't you excited?" Mills inquired. She wasn't thrilled at all and said, "I knew you would win." "How did you know I would win?" the Olympic champ asked. "I prayed for you this morning" the little girl answered.

Indians - They were the subject of Father Stan's first tape in 1971. The Indians were frank with the Benedictine priest and more than once he heard, "Father, all we ask of Christian people is that they live up to what they say they are. Be nice to people. That's all we ask."

The Indians' way of life, their recognition of the goodness of creation, their patience, their ability to love, and their feeling of community taught the missionaries a great deal. Father Stan learned much from his years on the reservations, including the answer to the question from the old Indian man: "Yes, God surely is nice!"

"They provided me with a point of view that could examine the culture out of which I came. A point of view that could weigh the theology that had been taught to me. A point of view that allowed me to watch the growth of people who have faith, hope and love. And the stagnation of those who have little faith, little hope and are afraid of love," he wrote.

"I'm grateful to the Indian people who were kind enough to smile at competition and self-righteousness, who were kind enough to forgive the arrogant and the judgmental, who were patient enough to let some wisdom finally take root in youthful men. I am above all grateful to those who can say to me, 'I love you.'"

Having spent almost all of his adult lifetime working as a Benedictine missionary among the Indians - more than 60 years - Father Stan could honestly say, "I am so grateful that my life has been spent on the reservations in the Dakotas. I fully believe that had I not been in touch with the spirit there my spirit would have long ago shriveled into a cancer for my body and caused my body itself to decay."

End

Bibliography
of
Eagle Man and More Missionaries

Books

Bowden, Henry Warner, American Indians and Christian Missions, The University of Chicago Press, Chicago, 1981.

Carson, Mary Eisenman, Blackrobe for the Yankton Sioux, Tipi Press, Chamberlain, SD, 1989.

Chittenden, Hiram Martin and Alfred Talbot Richardson, ed., Life, Letters and Travels of Father Pierre-Jeanne DeSmet. S. J., 4 vols., Francis P. Harper, New York, 1905.

DeMallie, Raymond J. and Douglas R. Parks, ed., Sioux Indian Religion, University of Oklahoma Press, Norman, 1987.

Duffy, Sister Consuela Marie, Katherine Drexel, SBS.

Duratschek, Sister Mary Claudia, OSB, Cruising Along Sioux Trails, The Grail, St. Meinrad, IN, 1947.

Enochs, Ross Alexander, The Jesuit Mission to The Lakota Sioux, Sheed & Ward, Kansas City, MO, 1947.

Government Printing Office, Papers relating to Talks and Councils held with the Indians in Dakota and Montana Territories 1866-1869, Washington, D. C., 1910.

Haefeli, Evan and Kevin Sweeney, Captors and Captives, the 1704 French and Indian Raid on Deerfield, University of Massachusetts Press, Amherst, 2003.

Hassrick, Royal B., The Sioux, University of Oklahoma Press, Norman, 1964.

Holley, Frances Chamberlain, Once Their Home, Our Legacy From the Dahkotahs, Donahue & Henneberry, Chicago, 1890.

Karolevitz, Robert F., Bishop Martin Marty, privately printed for Benedictine Sisters of Sacred Heart Convent, Yankton, SD, 1980.

Morrison, Dane, ed., American Indian Studies, Peter Lang, New York, 1997.

Nurge, Ethel, ed., The Modern Sioux, University of Nebraska Press, Lincoln, 1970.

Page, Jake, In the Hands of The Great Spirit, Free Press, New York, 2003.

Rahill, Peter J., The Catholic Indian Missions and Grant's Peace Policy, The Catholic University of America Press, Washington, 1953.

Sacred Congregation of Rites on the Introduction of the Cause for Beautification and Canonization and on the Virtues of the Servant of God, The Posito of the Historical Section on Katherine Tekakwitha The Lily of the Mohawks, Fordham University Press, New York, 1940.

Standing Bear, Luther, My People, Houghton Mifflin Company, Boston, 1928.

Tatum, Laurie, Our Red Brothers and the Peace Policy of President Ulysses S. Grant, University of Nebraska Press, Lincoln, 1978.

Tinsley, Ambrose, OSB., PAX: The Benedictine Way, The Liturgical Press, Collegeville, MN, 1994.

Unger, Steven, ed., The Destruction of American Indian Families, Association of American Indian Affairs, New York, 1977.

University of South Dakota, Who's Who Among the Sioux, Vermillion, 1988.

Vescey, Christopher, ed., Handbook of American Indian Religious Freedom, The Crossroads Publishing Company, New York, 1991.

Vestel, Stanley, Sitting Bull, Champion of the Sioux, Houghton Mifflin Company (The Riverside Press, Cambridge), Boston, 1932.

Utley, Robert M., The Lance and The Shield, Henry Holt and Company, Hew York, 1993.

Walsh, James J., These Splendid Priests, Books for Libraries Press, Freeport, NY, 1926.

Sources

Blue Cloud Abbey, http://www.bluecloud.org/

Diary of Rev. Stanislaus Maudlin, OSB, (transcribed).
Bureau of Catholic Indian Missions newsletter, articles by Msgr. Paul A. Lenz and Rev. Ted Zwern, S. J., 1998-2004.

Booklet, The Marty Story by St. Paul's Indian Mission, Marty, SD 1954.

Mother Katherine Drexel by Dennis M. Linehan, S. J., America, Sept. 16, 2000.

Manuscript, A Vicar for Indians: Rev. Stanislaus Maudlin, OSB, presented at South Dakota History Conference by Carol Goss Hoover June 3, 1994.

Columns by Rev. Stanislaus Maudlin, OSB in Turtle Mountain Times (various dates).

The New York Times, Dec. 23, 1997 p. 16, col. 1.

The New York Times, May 22, 2000, P. E1, col. 2.

Grand Forks Herald, November 19,1997.

Interview (telephone) of Rev. Stanislaus Maudlin, OSB, July 11, 2000.

Interview of Rev. Stanislaus Maudlin, OSB, July 14-15, 1998.

Interview of Rev. George Lyons, OSB, July 15, 1998.

Interview of Bro. Leon Smith, OSB, July 15, 1998.

Interview of Sister Irene Demarris, SDS, July 14, 1998.

Interview of Sister Charles Palm, OSB, July 11, 1998.

Manuscript by Rev. Stanislaus Maudlin, OSB, about Rev. Sylvester Eisenman, OSB and Tekakwitha Indian Conference, undated.

Short History of Kateri Tekakwitha Conference 1939-1997 by Rev. Stanislaus Maudlin, OSB, Sept. 14, 1997.

Manuscript, A Race in Peril by Rev. Villock, St. Francis Xavier Indian Mission, Herrick, SD, undated.

The Life of the Good Katherine Tegakouita, now known as the Holy Savage, by Rev. Claude Chauchetiere, from original manuscript in Archives of St. Mary's College, Montreal, Series A, Number 343.

Letters

Letters to Very Rev. J. B. Tennelly, S.S., D.D., Director of Bureau of Catholic Indian Missions, (various dates 1950-).

Letter from Stella Pretty Sounding Flute to author July 14, 1999.

Letter from Rev. Stanislaus Maudlin, OSB to Dr. Herbert Hoover and Carol Hoover, January 29 1999.

Letter from Sister Mary Brenden Kress, SND, to author June 26, 1998.

Letter from Brenda Morin to author June 15, 1998.

Letter from Ramon A. Roubideaux to author May 18, 1998.

Letter from Bernice Hopkins to author April 7, 1998.

Letter from Stella Monette Davis to author June 2, 1997.

Index

About the Author

This is the second book which William L. Maher has written. The first was the biography of U. S. Army Chaplain Emil Kapaun called "A Shepherd in Combat Boots". Father Kapaun was a prisoner in the Korean War and died in a North Korean prison camp.

Mr. Maher was a sports reporter on a daily newspaper before he became a lawyer. His articles have been printed in several Catholic and legal publications. He lives in Brookville, New York with his wife, Lee, and serves there as a village justice.

Printed in the United States
47826LVS00003B/193

9 781420 826555